DEMON UNBOUND

DEMON ENFORCERS, BOOK 1
JENN STARK

OTHER BOOKS BY JENN STARK

The Demon Enforcer Series

Demon Forsaken (coming July, 2018)

The Immortal Vegas Series
(series complete!)

Getting Wilde
Wilde Card
Born To Be Wilde
Wicked And Wilde
Aces Wilde
Forever Wilde
Wilde Child
Call of the Wilde
Running Wilde
Wilde Fire

One Wilde Night *(prequel novella)*

For Linda,

Who helped me shine the light.

CHAPTER ONE

"Welcome to be-a-*utiful* Acapulco!" The game show announcer's self-satisfied voice crackled in the hot, humid darkness, barely audible above the rap music that cranked out over the now-empty beach. Along this stretch of sand, however, no one sang, no one danced. The scent of blood hung heavy on the air, thick enough to taste.

Demons had been here, Warrick knew. Demons who'd murdered God's children.

So, of course, Warrick and the Syx were here too.

"Shut off your phone," he snapped at Finn. "If I can hear it, so can they."

Warrick stood evenly balanced on both feet, fists clenched, head cocked, as if he could smell the very night to find what he sought. Which, of course, he could. Every demon horde had its own particular stench, and Warrick had already come to know the Fuerza Negra's too well.

"It's not like they don't already know we're here." Finn, the Syx's youngest and newest member—which still put his age at right around six thousand years—crouched beside Warrick. He smirked as he pocketed his phone, then stood as well. With one thick-soled boot, he toed aside the spent rounds of ammo that littered the beach. "Looks like they've been busy too. Normally, we just have claw marks to go on."

"Raum?"

The third member of their team stepped forward, his face as bleak as winter, his eyes distant. Of all of them, Raum was the best at identifying the dead. He'd also always felt the weight of his sin the heaviest. But they'd each come to their present roles through their own disgrace, each with their own burdens to carry.

"Seven killed," Raum said, in a voice that had once made angels weep for its loss. "All males. All human."

"Seven." Warrick scanned the barren coastline. "I thought you said this cartel left their kill behind as a message."

"That's their standard MO, yup," Finn agreed reasonably enough. "Up to now, though, we haven't been the ones getting the message. They may be trying to hide."

"Or they're making a stand," Raum offered.

Warrick growled, the sound rolling dangerously over the quiet beach. "That'd be a bad idea."

Demons had lurked among humanity since the dawn of creation, the ragged remains of Fallen angels who'd been cursed by God for their sins. Most of them, however, were smart enough to stay hidden. If they kept to the shadows, they could survive — some even thrive — cheek to jowl with the sort of despicable humans who could give them a run for their money in a race to the bottom. Those demons spent their twisted existence on the fringes of society, victims of their own insatiable habits.

There was a catch, however. Demons couldn't kill a human, couldn't even harm one of God's children, and expect to avoid His divine wrath. That was where Warrick and the Syx came in.

Though they were themselves demons who'd been damned beyond the veil for their own sins, trapped in a bolt-hole created at the fall of Atlantis, Warrick's crew of enforcers had earned some measure of reprieve from their condemnation through their ability to rout out the worst of their kind. They'd spent millennia at the beck and call of humans who cried out for their aid. Now, that aid was in epically high demand, for two very good reasons:

One, it took a demon to banish a demon, and nobody was better at it than Warrick and the Syx.

And two, a shit ton of the bastards had just been set free to roam the earth. Again.

Not since before the fall of Atlantis had the world teemed with so many of the damned. Warrick had felt their return like a physical blow, a howling in his bones. But so far, this new influx of demons hadn't bubbled up to the top of the Syx's hit list.

The Fuerza Negra had.

"Four women were with the male victims," Stefan said, his voice floating through the darkness, rich and indolent. He didn't mean to sound like a hustler on the make, but old habits died hard. And of all of them, Stefan was most attuned to the females of God's chosen. He could beguile and be beguiled by them in equal measure.

"Not dead," Stefan continued. "Not hurt, at least not much. Scared, though. They know they *will* be hurt, probably killed, but they are brave." He sighed. "Very brave. They have expected such a death all their lives."

"How long ago?" Hostages, then. Distractions. The Fuerza Negra *were* making a stand, even after the Syx had been called. They had to know the reputation of Warrick's team — all demons did. And still they stood fast. Challenging Warrick. Disrespecting him.

Warrick felt the familiar fury lick through him. He

had old habits too. And he wasn't about to let them die.

"A half hour. No more." Stefan turned toward the music, frowning. "Something's not right, though. The research we've done — the Fuerza Negra cartel does its work and leaves, going to ground before the guns stop smoking. That's not what happened here."

Finn snorted. "If we'd been tapped earlier, it wouldn't have happened at all. Everyone waits until the last second, and by then, it's too late. Stupid."

The demon's phone was back in his hand. Since the Syx had been unexpectedly pulled free of their prison beyond the veil most recently, Finn had immersed himself in the technology of the current time. Before, they'd never been on this plane long enough to explore the technology of the era. Now Finn couldn't let the small device out of his sight.

But phones had nothing to do with the summoning of the Syx. That was a call in the blood, their bodies wrenched out of wherever they were holed up, their spirits bound to answer, however many the job required. For this task, on this beach, only four of them had been considered necessary, four of them dropped into the heart of this godforsaken —

"Welcome to be-a-*utiful* Acapulco!" Finn's phone chimed again.

Warrick hummed another warning, certain Finn was triggering the thing himself, but he kept his eyes on Stefan. "What is it?"

"They're still in there. The women. They—" He scowled, glancing back to Warrick. "They're being held. Drugged, now. Put on display."

"Maybe they think we won't strike with so many humans around," Finn put in. "Social media puts this party as a gig of Manuel Duarte's. According to what I'm reading, you get invited by Manuel, you'd best plan on coming to the party. You don't show up, it's a slam that he and his boys don't overlook. This time, though, I'm thinking Manuel should've double-checked the guest list."

"They invited the Fuerza Negra." Warrick was facing the hotel now too, its doors flung wide, bright light spilling out into half-moons on the sand.

"Yup." Finn nodded. "Someone apparently got cocky. Then someone got dead."

"Finn." Raum's voice was soft. "Respect for God's beloved."

"I know what they are," Finn shot back, his words now clipped, though his easy smile never wavered. "I was beloved once too. We all were."

"Where are the women?" Warrick asked Stefan.

"Where you'd expect bait to be," Stefan said grimly, pointing to the bright lights of the hotel. "In cages above the dance floor, each with a claw around her throat. We go in, they die. We stay here, they die. It's all the same to the Fuerza Negra."

"Three hundred people are packed onto that dance floor, my brother," Finn said, scrolling through his phone. "Dancing like there's no tomorrow." He cocked a glance up to Warrick. "We go?"

"We go," Warrick said, the usual heat spreading through him hard and fast. "And not alone. Summon Hugh and Gregori...right into two of those cages, I'm thinking."

Finn grinned. "It'll be a tight fit."

"They won't be there that long."

The youngest of the demon enforcers snickered, and a second later, his phone's tinny speaker flared again to life. "Welcome to be-a-*utiful*—"

The grab happened so quickly, Finn barely had time to blink. Warrick wrenched his phone away and crushed it into sparkling shards, dropping it to the

9

ground like so much sand.

Then, silently, they all started running toward the bright lights and music.

The hand on Maria Santos's arm was thick, heavy. It squeezed with the kind of coiled-up violence that'd always meant trouble, long before she'd become an undercover cop for the LAPD. In this dump of a strip club deep in south Compton, that trouble could be anything, but Maria had no doubt about what had Pablo so keyed up tonight. After five months of infiltrating the Guardia gang, Maria's test to become its newest member was finally here.

Pablo's eager words confirmed it. "C'mon. The lieutenant's ready for you."

The second newest member of the Guardia, Pablo was barely twenty, all arms and legs and manic nerves. He tried to play it cool, but there was no missing the excitement in his voice, the blood lust. They'd picked someone for Maria to kill. She'd have to make it look good too, if she wanted to remain in place on this op. It was either that or consent to something far worse. And while she loved her job with the LAPD, she didn't love it that much.

There'd be a hell of a lot of paperwork to process for discharging a weapon, though, despite the number of times they'd gone over it in advance, or how many approvals she'd gotten. It'd be worse if the Guardia didn't give Maria some dirtbag to shoot, but instead a civilian. That had been her biggest dread on this job from the beginning. Not getting killed. Not even getting raped, though she had a healthy fear of that with these assholes. But being asked to prove herself by taking a shot at some innocent bystander? Maria steeled herself for that, knew it was coming. Because it'd be exactly like the lieutenant of the Guardia to do that to her.

"Move it." Pablo's voice kicked up a notch, his excitement palpable.

"Yeah, yeah." Maria peered past the thug's shoulder and into the darkness of the back room, where she was pretty sure associates of her primary target were holed up, that target being Takio Soldaro, head of the gang for which the Guardia served as production hub—pulling in supplies, cooking drugs. A gang that made the Guardia look like a bunch of Cub Scouts. Takio was the whole point of this op, and Maria was so close—so damned close to nailing him. So close, after fifteen years of waiting.

From all she'd seen during the past four months, Takio and his goons rarely emerged from the hellhole that she and the other members of her police squad called the Citadel, four cinderblock-apartment high-rises that were proud to lay claim to one of the darkest patches of south Compton. Takio's top lieutenants worked almost nonstop, rumor had it, cooking something special inside those walls that Maria was desperate to uncover—some new strain of drug that she was sure would spiral the world even faster down the drain.

When Takio and his men did crawl out of their pit, though, it was to check out the wares at this club.

According to the whispers of the dancers, Takio liked his women soft, pliable, and above all, ghostly pale. So that avenue was out. No amount of cosmetics would take away Maria's dark features and muscular build. Most of the time, she had no problem with that. But when it came to taking down a bastard like Takio, it would've been a lot easier if she looked the part of one of the spun-sugar playthings that tripped his dick.

She'd done her best, though, with what she had to work with. Takio might like them young and blonde, but the lieutenants of the gang that served as his secondary muscle didn't so much care. After a quick recon of the Guardia's top personnel, she'd latched on to Jack — a one-time thug but currently more the brains of the operation. Three days earlier, however, Jack had been taken into protective custody, part of the longer-term sting that would place Maria at the heart of the Guardia operation. Without him, phase two of the operation could swing into gear.

Maria couldn't walk away from the gang, after all. She knew and had seen too much. That meant she could either hook up with another gang member, or officially become one of them.

She'd immediately chosen the latter. All of it part of the plan.

But the plan could go sideways in a heartbeat, depending on who they had waiting for her to shoot tonight.

Maria and Pablo moved casually down the hallway, the throbbing beat of the house music shaking the walls. The gold cross hanging in the hollow of her neck seemed to burn against her skin. It wasn't hers, of course. But it had brought her here.

Even as a little girl, Maria had never had much reason to believe in God. However, Cara, her cousin, had not only believed in Him, she'd believed that if someone pure and true begged it of Him, He would come and save Cara, no matter her own sins. And it'd been Cara who'd pressed the necklace into Maria's hand, beautiful Cara, wild-eyed and dying on the broken asphalt of the 7-Eleven parking lot, in her soft flowered dress and black patent leather Mary Janes, the hummingbird tattoo on her collarbone fluttering as frantically as her heart had been. She'd begged Maria to call on divine aid to save her—save her or find her killer right then, that night, that moment, because she did not deserve to beg God herself. But Maria, ten years old and nearly hysterical with fear, hadn't understood a word her older cousin had been saying. That night, Maria could do no more than hold Cara close, her own hands wet with blood as Cara had whispered deliriously of the terrible truths that God had shown her. Truths only she could see... truths that had gotten her killed.

No, Maria hadn't turned to God that night or any night after. Because even at the age of ten, Maria had known that God didn't give a shit about people like her and her cousin. God couldn't save her cousin from a knife wound to the abdomen. He couldn't make the blood go away. He couldn't ease the guilt Maria carried with her for not doing enough to protect Cara, either. No one could do that.

Instead, Maria had waited, watched. And above all, she'd forced herself to get stronger. She'd run. Lifted weights made out of bricks or milk bottles filled with sand. Picked fights with kids bigger than her. She'd even tried trolling the gangs, and those run-ins had left both permanent scars and lasting lessons. Eventually, she'd grown up and gotten out of Compton, become a cop far north of the heart of the city, done her time. And all the while, she'd tracked la Noche, Takio Soldaro's gang, her cousin's killers. She'd watched them for fifteen years, until she knew everything about them and was in a position to do something about it. When the undercover job in her hometown neighborhood had come up, as she'd known it one day would—she was more than ready to take it.

And she was *so close*.

Maybe now, she'd be able to finally get justice for Cara...maybe now, the nightmares would stop.

Maybe.

Pablo stepped aside, then shoved Maria into the room, hard enough to send anyone else sprawling. Instead, she took his momentum, went with it, then drew up tight and ready.

"Maria," the lieutenant said, nodding to her.

"Lieutenant Cedo." Maria kept her expression flat, not betraying her instinctive reaction to the man. Tall and burly, he was just going to fat, but there was enough muscle layered over his frame and enough precision to his manner that she figured he had to have military training. Add to that his endless supply of guns, not all of which were street weapons. Unfortunately, the LAPD couldn't get a fix on how connected Cedo was because no one knew where he came from. His background had proven impossible to track down. The name Cedo was obviously an alias, but there was something more to Guardia's top lieutenant, something she couldn't quite track…something that legitimately unnerved her.

Most of the time, Cedo looked like any of the other hard-eyed gangbangers that bit into the heart of south Compton like a twisted coil of barbed wire. Cedo's eyes were slightly crazy, sure—but that went with the territory. Every once in a while, though, if Maria looked at him the right way, she could see something more in Cedo than simply wild eyes. The rippling of his face, the shimmering of his skin. And it was those times that she remembered what Cara had whispered to her, the "terrible truths" she'd seen: men who weren't men at all, but howling monsters with elongated snouts and hands that erupted in claws and—

"Maria. Good. I'm glad you're here." Maria yanked herself back into focus as Cedo grinned, then handed her a gun. She knew without asking it was clean, stolen, its serial number filed off. It'd probably be sold after she did what she needed to do.

"We got us a special treat today."

Cedo stepped back, and a murmur of laughter snaked through the room. Several of the men along the far wall shifted their position to reveal what was hidden behind them.

Maria froze.

Standing in the opening was one of the club's dancers, her eyes half-closed, her limbs loose, her mouth slack. Unbidden, Maria's hand stole to the cross around her neck before she ruthlessly dropped it again.

She couldn't stop the words from springing to her lips, however. "Sword of God, hear me, I pray," she muttered automatically. As if Cara was right in front of her once more, bleeding, dying, her cousin's whispered, anguished prayer flashing easily into Maria's mind, all these years later.

Cedo probably couldn't hear her words, but if he did, good. If he thought Maria was squeamish about shooting a helpless woman, it'd add weight to her act of pulling the trigger. But the dancer wasn't the problem.

The problem was that Maria knew the man who *held* the dancer. She was almost certain of it. She'd seen him fifteen years ago, lurking in the crowd of bystanders as Cara had bled out in her lap.

A man whose eyes had looked a little too crazed, a little too wrong, staring at Cara. A man whose eyes looked a little too wrong, now.

"Sword of God, defend us." Maria breathed again, staring at him. She lifted her left hand once more to the cross, clutched it tight. Because the man's eyes weren't simply crazy…she'd almost swear they were *glowing*. A faint, undisputable green. "Defend us all."

She raised the gun.

Warrick jerked his head up, the call so urgent, so visceral, it penetrated his killing fury. He spun to his left, his blade cleaving the nearest demon from shoulder to spleen. Blood geysered out, coating the floor, the wall, far too much for any normal human. It also immediately coalesced into a sooty black slime that would leave the human crime techs unsure, aptly enough, of what the hell had happened in this place. Because for all the residue, there'd be precious few bodies left behind when the Syx were done.

Warrick's gaze swept the dance floor, his ears picking up the sound of the not so distant sirens. Time to go. There wasn't much left for them here anyway. As planned, Hugh and Gregori had hit the room first, their daggers gutting the demons who'd held two of the captives, exploding them into sooty black sludge before they could get their bearings. Then the remainder of the Syx had crossed the threshold of the night club, and with a low command, Raum had dropped all the humans in the room flat. That'd left the Syx squaring off against the Fuerza Negra—forty of them.

Ten-to-one odds, at least until Hugh and Gregori had recovered the second set of hostages. But that was okay. They'd needed the exercise.

And in the end, the Fuerza Negra hadn't been the pushovers Warrick had been expecting. Their humans fought alongside them, bullets ripping open skin and shearing bone, but ultimately not harmful to the Syx. But they were distracting, and that made fighting the horde more challenging. More, the Fuerza Negra battled with a frenzy he normally didn't encounter in his own kind. Something here was different. Dangerously different. Different in a way he'd have to figure out before too much longer, though not in a way that mattered for this particular horde.

But now —

The call came again. *"Sword of God, defend us — "*

The words were ancient, arcane. And he could no more ignore them than he could stop breathing in this plane.

Lots of people prayed for deliverance from the hands of their oppressors. Most of the time, it did them no good. Death dealt by the hands of the children of God unto their own kind was their own problem. But for Warrick to hear this call meant there was a demon in the mix, a demon who was either in the process of killing a human or who'd brought one to harm. And that was all the requirement needed.

"Defend us all."

Warrick burst out of the gore-soaked Mexican nightclub and shot through time and space toward another pit of death, this one a cramped room crowded with men who stank of adrenaline, their bodies decaying with booze and drugs. There was nowhere to hide in this room, so Warrick poured himself into the thin air behind the summoner.

Demons could change their appearance at will, adopting whatever façade, or glamour, worked best for the situation. Right now, what worked best was for him to be invisible. Further, the bright light of the mortal soul who'd called Warrick blocked his shadow from his own kind; as long as he was with his summoner, demons couldn't see him.

But he could see them.

There were two demons standing in close proximity, but only one that he had the right to obliterate this night. Warrick narrowed his eyes, took in the other details of the room. The woman in front of him — her head coming up to his chin, her long hair smelling of sky — held a gun in a rock-steady hand, her aim unflinching. Warrick sighted it, saw the trajectory. He'd assumed she was going to kill the bound human, but she wasn't aiming at the human. She was aiming at the demon.

That wouldn't do her any good. The demon wouldn't fall. Wouldn't die. Would barely notice the impact.

"Sword of God, defend me –" The words rang in Warrick's mind, demanding. He didn't know what this woman was doing in this cesspool, or why she had the gun. Everything about this felt wrong.

He reached out with a flick of his senses, touching the mind of the shooter—and was instantly rebuffed. She was shielded from him, the cross at her neck an effective ward. Still, because she'd summoned him, he could see at least snatches of her thoughts. This club, this room… It was a cesspool of humanity, not just drug runners but drug manufacturers as well, creating some new flavor of poison to unleash on the world.

The shooter's mind held other memories too, vivid enough to leak through. A girl bleeding to death in her arms. Fear, loss…shame. So much shame that she hadn't done what she could have—what she should have—to save someone she loved.

And, Warrick realized, *this* was why the summons had come to him, not the others. Because he also should have done more to save someone he loved, six thousand years ago. He hadn't. Instead, he'd committed the sin that had damned him for an eternity as a demon. Which made this call a brutal, mocking reminder of his failure that night so long ago.

Rage crackled through him.

"Go ahead, shoot," the demon to his right said. He was watching the human hungrily. Eagerly almost. He wanted her to commit the sin of murder. Wanted it bad enough that he was vibrating with the desire. He was smart, clearly. More than that, he was ancient. He'd learned how to avoid harming humans directly. Instead, he'd yank them all the way up to the brink, then let them damn themselves. Smart.

But the woman... Warrick focused on her. Her hand didn't shake, but her stomach roiled. She was no stone-cold killer. She didn't know she couldn't harm the demon in front of her; she was going to take the shot anyway. And she was going to fail.

But he wouldn't.

Warrick lifted his own arm, wrapped his hand around the woman's as she took final aim. A hard grin flashed across Warrick's face as the demon across the room blinked, surprise touching his flickering green eyes—

They fired.

CHAPTER TWO

Maria almost jumped out of her skin, but though she hadn't fired the first shot—*knew* she hadn't—she saw the bloom of blood at center mass of the man's chest. She shot again, twice, in quick succession, both shots deliberately high and wide. Partly in reaction, partly to discharge the firearm so it wasn't cold when Cedo took it from her. But as the man collapsed, the dancer he was holding screamed, abruptly coming out of her drug- or alcohol-induced haze, some feral instinct toward self-preservation finally kicking in.

As the members of the Guardia standing near the woman grabbed her and surged back, not expecting the cascade of bullets, Maria spun. She caught sight of something hazy shifting quickly between her and Cedo, glowing amber lights flashing bright. Then that was gone too, and only Cedo remained.

Cedo, for his part, was staring dumbfounded at the hole in the man's chest. Then he snapped his gaze to Maria. "Who *are* you?" he asked, though his tone was more surprised than accusatory. He shook his head, hard. "You can't do that."

"You wanted me to shoot, I shot. You didn't say who," Maria said, pitching her voice loud with a bravado she didn't feel. The man on the floor writhed in what seemed like real agony, but no one leapt to his aid. No one got close, in fact. *What the hell?* "Who is he?"

Cedo's lips twitched into a grim smile, but his skin stayed firmly on his face, thank God. "Not one of ours, not officially. He latched on to the boys, wanted in on the party. Even picked the girl."

The dancer was being hauled out of the room, passed out. Whether she got that way on her own or someone helped her, Maria wasn't sure.

An unholy gargle of pain came from the floor. Maria looked back, then stared. "What's wrong with him?"

Cedo snapped some sort of order, his voice harsh in her ears, but Maria was no longer focused on the lieutenant. Instead, her attention was arrested by the guy on the floor. The guy who would be dead if no one did anything about it. But nobody was moving toward him, the other men hanging back, all of them staring with the same level of confusion she had. Confusion and horror, really, which made Maria want to sag in relief. She wasn't the only one seeing what was happening to this guy, at least. Watching the blood that spouted from his chest turn black and strangely…thick.

Another man burst into the room, ran right up to the injured guy, knelt down. But he didn't touch the guy either. A few of the Guardia's lower-ranking thugs slipped out the door. Cedo didn't make any move to leave, and Maria couldn't leave if she wanted to. She was frozen in some kind of thrall.

"What in the…" Despite herself, Maria edged forward, closer to the fallen man, her hand stealing once more to the cross around her neck. As the man twisted and writhed on the floor, his pain obvious, his skin didn't just shift, it seemed to *evaporate* for whole seconds at a time, leaving the body beneath it exposed. A body that was far more monster than man, withered, white, covered in scars, with three sets of arms and two sets of legs and—

Focus!

Maria ruthlessly jerked her attention back in line, and the man once again appeared human. A human in grave condition, which put Maria in a bad position. Even if she couldn't admit to it, she was a cop. She couldn't let this man die on the floor, no matter how much of a scum sucker he was. But she also couldn't help him, not without Cedo's tacit permission. Otherwise, this entire charade would be for nothing.

She turned to the Guardia lieutenant. "You want me to finish him off?" she asked, pointing to the gun he'd pulled out of her hand.

"Yeah. No need for that, I'm thinking," said the guy crouching beside the bleeding man. "Son of a bitch."

Maria glanced back, then stared. The injured man had stopped moving, but that didn't mean he was done changing. Something dark and foul rose up out of the blood that had spewed from his body, as toxic as city smoke. It shuddered in the air, then dissipated—but it left something behind too. A thick black stain now surrounded the man, as if he'd fallen in tar.

Maria recoiled. "What in the *hell*…?"

"Hey! I've seen that before."

Pablo, the overeager recruit, was one of the few men remaining in the back room. He stared, wide-eyed, at the corpse on the floor, and his mouth started going a mile a minute. "Down on Seventh, at Jackal's, there was a big fight two, three days ago. Bunch of new guys hit the bar, acted like they owned the place, only, you know, that's already the Cinquo's turf. And they didn't appreciate the competition, took 'em out cold. That— that stuff that's on the floor there? That shit was *everywhere* at Jackal's. The next day, it was still there. Took all weekend to get cleaned up, and the guy at

Jackal's said it wasn't because they found something that finally worked. They'd simply shut up the bar for a couple of days, locked the doors to let things chill out. When they came back, it was gone."

"They know what it was?" Maria asked. She edged forward, dragged her boot across the thick puddle of residue. It left an oily streak across the floor.

"Not a clue." Pablo shrugged. "Maybe there's something's in the water."

She snorted and could feel Cedo's gaze on her. She needed to play this cool, but she was mostly confused. Between what she'd seen and how she felt about killing, if she'd actually shot the guy, Maria was pretty sure she'd be throwing up right now. She hadn't shot him, though. She hadn't pulled the trigger the first time, no way. Someone else must have shot the guy at exactly the same time.

But who?

The man on the floor leaned back. Then he raised his head, his gaze shearing off Maria's face to focus on Cedo. "You see it happen?" he asked, as if anyone could've missed it.

The two exchanged a look that Maria couldn't interpret.

"I saw it," Cedo said. "And I want to understand it." He reached out and grabbed Maria by the arm, yanking her around to focus on him. "How the hell did you do that?"

She stared back, fresh panic knotting in her gut. She couldn't tell the story of a second gunman. That would make her sound insane. But Cedo wanted an answer, and for once, his eyes weren't wild — merely furious.

"What are you talking about?" Maria blustered, to buy herself time. "You gave me the gun. What did you think I was going to do with it?"

"I *thought* you were going to shoot the girl."

"Well then, you should have told me that. This guy looked like the bigger scumbag, and I didn't recognize him. He's not one of yours, you said."

Cedo scoffed a short laugh. "He sure as hell isn't. But he also isn't one to be dropped easily."

"He shouldn't have been dropped at all." The other man was still on his knees, but he'd scooted at least three feet away from the wounded man, probably to avoid the spreading black stain. He glanced back at Cedo. "This ain't gonna look good, if we get asked."

"We're not going to get asked." Cedo's voice had abruptly shifted into tones of cool calculation, the mark of a practiced problem solver. "If we do, you're the one who took the shot. Say the guy was spilling his guts to the wrong people."

"That'll work."

"He had to be on something," Cedo mused, shaking his head. "Only way it's possible. If he was high...sick..."

"That's gotta be it." The guy on his knees now stood, his voice taking on an eager edge. "No way to explain it otherwise. Gotta be it. Sampling the merchandise."

Maria shifted her gaze between them, utterly lost at their byplay. "Look, um, I'm sorry I shot the wrong guy."

"Don't be," Cedo said, turning to her. By some miracle, he'd lost the scowl, though his gaze remained far too curious. "Bonnie was an asshole. And, bottom line, you took the shot. You passed."

Maria felt an almost queasy sense of relief spill through her, and she offered up a grateful smile of her own before remembering to shutter her face. Too late, she caught the flare of interest in Cedo's eyes. *Uh-oh.*

"If you're done with me, then, I'm out," she said. "You need me, you can find me at the gym."

The subtle reminder wasn't lost on him, she knew. Lucy's gym was where she'd met Jack. Jack, her *boyfriend*, as far as Cedo knew. But of course, Jack was gone, picked up by the cops. No one was worried he'd spill, given the number of times he'd gone to jail and the number of years he'd been with the gang, but no one expected him back anytime soon either. Which changed things.

"I'll find you at the gym," Cedo said, and his smile had morphed into a slow grin now, slow and a little too meaningful. *Great.* "And you better believe we're going to need you. But for the next few days, you watch your back. You see anyone following you, you let me know. I'll put some guys on you to watch."

Maria frowned. That was an unusual display of camaraderie, even if she had just shot at someone to prove her worth. "Why?"

Cedo nodded toward the guy on the floor. The guy who was no longer moving, Maria tried not to notice. "Because like I said, Bonnie here, he isn't one of ours. He belongs to la Noche. And even though I'm willing to bet he was doped up on something, you *did* drop the guy, and you shouldn't have. If Takio asks the wrong person about it and gets an answer he don't like, he might come looking for you."

Excitement and panic squirreled through Maria at the sound of Takio's name. "Maybe, um, maybe this Bonnie guy wasn't expecting the bullet." She shrugged, trying desperately to sound calm, controlled. "He zigged when he should have zagged."

"Don't matter what the reason is so much as what *Takio* believes the reason is." Cedo said. "We're gonna let everyone know the story, but that'll take time. Until then, watch your back, yeah? And I'll watch your front."

Cedo's gaze dropped to Maria's chest, lingered there for a long moment. Beside her, Pablo snickered loud enough she wanted to punch him. Cedo had three or four girlfriends already on his string...but it certainly looked like he was about to go fishing again.

"Will do." Maria turned on her heel. *Just freaking great.*

The city of Las Vegas in December glittered even more than it usually did, the desperate flash and sizzle of the Christmas holidays turning the garish neon lights into violently shifting shades of red and green. It wasn't bad during the day, but at night, it was madness.

Warrick stood in front of one of the older casinos on the Strip, a slightly tired-looking Treasure Island. He wasn't there for the gambling, though. He wasn't even there for the casino but for what stretched above it. A phantom white tower most humans couldn't see, at least those who didn't possess any psychic skills.

When he and the rest of his team had forced their way back to this plane the previous summer, on the back of one of the strongest living human psychics on Earth, they hadn't known what to expect. It certainly hadn't been the glitter ball of a city that Vegas had provided, though Warrick and the Syx had holed up on the Strip easily enough. The psychic who'd sprung them wasn't the only sorcerer in town, it turned out. There was also the man who'd sent her into the Syx's bolt-hole beyond the veil, Viktor Dal—also known in this plane as the Emperor.

Not any ordinary emperor either. No, this guy was part of a council of sorcerers whose magic was tied to the metaphysical power of the Tarot. So when Viktor said he was the Emperor, he meant the *Major Arcana* Emperor, with all that card's attendant skills: charisma, dominance, brute force. Over the millennia, there'd been as many as a dozen members of the Arcana Council, each of them tied to a Major Arcana card. They represented the most powerful sorcerers on Earth. When they worked together, some whispered, they were more powerful than the gods.

Warrick snorted, thinking about that. The gods, maybe. But not his God.

Still, that didn't mean that these sorcerers weren't trouble, and the Syx knew the Emperor well. Knew him and had been screwed over by him already once in the past century. That wasn't going to happen a second time.

Given his highly inflated opinion of himself, the Emperor had fully expected to keep the Syx under his thumb during their stay in Vegas, at least until he could figure out how to double-cross them again. But Warrick had bigger problems than Viktor Dal, now. Yes, he and his team were back, temporarily freed from their prison to walk the earth anew. But as he was quickly learning, on this plane, there were still two entities he needed to worry about—both of them members of the Council, both of them heavy hitters of the Tarot. Both of them powerful enough to stuff him and the Syx back beyond the veil with the barest twitch of their fingers.

Death and the Hierophant.

This incarnation of Death, a former druid priestess, had served on the Arcana Council for two thousand years. She'd mostly left the Syx alone, though by rights, in her role as Death she could command them to hunt demons at will. The Hierophant, however, had been around longer...a lot longer. And his connection to the demon horde was most definitely personal. So, with the recent release of so many more demons into the back alleys and dark corners of the planet, Warrick had known the Hierophant would come calling soon enough.

And now it was apparently time.

Warrick twisted his lips into a sneer. *Hierophant.* Why the archangel Michael, God's most favored warrior, had bothered to join the largely human construct of the Arcana Council, Warrick had no idea, but damned if he hadn't served in that capacity for thousands of years now. The archangel had taken on the role of Hierophant of the Arcana Council at the breaking of the world, when Atlantis had fallen and the sorcerers of the planet had surged together to push out the gods and goddesses that had sought to rule them so tightly. It'd worked too, against all odds. The Arcana Council had formed a protective veil around the world, then banished beyond that veil not only the deities but their minions and lieutenants as well, including most of the hordes of demons that had run rampant over the earth. Most of them. Some demons had gotten lucky and missed the purge, hiding out for centuries until it was safe enough to creep out of the shadows. Some, like Warrick and the Syx, had agreed to track down and eradicate those who stepped too far out of line. It'd been an imperfect solution, but the only one open to them. Warrick and his team had always known they were living on borrowed time, able to taste the sunshine of this earth but not savor it. Constantly forced to remember that theirs was not a life to be lived as one of God's chosen.

They'd given up that privilege long ago.

But he and the Syx had served ably and well, never ignoring a single call, no matter who had uttered it.

And in all the millennia since the veil had first been cast between the humans and the gods, never once had the archangel summoned him directly. Any of them.

Until now.

"Trap?" Raum murmured. Warrick shrugged.

"No point. He can send us back with a blink. A trap might entertain him, but I don't think so."

"Well, he's not going to simply let us walk free."

Warrick snorted. "Not likely."

They entered the lobby of Treasure Island, not drawing the attention they should have, given their height and bulk, but that was by design. If someone glanced at them and they had no problem being seen, they appeared to be men of above-average size, walking easily along the brightly lit gold-toned carpets and glittering tiles. If someone focused harder, they would see the demons' added height, stouter frames. If the Syx didn't want to be seen by humans—they simply weren't. That level of discretion had long served them well, but life was proving more complicated to navigate now that they'd been on this plane full-time for the past several months. If they stayed, they'd need to come up with more consistent protocol.

If they stayed…

Warrick grimaced. There was only one person who could grant them that benediction, and he was the avowed enemy of their entire race.

Again…not likely.

They didn't stop until they got to the corridor of elevator bays. The casino opened up at the far end of the hallway, but that wasn't their target. Warrick and Raum needed to go up—way up. It didn't take much to find the elevator they needed. The bay was between two light-gold-toned elevator doors and was an eye-searing white. It would've blinded most humans, if they could see it. Fortunately, only a few of them could.

The doors opened before they reached them, and without looking around to see if anyone was watching them, Warrick and Raum stepped inside. The portal whispered shut, and the carriage shot skyward.

A blink later and the doors opened onto an austerely simple chamber. Onyx-toned floors, gray walls and ceiling, a fire burning in the grate at the far end of the room. No windows. The archangel stood next to the fire, but to Warrick's surprise, he wasn't alone.

Raum muttered something low beside him, but neither of them hesitated as they stalked forward. If Death wanted to sit in on their summons, that was her right. Again, she was a member of the same Council that had once successfully banished more than ninety percent of demons from the earth. Since then, though she didn't like to noise it around, she'd been the first line of offense on the ground for humans facing demons, giving mortals the words they needed to summon the Syx. Now, the Syx were on the ground as well.

The sooner they got this meeting over with, the sooner Warrick could get back to the demands of those humans. Demands that were coming in at an ever-increasing clip. Neither the archangel nor Death would do anything that would keep the Syx from their job, surely.

Warrick stuffed that thought back down as quickly as it rose, willing himself to indifference. If he'd learned anything during his millennia of service, it was that nothing was assured.

He and Raum reached the far end of the room, then stood at attention before the archangel. They didn't bow, and they sure as hell didn't kneel. Neither did the archangel expect them to.

Instead, the Hierophant regarded them with his eerily light eyes. Everything about the man was light, from his alabaster skin to his pale blond hair to his bloodless lips. He didn't sprout wings, but he didn't need to. He was as stainless and blameless as one of God's warriors should be.

In contrast, Warrick felt like the sins of his brethren were soaked into his bones.

"You were noticed." The archangel's voice was low, resonant. His words rolled along the stone surfaces of the meeting chamber, then back again, echoing onto themselves. Warrick tensed. The ancient trick of demon entrapment was still successful all these centuries later.

"We weren't trying to hide," Warrick said, his own harsh voice cutting through the shushing echoes of the archangel's rebuke. "The more the horde knows we're here, within easy reach, the more they'll think twice before taking another life."

"The more they'll hide as well." It was Death who interjected, her arms folded over her chest. Warrick shifted his gaze to her. She was beautiful in the ways of the ancients, her clear eyes and hard jaw unforgiving, her body straight and tall. She was dressed in ripped jeans and a paint-stained T-shirt, her feet shoved into heavy work boots. In contrast, the archangel's robes were pure white, like everything else about him. To interact with the modern mortal world, Death had taken on the guise of a tattoo artist and some sort of painter. Warrick didn't understand it, but he didn't need to.

"We assumed the demons going to ground would be preferable to them taking the lives of the innocent."

Michael interjected. "For now, yes. But there are too many of them. Too many of the filth set free."

Warrick eyed the archangel steadily—Michael couldn't blame the Syx for summoning the demons. They'd been as surprised as the rest of the world. "That's not our doing," he growled, remembering the strangeness he'd felt as the new hordes had breached the veil. "But their arrival changes things. We noticed it in Acapulco. The entire demon population on Earth is amping up."

"Then all the more reason for you to amp up as

well," Death said. The archangel looked mutinous, but he didn't speak as she continued. "You must redeem yourself, Warrick, you and your team. If you gain that redemption, you can stay on Earth to tackle the new hordes that have invaded this plane. If you don't…" She shrugged, her gaze not leaving him. "We don't have the luxury of time. We'll find someone to replace you."

Beside him, Raum hissed.

"Replace us?" Warrick said. "No one else has fought so hard or so long."

"And no one else is as close to repaying their debt as the Syx," Death agreed. "It's the only reason you're being given the chance. But trust me, you're not the only demon who craves a return to this plane. A permanent return. We would give you that and the knowledge that you cannot be banished by anyone's hand—*anyone* on this earth," she said, sending the archangel a cold look. "But you must each repent of your sin. And you must be forgiven."

Warrick could hear a low rumble of anger, realized it was coming from him. "There is no repentance for our sins," he said, his words little more than a snarl. "So we have always been told, so we have always known as truth."

"Careful, *Warrick*," the archangel said, his cold gaze now narrowing. "You ever want to return to the full name the Father gave you, you will open your mind and your heart to the task we set before you. Because if any one of you fails—all of you fail."

Death stiffened, clearly surprised, but she didn't speak. Warrick clenched his hands. He had given up his creation name when he had fallen. There was no going back to that.

However, there was also no denying how still Raum had gone beside him. Raum, once one of the heavens' most beloved of angels, who'd been cruelly torn from the celestial ramparts for a crime he could not help but commit. For Raum, for the rest of his team, Warrick could do what was necessary.

"What do you require?" he asked levelly.

"I require you to do your job," the archangel retorted. "Your last summons, the job was not complete. You'll return."

Warrick frowned. "The last... We left them all dead."

"Not that one." The archangel waved his hand. "Los Angeles. The drug lord filth known as Takio, the demon whose lieutenant you killed. The new technoceutical this Takio is producing must be destroyed—and he must be banished as well. Once and for all."

"I don't understand." Unbidden, the images flashed before his eyes, barely out of reach, the images in the mind of the female with the hair that smelled of sky. But she'd been warded by the cross at her neck, and Warrick hadn't been able to see much of her thoughts. Certainly nothing about a technoceutical, which were quasi-organic, quasi-synthetic drugs popular with a particular cross section of present-day Earth's population—the very rich, and the very psychic. Still, he could feel Death's gaze on him, and he glared at her. "Who is Takio?" he growled.

Death held his stare. "You would know this demon as Holkeri," she said quietly.

Warrick's sight went white.

CHAPTER THREE

Maria slung her bag to the table, then wearily stumbled past the counter and into her kitchen, which was about the size of a sneeze. The third-story walk-up was short on character but long on security, perfect for her cover story of high school dropout and abuse survivor who was making ends meet and both exercising and exorcising her demons in a minimum-wage job at Lucy's boxing gym. She pulled out a bottle of wine from the cabinet, then grabbed the carton of leftover Chinese food from the fridge, settling both on the counter with a clatter. A stack of envelopes lay unopened, untouched, and she swept her gaze around the rest of the apartment, taking it in with practiced focus.

No one had been in her place. She knew it, had known it the moment she walked in, but she still double-checked every time, if only to keep herself honest. She was a big proponent of using her innate intuition as part of her chosen profession, but she never wanted to rely too heavily on it. Not when she also had eyes in her head to see, a nose to smell, ears to hear.

She poured a glass of wine, her hair still damp from her hasty shower at Lucy's. After all these years, she still didn't like showering in tight, enclosed spaces. Give her a concrete block with a row full of spigots and a second exit door every time. She could move in that kind of space. She could kick and fight. She could escape.

She never again wanted to be in a place where she couldn't again.

Maria pulled a set of chopsticks from the cup on the counter, then carried her dinner to the threadbare couch. She couldn't afford a computer — too easy to steal when she wasn't around, and probably not something her pay grade would allow. Her basic tablet was mainly for show, something to surf the internet with, little more.

Now she eyed it. No one would question her for a search history on what she'd seen yesterday. No matter how hard she'd pounded the bag at the gym, she couldn't get it out of her mind. All that black goop... It had to be the Bonnie guy's body releasing toxins of some sort, like Cedo had said, and that had given her an idea. An idea she'd latched on to with both hands.

Though she was willing to believe she'd imagined Bonnie's crazy eyes because of her own fear and adrenaline, the changes she'd seen happening to the guy's body...maybe that *was* the result of the drugs Cedo and his goon seemed to think Bonnie was taking. That made a certain sort of sense. If Bonnie's blood had been doped up and emitted toxins into the air that caused hallucinations, that could explain what she saw — particularly the extra arms and legs bit. And maybe the drug Bonnie had taken was this mysterious concoction that everyone thought Takio was cooking up.

"Toxins," Maria muttered. She bit her lip, thinking it through for the fifty thousandth time as she slurped up the cold, salty noodles...and liking the explanation more and more. It could be possible.

If so, it made her job more important than ever. She wasn't the only one who'd seen the goop in Bonnie's blood. Pablo had too—and not for the first time, apparently. That meant it had gone public—at least in this very tight-knit community. Maria needed to let her superiors know that they might be on the verge of a major outbreak of something seriously bad…and that they needed to contain it, whatever it was. She also needed to make sure it hadn't already made an appearance somewhere else.

Maria pulled her ancient tablet over, engaged her hotspot, and painstakingly keyed in a search for unusually dark or black blood. Then she started clicking links. Ten minutes later, wine in hand, she was still clicking, but she was so far down a rabbit hole, she gave up.

"Stupid freaks," she muttered, taking another swig. It was something out of a low-rent Comic-Con—possessed humans, spaceship abductions, demons walking the earth. All she wanted was a straightforward drug reaction, and instead she got the X-Files.

Her phone beeped then, and she set down her glass, studied the device. Text, not email. You couldn't recover deleted texts without a warrant, and even then, it was sketchy on certain devices. The text was from a department store, announcing a 20% off sale, and Maria pursed her lips at the coded message. Stan, her contact inside the LAPD, wanted to see her. She wasn't due for a check-in for another two weeks. Why would Stan need to meet with her so close to Jack's pickup? It didn't feel right.

Did Jack rat me out? There was no way to know, but she didn't think so. She hadn't been under all that long on this job, and if Jack had turned, she'd likely have already been taken out. As quickly as people died in this neighborhood, turnover in the gangs was quick and often brutal. But Jack had been with the Guardia for a long time. He'd vouched for her, and that had carried weight. In truth, given how well respected he was, Maria had expected it to be harder to flip him. But Jack had been spooked about something before Maria had even shown up at his door. Big-time spooked.

Now she thought about the black goop on the floor at the nightclub. Had Jack seen more than he'd let on? Here she'd thought she'd scored a coup getting him off the circuit, pumping him for intel. But had he been so ready and willing to break for a reason?

Maybe police protection had been the answer to his prayers.

Maria went over it all again in her mind. She'd started working in the gym five months ago, instantly catching Jack's eye as she'd planned. But she'd had to beat him flat twice before he'd so much as talk to her. It'd taken another four months to get the Guardia lieutenant to turn. Four long months of sparring that had shaped her already lean physique into hammered iron. Jack had liked that, had liked her. Drugs had ruined his ability to make love and had also tanked his libido, but that was a secret no one in the gang knew. And once Jack had told Maria that and had found in her a sympathetic ear…the other secrets had come fast and furious. He'd been the biggest break she'd gotten in her search for Takio in years. Because after she'd been given approval to reveal that she was a cop and she'd brought Jack in, Jack had given up intel on anyone and everyone in the gang. In return, he'd get to walk free when this was done. Thanks to Jack, Maria was that much closer to the man responsible for killing Cara.

Or was she? What was really going on with this gang?

No response was needed to the text, of course. This was a one-way communication. Instead, Maria found her hand lifting to Cara's necklace. Almost without thinking about it, she stood and drifted over to the plywood bookshelf, then pulled out the box of photos she kept there. The photos were a nice touch, she thought. For anyone who'd come snooping around, they showed that Maria was a simple girl from this same neighborhood, and that she cared about family. No one would ever look too close, but if they did, they'd see her as a young girl, playing with her friends, her family, her...

Maria paused as she stopped on a picture of Cara. Cara had been barely ten years old in the photo, five full years before she'd died, already in and out of trouble. But beautiful — so beautiful. She'd fairly radiated with life and energy. And this picture had been taken at a park not ten blocks away from where Maria was sitting now. The place was now gang territory, but back then, it'd been an oasis. Clean and open and remarkably trash free, at least on that morning. The kids were all in dresses, even Maria, bouncing around, little more than five years old. Cara had a basket filled with brightly colored plastic eggs. Maria couldn't quite remember that day. She'd been so young, and so much had happened after it. Her mother's death, moving in with her aunt. Cara dying in her black patent leather Mary Janes. Everyone drifting away like ghosts on the hot breeze.

But on this day, everything had been good and full and...

Maria stopped, then picked up the photo, studying it more closely as she fingered Cara's cross with her other hand. Cara wasn't wearing the cross in this photo — there was no sign of a tattoo on her either. But then, she'd been only ten. Behind her and Maria, there was a crowd of parents — what she assumed were parents — standing in the background, watching the kids. Laughing, chatting.

And there was a man in their midst too. He didn't look out of place, exactly, though his suit was all wrong. Where every other adult in the picture wore khakis and pastel or white polo shirts, this man was in a suit with an actual tie. That seemed a little intense. Everything about the man struck her as a little too intense, actually. Intense and…weirdly familiar.

She blinked, making the connection. It was his eyes…he had the same weird eyes that Bonnie had, that she'd seen — maybe — in Cedo as well. Were they all on the same kind of drugs? Maybe not the newest strain that had damaged Bonnie so obviously, but something that affected their eyes? Something she'd seen…and that Cara'd seen too? Maria frowned, looking from the picture back to her tablet, then realized her other hand remained lifted, her fingers still playing with Cara's tiny gold cross. She dropped the pendant back to her neck, ran her hand through her still-damp hair. Tonight wasn't a good night for her to be thinking of the past like this. The girls and boys in their brightly colored Easter outfits, the parents laughing, clearly relaxed, having a good time. In this picture, Cara still looked happy and Maria's mom was still alive. It was the kind of picture that made you believe everything was going to work out fine.

Maria sighed, then dropped the picture back in its box. She was tired, she thought. She needed to get more sleep — especially with Jack picked up and given Maria's new status with the Guardia. She needed to be extra careful going forward, and she needed her sleep.

"I miss you, Cara," she whispered, putting the box back on the shelf.

Then she went back to her bottle of wine.

Warrick crunched across the broken glass in the parking lot beneath the hot Los Angeles sun — unusually hot for this time of year, he was given to understand, especially for LA at Christmas. He had been to the city so many times in the last two centuries, he should have an opinion on it. But the truth was, his times on Earth all blurred together, even when he didn't want them to. He remembered moments, crystalline shards of time, that stuck out like diamonds amid the endless sand falling through the hourglass. A mother's face wet with tears and hope, a father falling to his knees, the surprise — and it was always surprise, in the end — of one of the horde realizing that Warrick was going to make good on his threat of banishment after all. That he wasn't going to change his mind at the last second and go dark.

He'd gone dark a long time ago. He still was dark. That didn't change his job.

A horn blared too close, and Warrick turned and scowled as the car he'd cut off screeched to a halt. As usual with these things, time slowed, fragmented. The horn becoming separate motes in the air, floating almost casually forward. The rush of the vehicle reduced to the barest inching forward, the movement scarcely detectible, while Warrick turned easily, taking in the two males in the vehicle. They were young, laughing, hats askew on their heads, bulky jackets obscuring too-thin, almost emaciated bodies, gaunt cheeks, hollow eyes, the stain of ink crawling up their necks and playing over the fingers of the hands grabbing the wheel. The driver was grinning, his teeth mottled and broken, already showing the impact of his meth addiction.

God's children.

Warrick curled his lip. He extended a hand, flipping

his fingers slightly — only slightly. He wouldn't kill the idiots. They were doing a good enough job of that on their own without his help. But neither could he tolerate their foul weaponized vehicle distracting him from his path. He had too much on his mind.

The car spun away from him, executing a full one-eighty that should have been impossible in the tight lane between the stacked-up vehicles. But nothing was impossible for a demon. Almost nothing, anyway.

Not everything was illusion.

Time rushed forward once more, and there was a scream, the release of ammonia in the fetid air, the screech of brakes too late applied as the human's car bucked and coughed. Some of the humans in the lot had seen. Warrick could feel their shocked gazes going from him to the car that now lurched away at increasing speed. He didn't care if they saw. He hadn't fully worked out his glamour yet, but when he did, they would remember what he wanted them to remember.

Not everything was illusion. But when it came to human perception, most of it was.

He entered the cavernous mall and tasted decay, depression. Less death, he thought, than the precipitous human decline of the will to live. Several stores down the long, brightly lit corridor were empty, gates of twisted metal spires shuttering them off from the remaining life in the mall. There were more people inside than he expected, but still fewer than there should have been given how crowded the parking lot was. Too many people were jammed together in this city, he thought. Jammed together and broken apart at the same time.

The large anchor store at the far end of the mall carried the heat signature he was looking for. Male, thick and marbled with fat, his heart muscle strained nearly to the breaking point with too much sugar and too much caffeine, disease only now beginning to worm through it. Wouldn't even be noticed for a few more years, Warrick thought, and picked up the twitchiness of Stanley Harris's hands. The police sargeant wasn't carrying, and he wasn't used to not carrying. And the mall cameras made him nervous. He was worried about the cameras catching his image.

Warrick shifted glamour midstride, assuming the appearance of a middle-aged woman in nurse's scrubs as he stepped closer to Harris and the woman who was nearest to him, the shooter from the other night. Both of them pawed through a rack of men's clothing.

Warrick had gleaned a lot of information from his brief interview with Stanley Harris — and from his even briefer interaction with Jack Mangia, once Harris had gotten him in to see the Guardia thug, still in police custody. The undercover cop's name was Maria Santos. Warrick would need to figure out what she knew more in depth before this day was over, but the cross was going to make that difficult. It was more than a typical cross, he'd realized, probably specially blessed somewhere along the line.

Fortunately, he didn't need to worry about the woman quite yet. Warrick shifted his gaze to Harris and focused.

The man's demeanor changed immediatly. His features smoothed out, his heart rate dropped, his fingers relaxed their death grip on the light gray men's shirt he'd grabbed from the rack. Slowly, deliberately, he replaced the shirt, then pulled a long-sleeved blue pinstripe free.

"Pardon me," he began, and Maria looked up, her dark eyes flashing despite her easy smile. She wasn't happy, Warrick decided. "Can you help me out with this? I need to make sure it's a good color for me."

She tilted her head. "I think you were better off with your first choice."

From his vantage point in the center of this section, Warrick got his first look at the woman who'd summoned him only two days earlier. Maria Santos was bone-achingly beautiful — though not in any traditional way. Too thin, with a body that looked hard and functional, she currently wore her thick black hair braided and hanging down her back. She was deeply tanned, with a veneer of sunburn in places. Her hands were abused, the knuckles scraped and bloody, the skin bruised.

She stepped closer to Harris and pulled a different shirt. "Or this one."

Now that she was close to him, she lowered her voice and spoke rapidly, but Warrick could hear her without issue. "What's happened?" she demanded. "They bought that Jack was picked up, bought that he was going to be in the tank for a while. If you guys have finished questioning him, he should be halfway to Florida by now."

"It's not him. There's a new operative in play," Harris snapped back, parroting the words Warrick had fed him the day before in his office. "Trained infiltration expert. One of the alphabets sent him down, wanted him dropped in cold."

Maria jerked as if struck. "A *plant*? Are you insane?" she hissed.

"Apparently, whatever la Noche is cooking in that drug lab has people concerned at the highest levels. They want their guy in there to assess the situation. His cover is that he's a buyer from another organization, the Red Spider. He's there to check out the merchandise."

"No way," Maria said, but Warrick could hear the waver in her voice. He'd done his homework. The Spider was an infrequent but high-dollar customer of la

43

Noche. If the gang was creating something new and hot, they'd want in. And it wasn't unreasonable they'd want to know exactly how new and how hot the product was.

Still, Maria wasn't quite ready to give up. "These guys do not play around, Stan. They'll spot a Fed trying to act like a high-level lieutenant in thirty seconds. They'll pop him before he clears the first door."

"Which is why you're getting him through those doors. He says he can convince them once he's in, and I've met him. He can." Harris fixed Maria with a hard gaze. "It's not like you don't have a mess of your own to fix. We got word of the casualty. Guy died right on the floor of that club. In front of you, word has it."

"Not my fault, not my gun," Maria asserted emphatically. "You won't have any way of checking, but my conscience is clear. I did not kill that man." She shook her head. "Honest to God, I don't know who did. He bled out way too fast, and then…"

Harris looked at her sharply. "And what?"

"There was something…weird about the way he died. You guys getting wind of any sort of drug interaction that messes up the blood? I mean, really messes it up?"

"That would be every single drug out there right now."

"This one's different," Maria countered. "And since you're saddling me with this new guy, you owe me. Look up incidences of deaths with evidence of thick black emissions from the deceased, like blood that's been mixed with crushed coal. Check the coroner's office. They'd know."

Harris still held the shirt, narrowing his eyes at her. "And this matters why?"

"Because the dead guy didn't simply go down. He dropped way too fast, then spewed enough blood for three guys. On the heels of the blood that spilled out of his chest, there was…" She flapped her hand. "I don't know how to describe it other than as black goop. But I saw it with my own eyes, and another guy in the room said that he'd seen it a few days earlier at a club called Jackal's. I think we may have a bad strain of pills or crack or — something, in the city, and it's going to incite panic if we don't brace people for it."

Harris made a face. "I don't see how — "

"Just check it, Stan. Least you can do if you're asking me to walk some Fed into the belly of the beast to pass him off as a legit buyer. Where will he make contact, anyway?"

"The gym." Harris sounded like he was surprised to be saying it, but Warrick didn't miss the gleam of interest in Maria's eyes. He'd guessed correctly. He'd show up, spar with her, get them both straight that he wouldn't cause her a problem. Then they'd make a plan to go in.

"Right, okay. Fine." Maria glanced at Harris. "I still think it's a mistake, but with enough confidence, you can pull off anything, I guess." She pointed to the shirt, spoke more loudly. "You going to buy anything else to go with that?"

"No, that should do it," he said, and she nodded as if this was a routine exchange between them, indicating there was nothing more to say. She turned to make her way down the clothing aisle. At the last minute, she stopped and looked back.

"When?" she asked, and Harris shrugged, still looking down at the button-down he was holding, as if now seriously considering the purchase.

"Give it a few hours. He'll be there."

"Fantastic," Maria muttered. And despite himself, Warrick grinned. She thought he was going to be a liability, but that was only fair. She hadn't met him yet.

He wouldn't need long to change her mind.

CHAPTER FOUR

Maria sagged against the heavy bag, her lungs heaving. She'd long since figured out that Stan's "few hours" apparently meant "whenever the Fed feels like showing up."

It wasn't so much that she was eager to meet the guy, but she was eager to figure out what the hell it was he thought he'd accomplish. A buyer for the Red Spider? She'd barely heard of the organization, and she wasn't about to bring up the name to Cedo before the guy made his appearance. She'd have to be doubly careful, especially if Cedo's warning from two nights back was true. She'd taken out one of Takio's guys, and apparently, that was a coup of some sort. Though she hadn't seen anyone tailing her, Cedo'd been pretty sure that Takio would be pissed. Maybe pissed enough to want to see her. That could be her chance to get inside his inner sanctum, into the heart of the Citadel. Once she got there, she needed to find something big enough, damning enough, that Takio couldn't talk his way out of, despite all his money and guns. Maybe evidence of a drug that turned its victims into black-goop-filled aliens.

Maria grimaced. She had no doubt that someone

else would take up residence in the Citadel the moment Takio vacated it, and in most cases, the new guys ended up being bigger assholes than the old guys. But not this time, she thought. Forget this newest drug—from everything they'd heard on the street, though they could prove nothing, Takio had killed the leaders of at least three rival gangs in the area, and he was rumored to have their heads displayed in the Citadel to keep the locals in line. He'd trafficked women and children into the sex trade. He'd run enough drugs to light up half the northern hemisphere. He was mysterious and deadly and seriously bad news, and he clearly got his rocks off burying himself in the Citadel, where law enforcement would have to come at him through concrete blocks and machine guns instead of driving their cruisers up a long manicured drive and through a stately private gate.

Suddenly, a voice cracked across the stillness of Lucy's, old Charlie's unusually cheerful cry of welcome bouncing off the concrete walls. "Hello, friend. You Warrick?"

"That I am. You must be Charlie."

Maria stiffened, hearing the voices but not processing them correctly. Charlie was as much of a permanent fixture in Lucy's gym as the sweat-stained concrete floors, an old boxer who'd gone from fighter to trainer to cleanup patrol as his body had grown more bent and wizened. He'd never lost his love for the sport, though, and his eyes were still remarkably sharp, despite all the knocks to the head he'd sustained.

He also wasn't big on new faces in the gym. It'd taken him a full month to even acknowledge Maria, yet here he was laughing and chatting with the newcomer as if he was his long-lost friend.

Maria pivoted and focused on the speaker, who stood easily with Charlie while the old man grinned and rubbed his bald head. It was one of Charlie's most endearing habits, as if he was always a little surprised that he didn't have hair anymore. It also showed that Charlie was completely comfortable around the stranger, who hovered over him at easily six foot six.

Definitely no one she'd seen before.

The guy who'd entered Lucy's was a brawler, all right, but unlike most of the boxers who frequented the gym, he looked like he'd been professionally trained. His body was big—and not barbell big. The kind of big that made you think he could just as easily haul himself up a mountain as throw punches into a heavy bag or another man's jaw. Long, sinewy muscles, broad shoulders, powerful legs, tight abs. Which she knew because he was wearing a tank top that was little more than a few artfully arranged strips of cloth that had been ripped to reveal the impressive swath of muscle underneath.

Jack had favored the same kind of tank tops...but this guy carried it off way better than Jack. Maria lifted her hand self-consciously to Cara's gold cross. Was *this* the Fed plant? Because he sure did look like a badass, she had to admit.

As if hearing her thoughts, the man glanced over to her—and practically drilled her to the mat with the force of his eyes. They glowed almost as intently as Bonnie's had in the club. Not quite as crazily—the newcomer's eyes were a steady golden amber, intense and unflinching—but enough that she sure as hell noticed the similarity.

Then the moment passed.

Maria rubbed her hand through her hair, going for nonchalant and failing miserably. This guy was going to be her partner? Mr. Tall, Dark, and Death Row? And what had Charlie called him, Warrick?

Yeah, well. The guy *looked* like he was ready to go to

war, anyway.

With a slap on Charlie's shoulder that left the old man grinning, Warrick turned and sauntered toward her, taking a second to greet the other boxers working out or warming up with the same kind of collegial cheer Jack had always effected so well. Everyone seemed to respond to him the same way Charlie had — open faces, welcoming smiles, easy banter back.

"You must be Maria," Warrick said as he approached.

When she didn't answer, he leaned on the ropes that cordoned off the mat area, glancing around appreciatively. There were two boxing rings shoved into the tiny gym, but those were strictly for sparring. Still, roping off the area where the heavy bags stood gave you the impression you were in the ring, which was good for motivation and keeping boxers in the zone, as well as doubling as extra sparring space.

"I heard you were a good sparring partner," he continued.

"You did, huh?"

"I did. You up for it now?" Warrick pushed down the top rope and swung a leg over as Maria watched. His legs were thicker than those of most amateur boxers too. That group tended to be firm believers that only upper-body workouts in the gym were worth their time. Otherwise, legs were best served with fast-twitch workouts that helped drive speedy footwork. Warrick clearly hadn't gotten that memo, though. The long slabs of muscle that defined his quads and made his calves look like he was a pro cyclist were…impressive.

"You're making me shy." Warrick chuckled, catching her mid-stare.

Maria jerked her gaze back to the guy's face and, partly out of habit, partly out of nerves, she brought her gloved hands up. Warrick had his own powerful fists wrapped, but he wasn't wearing gloves. She and Jack had practiced like this hundreds of times, however, with Jack taking her blows with his wrapped hands. Warrick dropped into a similarly relaxed stance, following her as she circled him.

"You new in town?" she asked. "I'd know if I'd seen you before."

Warrick shrugged and winked at her. "New enough. Care to show me around?"

"Maybe, maybe not."

"Fresh blood!"

Warrick turned at the sound of Lou Celio's voice. The burly man's face broke into a wide grin as he came toward them. "You clearly aren't an idiot either," Lou continued. "Maria's one of the best sparrers we got here. She'll put you through your paces."

"I'm counting on it." Warrick said. "I'm only in town a few days. Heard this place was the only gym worth a damn."

"You got that right."

Warrick sent Lou such a disarming smile, Maria found herself believing that someone *had* told him that, that he really was some random guy looking to blow off some steam. Lou certainly did. The crusty old gym rat stared back at Warrick, as rapt as a thirteen-year-old girl with her first crush. What the hell was going on here?

"You got anything needs doing, Lou?" Maria asked, trying to keep her voice from sounding abrupt and almost succeeding. "I can clean up if so."

"Nah, nah. You two work out. I got things covered today. Nobody'll try anything screwy with Charlie on watch."

"I heard that!" The old man chortled from the back, and despite herself, Maria's heart gave a little tug. Compton wasn't her patch anymore, wasn't anywhere near her patch, but that didn't change the fact that she'd grown up in this area. She'd never stepped foot inside Lucy's gym when she was a kid, but the place still felt a little too much like home.

Maria took a step back, avoiding Warrick's intense gaze. "I'm pretty much done working out," she said. "You should lace up with someone more your size."

"And yet I have my heart set on you. Got some kinks I need to work out." He looked over at Louie. "Can I borrow a spare pair of gloves?"

"That you can." Lou beamed. "Let me get some for you."

Warrick tried not to stare at Maria Santos as he laced up, the gloves a slightly tight fit but nothing he couldn't manage. He wasn't going to be throwing punches so much as taking them, if everything went well here. He mostly wanted to see how the cop handled herself. So far, he wasn't happy. Not because she didn't seem competent...but because she was eyeing him with way too much mistrust.

That rarely happened—had never happened to Warrick, in fact.

He'd taken some time to get as many details as he could about Maria out of Jack. The Guardia lieutenant was a bruiser, a thug, and an alcoholic, but he was mostly tired at this point. He wanted out of the life, and he was grateful for the path Maria had given him. He planned on moving across country and living with his sister's family until he could get on his feet, an offer that had been on the table for some time, or so he'd told the police piously. And in truth, though he'd been in and out of jail often enough over the past two decades, it'd all been for comparatively petty stuff, and he'd served his time. For everything he hadn't, the cops had been willing to look the other way in exchange for information on the Guardia.

Warrick, of course, knew more about Jack than anyone, now. Stan Harris had allowed him thirty minutes with the lieutenant, but he'd only needed five to read the man's mind. Now he knew Jack Mangia's sins, his appetites. Knew his weaknesses too. A lifetime of drugs had taken its toll on Jack's body, but his mind had still been more or less sharp. Warrick believed he'd make good on his promise to the LAPD of good intel, but not because of his sister in Florida.

Florida was simply closer to where Jack had stashed his money.

But now that he was in front of Maria, Warrick could tell she still considered him a problem—a Fed who would no doubt blow her cover. She also wasn't apparently falling for his charisma glamour with anywhere near the same wide-eyed acquiescence that Stan Harris, Charlie, and Lou had. She remained skeptical of him, even after meeting him, and that was…unusual. Unusual and dangerous. Normally, only high-level demons were so discerning.

Since Maria Santos clearly wasn't a demon, that left one of two options. One was that she was an exceptionally skilled psychic, what members of that community currently called a Connected. But Warrick dismissed that possibility out of hand. While he didn't doubt that Maria had some level of intuition, the kind of psychic ability she'd have to have to block his charisma glamour would be fairly epic. If she was that kind of a Connected, she'd be able to levitate school buses.

Which left Warrick with the little gold cross around her neck. Not a completely plain cross either, but one that had a small circle of gold behind its crossed bars.

All religious symbols held some sort of power, but this…this was something different. It had to have been blessed by a holy man or woman, someone of pretty impressive faith too. There was simply no other explanation.

"You ready?" Maria asked brusquely, already up in one of the main fighting rings.

"Always." Warrick said. He hauled himself up into the ring and didn't miss the flare of heat in Maria's eyes. She wasn't *entirely* studying him with irritation, that was for sure.

They began circling almost immediately. "Whaddya want?" Maria asked, the tone in her voice wry, as if she had no idea what he might hit her with.

"You strike," he instructed. "Whatever you got, I want to see."

Her eyes narrowed as she took a couple of experimental shots, which he blocked easily. "I'm not the one on trial here," she grumbled. Warrick watched as Lou and Charlie moved toward the front of the gym. The other guys had cleared out, so now, other than the owner and the caretaker, they were currently alone in Lucy's. Still, that didn't mean he could let his guard down. Anything they said could be overheard.

Maria seemed to think so too. Her next question was carefully vague.

"So, Warrick, huh? You're just gonna waltz on in and take a look around, see what there is to be seen?"

"That's sort of the idea. Jack and I chatted, and he said you'd be cool with it."

That information made something flicker in her eyes. Disbelief? Yet more wariness? "Uh-huh. Why now? The Guardia and la Noche have been cooking this new dish at the Citadel for well over a year. Why is the Spider suddenly interested?"

Warrick shrugged, improvising his answer. "You can thank Jack for that. The intel he shared clued us in that la Noche was much further along in their production cycle than we realized. Now that we know, we need to—"

He saw the shot before she threw it, which was the only reason he was able to avoid a solid blow to his jaw. As it was, Maria's competent strike was no match for his speed, and he dodged it easily. She'd thrown so much into it, however, was so sure of her trajectory, that she fell off-balance, careening into him. He didn't adjust his speed for that, and as a result, he was body slammed with nearly five feet ten of lean, toned human female— her skin warm and damp, the scent of her rising to wrap him with an intensity he'd determinedly avoided for more than six thousand years.

Need flared within Warrick, so sharp, he gasped, his blood raging through his body and pooling in his groin. Every single one of his muscles engaged, and a few of his organs too—though sadly, not his brain for the scant, glorious seconds that he allowed himself to hold Maria Santos close, to draw in her heat, her fire, and to feel the impossibly perfect length of her body along his.

Warrick's eyes squeezed shut for a long moment, all the years falling away, all the thousands of years to when he'd first fallen to the earth, a Watcher, a Nephilim, apart from God but still blessed, still gloriously blessed to taste both the human and the divine. That was the true gift of the Fallen that no theology had dared share. That God the Ever Merciful had *let* them fall and not cursed them, not at first. Not until they'd let their glorified status go to their heads and they'd sought not to teach the mortals, but to run roughshod over them. Warrick had been one of the worst—not a ruler, not seeking to subvert, control…but merely deciding to vent his divine rage upon those who could not withstand it. He'd allowed his need for revenge to consume him in a moment of pure, unholy fury…and he'd paid the price.

Maria pressed hard up against him, and he came back to the moment in a flash.

"Got you — got you," he managed, angling away from her so she didn't realize how much his body had reacted. As he did, his mind clamored that most men in this situation wouldn't have done that, would probably have taken Maria to the mat to show off for the small audience they had — but there was no way he'd be doing that.

"I'm good," she said, bouncing lightly off his body as if she hadn't noticed anything wrong. Her face was flushed now, her own breath coming fast. She started circling him again. "You're not bad either."

"I'm working on it."

"Charlie and Lou already like you. And they don't like anyone."

"You don't like me." Warrick grunted as he took a blow to the stomach, barely turning to the side to absorb the impact.

"Yeah, so maybe I've got better taste. How long are you gonna be in my face?"

"Defend," Warrick growled, and they changed positions, Warrick delivering new punches for Maria to parry. They continued to spar, Maria taking shots at his chest, his face, his stomach. He broke most of them, but she landed enough that she wouldn't get discouraged and quit. He wasn't really checking her punching skills, but her endurance, her resourcefulness. And she had plenty of that. She quickly adjusted to Warrick's clear dominance and altered her own strike style, going for the unexpected, even the unwise. That was good. She wouldn't be in a situation where she truly had to defend herself, but he needed someone who could think on her feet. Because what they were going into—

Another of Maria's misdirections sent him spinning to the right, but this time, he snaked out a hand to grab her and pull her with him so the two of them dropped heavily to the floor, her long, athletic body splayed over him, her legs straddling his hips. In this position, there was no denying the fact that his body was rock hard. He barely kept from hissing out a sharp breath at the intimate contact. *Focus.*

"Okay, *Warrick*," Maria said, her words tight and low as she tilted her hips forward to grind into him. "Anything else I need to know before we start working together?"

"Sure," he said, holding her gaze. "We need to stick together. Like right next to each other, together, at all times."

Her brows shot up. "Why? I can handle myself."

"I don't doubt you can. But you know these people, and I don't. You can tip me off if anything seems like it's going sideways. That might come in handy." This was all true, but it wasn't the real reason why Warrick needed Maria close.

Because she was the human who'd originally summoned him, whatever glamour Warrick chose to effect would be ironclad whenever Maria was nearby— even to another demon. If they were separated...that glamour might not hold up as well. He wasn't worried about humans seeing through his glamour, of course. He'd convinced Stan Harris and Jack Mangia easily enough, not to mention Charlie and Lou. But demons were a different story.

Maria stared back at Warrick, then she nodded once, definitively.

He thought she'd roll off him then, but instead she leaned down, her face close to his. "I'm going to do you one better," she announced, her words quiet and fierce. "Everyone at the Guardia knew Jack and I were involved, and that protected me. Now he's gone, and that protection is too."

Warrick felt anger curl deep in his gut. "You've been threatened?"

She shook her head. "I haven't, but I don't want to be either. So we're going to add a new wrinkle to your cover, right now. You showed up to the gym looking for Jack, found me instead, liked what you saw. With Jack on ice and none of us sure when he'll be back, given how many times he's been jailed, I decided I liked what I saw too. You and I pick up where Jack and I left off—and as far as anyone knows, we left off hot and heavy." She rocked against him again, and this time he did hiss in reaction. "I think you can pull that off okay."

Warrick held Maria's gaze, but when he spoke, it was through gritted teeth. "One problem with that. I know Jack couldn't have sex. Couldn't even react this way."

Maria narrowed her eyes at the admission, clearly not expecting Jack to have shared that little nugget of information, but she remained undeterred. "Aren't you the crack interrogator? That doesn't matter. He was all over me, and now you will be too—starting right now. There are eyes and ears everywhere in this gym, except in the showers. That's the only place here Jack and I could have a decent conversation."

Warrick blinked. "The showers?"

"Hot and heavy, baby. And we gotta talk." Not saying anything more, she slid off his body and rolled to her feet. Warrick found he instantly missed the contact.

"I'd say Maria won *that* decision." Charlie called from the far side of the ring as Maria held out a hand to

Warrick.

He took Maria's hand and allowed her to pull him upright, blinking away a thin line of perspiration that dripped from his brow. How long had it been since he'd even worked up a sweat?

"I'd say you're right," he called back, and the old man went back to sweeping the nonexistent dust from the floor.

Then Maria grinned at Warrick, her smile all teeth. "Showers," she said, cocking her head toward the back.

He grimaced as she spun away from him, then forced his expression to relax into one of keen male interest...exactly like he was supposed to. *Showers.*

God help him.

CHAPTER FIVE

Maria stamped down the narrow hallway of Lucy's the way she always did, then banged her fist on the heavy door to the locker room. When there was no response, she pushed through and kept walking all the way to the concrete shower room. There was no door on that room, but the showerheads were deep enough inside that nothing got wet that wasn't supposed to.

She yanked off her gloves, T-shirt and bra, then kicked off her shoes and socks, making quick work of her hand wraps. She deposited the whole mess on the short bench inside the shower room and stalked to the second spigot from the last. There was nothing magical about that spigot, but it was habit. She'd gotten through a lot in her life with habits.

She turned the water on full blast and waited.

Though there were two individual bathrooms that Louie kept remarkably clean, there was only one locker room at Lucy's. Other than her, very few women ventured into the boxing gym, and then not for very long. Rather than figure out how to accommodate a female clientele, Lucy had made the locker room more or less female-first. If there was a female who wanted a shower, the guys needed to clear out and wait until she came out. Anyone so much as gave a hint of complaint, the men who bothered her would lose their membership privileges.

There'd never been a problem. This was a group of guys who valued their workout space far more than they cared to hit on a woman who knew how to throw a punch.

But Maria had introduced a caveat to that system — that Jack could, should, and damned well better be in the locker room with her. When she'd started, she'd claimed she wanted the added layer of security, and Jack had quickly agreed. He didn't realize how much she'd known about him, and he was happy for the illusion their relationship provided.

An illusion that had included him hanging out with her in the locker room while she showered...the locker room and then the shower itself. Which worked out fine for her, because she didn't trust that her apartment wasn't bugged, or the public spaces of Lucy's, or even the locker room. But standing underneath a blast of water, they could talk. And they did talk...a lot. It had proven to be the best possible arrangement for safety.

Maria jumped involuntarily as she heard Warrick slam the door of the locker room, announcing his presence. She fully intended to carry on her same conversational precautions with Warrick, making him stand bare-assed naked in front of her, to make sure he wasn't wired, wasn't carrying, wasn't a threat in any way...and once she was assured of that, they could talk more directly.

But now that she'd seen the guy, she wasn't so sure that was such a great idea. Jack had been a big lug, startling in his anger when he needed to be, but an oversized, rough-hewn teddy bear the rest of the time.

Warrick was no teddy bear. He was more like a wolverine with anger management issues.

"You good?" he called now, with his gruff voice.

"I'm good," she shouted back. If Warrick had truly chatted with Jack and gotten the full scoop, he'd know that Jack no longer waited in the locker room for her but showered up close and personal, and he'd no doubt understand the conversational advantages of that arrangement. But showering next to Jack was one thing.

Warrick, on the other hand…

She steeled herself as she turned, peering out through the blast of water. Sure enough, he was heading toward her. And sure enough—

Oh, *damn*.

Maria reached out and fiddled with the hot and cold handles, turning the water into pounding jets. She didn't hate herself enough to turn up the cold as high as it could go, but she regretted that decision instantly as Warrick strode across the open shower room in all his pure, unmitigated man-ness. He was completely naked, his six-foot-six frame somehow managing not to look monstrous because every inch of it was in perfect proportion. His massive shoulders and long, heavily muscled arms tapered into beautiful, long-fingered hands, his thick chest whittled down to a six-pack that would have made Jack howl with envy, the whole of it brushed with a spray of dark hair—and as her gaze dropped further, she turned away abruptly, staring up into the spray.

He was still aroused. Obviously aroused. Like, a lot.

"Sorry," he said. His voice was low but still carried over the water, and to his credit, he sounded thoroughly embarrassed. "We could have—we could have waited until we got to your place. I could have checked for cameras there. There aren't any here."

"I don't think so either," she said. "But if there are, I wanted us to start our arrangement here. You suddenly showing up at my apartment would look suspicious otherwise, you know?"

Warrick didn't respond, and she realized she was talking into the water, not his ears. She turned slightly toward him, keeping her gaze on his face. "Hold me — close," she said. "Otherwise, I'll have to shout."

"If you're — "

"I'm sure," Maria snapped as she turned back forward, now embarrassed herself, though she knew her idea made good, solid sense. She wanted the protection of Warrick's supposed interest in her — and he wanted her to stay close. A sudden, hot affair between them solved both problems, immediately. The Guardia men went through women like Doritos, and the few women gang members were every bit as active. None of them would think twice of Maria trading Jack for the newest stud on the scene, especially since Jack was in lockup. Still, Maria had been nowhere near this awkward with Jack — though, admittedly, they'd known each other a month before she made this move. She'd known Warrick, what...fifteen minutes?

Good Lord, what had she been thinking? Why had she been so sure, so bold? At least Charlie and Lou had merely seemed to like the guy, bro to bro. Here she was asking him to take his clothes off and hold her tight after barely having a *conversation* with him.

Maria's cheeks burned, but before she could come up with another idea to dig herself out of this hole of mortification, Warrick's arms closed around her from behind.

She expected to go stiff — with anxiety, fear, even latent PTSD from the assholes who'd tried to take advantage of her when she was young and stupid and running the streets. But even more so than she had around Jack, Maria felt completely and utterly safe with Warrick standing so close to her. As if she'd somehow merited her own guardian angel without anyone passing along the message. Probably because he was a Fed. A professional. Someone on her side, regardless of the way his body reacted to her—whatever it was, she was grateful. It'd been a long time since she'd felt anything close to safe, and she'd take it.

After the barest hesitation, she leaned back into Warrick's body, feeling the hard length of him against her back, her hands naturally coming up to grasp the beefy forearms that crossed over her breasts. For as intimate as their position was, Warrick didn't press in, didn't cop a feel. He held her almost like he thought she was going to break. It was—incredible, if she was honest with herself.

And it was also very much beside the point. This man wasn't her new boyfriend; he was a colleague. A cop—or a Fibbie—or some other special ops something that had been sent here for a reason.

Pull yourself together, girl.

"So this is how this is going to work," she finally continued, tilting her head up so that the back of it rested high on Warrick's chest. She shifted her stance under the water and felt the still super obvious evidence of his arousal against her ass. The rush of heat and need came unbidden, and she ruthlessly forced it down, struggling to focus. This man was a *cop*. A *colleague*. "We talk straight in the shower, and in noisy, crowded places. Maybe in my apartment, if we sweep it first. Otherwise, it's all bullshit."

"Noted," Warrick rumbled over her head. "What do you need to know that I can tell you?"

The question seemed too carefully formed, and Maria hesitated. She needed to use this time wisely—they could talk more in the open, but it would be in code, nuanced. Brutal honesty here wasn't merely a luxury, it was a requirement.

"Who the hell are you, for starters?" she asked. "Not your cover."

The snorted laugh sounded rueful. "My name *is* Warrick, actually. I kept it because I don't pull undercover work all that much."

"Oh, great." Of course, Maria had used her own name when she'd gone under cover, but there was a reason for that. She was a broken girl coming home—no one in this neighborhood would've ever believed she'd grown up to become a cop. As a result, she'd been instantly accepted.

He continued as if he didn't hear her. "I was sent here to track down what exactly la Noche is cooking in that lab of theirs. Nothing more."

"Fine. Then explain to me why Lou and Charlie are acting like you're their most favorite long-lost buddy. Because they don't do that."

"As to Charlie, he and I had a nice long conversation on the phone before I arrived. I told him I was looking for Jack, and he gave me an earful. By the end of our chat, he invited me down to check out the club."

"Really." That was totally not-Charlie behavior. Then again, at least Charlie wasn't standing in the showers with a naked stranger.

"As far as Lou's reaction," Warrick continued. "What can I say? I must have a friendly face." The wry comment was so unexpected, Maria jerked her gaze up to meet Warrick's eyes. This close, with water dripping off his chin, he took her breath away. He was not the most classically beautiful man she'd ever seen—this was LA after all—but he was easily top three in most memorable. His jaw and cheekbones were heavy, harsh, and his brows winged up in thick, arches over his straight nose that, unlike Jack's, hadn't been broken several times. But the most arresting feature about him was his eyes. She'd never seen anything like them — they gleamed at her with an almost golden cast behind their light brown veneer, so intense that she almost forgot to breathe.

Which was a problem, because when she did gasp a response, she barely avoided taking in a mouthful of water. "Okay, what drug?" she managed, trying to get back on point. "What is it you think they're making here?"

Warrick blinked as if that wasn't the question he was expecting, but he shrugged. "You've heard of technoceuticals."

Her eyebrows winged up. She had heard of them, kind of. Some sort superdrugs purported to do everything but help a man fly. The drugs were particularly popular among the fringes of society, well-heeled metaphysical gurus and Om-chanting healers. In LA, even up in her little burgh north of the city, they'd been fighting more traditional drug mixes — the heroin variants, fentanyl and carfentanil, as well as a million different degrees of laced marijuana. Maria hadn't even begun to do the research on technoceuticals. But she'd been hearing rumors...

"I thought those were fakes."

Warrick's smile was harsh, and his eyes shifted dangerously, unnerving her. "Everything's fake until the government has a use for it. Supposedly, Takio is cooking up a particularly vicious strain that has the powers-that-be worried. I need to find out more about it."

Maria scowled at his pecs. They were really nice pecs. "Okay, so let's say I get you in. What makes you think they'll let you walk in and take a peek?"

He shrugged. The simple movement made his chest and shoulder muscles ripple in a way that made her blink rapidly. "Because we've got operatives in the Red Spider that will back up my story of coming out to check the merchandise, and we've let it be known through other unofficial channels that the Spider's got a lot of money to burn on this drug, if it's anything interesting. With the kind of cash we're talking, I suspect someone in either Guardia or la Noche is going to want to talk to me."

"I hope so." Maria forced her focus away from his chest, met his eyes again. "Because if not, that friendly face of yours isn't going to stay so pretty for very long."

As Maria Santos gazed up at him, Warrick struggled to keep his body from spontaneously melting. This was a human, and he'd interacted with tens of thousands of them—he had been alive for millennia, after all. And yet, he couldn't help but stare at this one as if he'd never before held a naked woman in his arms.

In his defense, it had been a while.

Now that he'd seen more of her, however, he confirmed his original assessment that Maria Santos was long, lean, and built for action, her arms tanned to a deep bronze that ended at her shoulders while the tan on her legs ended at her mid-thighs. The rest of her skin was slightly paler—and not flawless either. Scars crisscrossed her body, most of them so light that they had to have been received when she was barely a child, but the newer ones made up for their small numbers in their length and thickness. This wasn't a woman who shrank away from pain. Her breasts were high and not as full as they probably should be, given her frame, but Maria also looked like she hadn't eaten a real meal in weeks. Part of her undercover disguise?

All that merely added to her sensual appeal. Her

thick ebony mane, streaming with water, framed a face uncompromising in its ferocity and beauty. And her long-lashed dark eyes stared at him above a long, straight nose and full lips — lips that were now tightly pressed together as she watched him.

He shrugged again, liking too much how it distracted Maria Santos. Liking everything about Maria Santos, in fact, far more than he should. "I'll do whatever I need to do, if it gets me inside their operation," he said.

Her lips twisted into a wry grin. "I'll keep it in mind." Still, she seemed to accept his explanation, which was a miracle in itself. "Okay, what do you know about the Guardia? Anything?"

"They've worked this area for decades," Warrick replied. "At first side by side with la Noche, but that changed about fifteen years ago. Now their entire drug operation flows up through la Noche." Another shoulder roll, another flicker of Maria's eyes, a softening of her lips that made him long to feel them on his skin. "Jack gave me the name Cedo."

She nodded. "Guardia's head lieutenant. Bad news, but no more so than most of them. He's at the top of the food chain, and he's the one with access to the Citadel, which is where all the magic happens. You want to see la Noche's drug operation, you gotta go through Cedo." Her eyes narrowed. "What is it you think this drug will do, exactly?"

Warrick flashed a smile. "Frankly, we don't know. I don't even have rumors to go on, other than whatever it is, it's bad. Suffice to say, though, we have a long-standing beef with Takio. I understand you do too."

"I do." Maria's eyes went slightly cold, despite the fact that she remained warm and vibrant and soaking wet in his arms. "But I'm already embedded in this op, and I have been for a while. You're only *now* figuring out Takio's dealing designer drugs? Why?"

"Let's just say he's good at hiding in plain sight."

"Yeah, he's good at a lot of things." Once again, Warrick heard the steel in Maria's voice, noted the stiffness in her body as she sized him up. She still wore the gold cross around her neck, which kept him from completely rifling through her thoughts, but it didn't take a demon's touch to know this human had suffered a great deal at the hands of the man she knew as Takio Soldaro. But Warrick knew his true name.

Holkeri. The name sent a shiver of dangerous rage through him, rage he knew better than to give in to. He forced his jaw to unclench, his words to keep coming.

"Now that we've tracked him down, it gets easier. We need to place him with those drugs, with the dealers—with anything. With that hook, my guys can move in. Now that you're this close, we're going to do it fast."

"What do you mean, fast?" This part was new to Maria, something Warrick hadn't worked into his conversation with her handler, but it was critical. The longer he stood toe to toe with this particular demon horde, the more at risk he would be for being identified as something other than a high-level buyer from a cash-flush gang. He wasn't worried about the humans figuring out his true nature, but the demons in this area were old. He could feel it when he first set foot in the neighborhood. You didn't survive so long on this earth without developing highly acute survival skills.

One of those skills was being able to recognize a fellow demon when he was standing right in front of you. Especially a demon who was a member of the Syx, and more than likely here to take you out.

"I mean, the sooner we get into the Citadel, the better, and once we're in, we're going to have to move.

Jack said he gave you all the details you need about what's inside those buildings, but can you trust him?"

"Of course. He had the best memory of anyone I'd ever met. I've been into Buildings A and B a few times, and everything he said I'd see in them has panned out so far. The other towers are built on the same plan. D seems to be the important one, but I've never been in there."

"Jack's also an addict whose brain is suffering the long-term effects of a debilitating dependency on drugs," Warrick countered. He wanted to believe Maria—he did. If he could, he could walk into the Citadel himself, based on the information Jack supplied him, both by answering Warrick's questions and through his thoughts that Warrick had so easily read. But he couldn't—Jack's mind had been fraying even as Warrick had plumbed his memories. His intel wasn't a lock. He needed Maria for that alone...not to mention her involvement had been a condition that the archangel Michael had insisted upon.

Maria shrugged. "So that means you need me for more than just your lookout. Good. But I still don't get the rush."

More improvisation. Good thing demons had no problem with lying, or this job would be a bitch to get through. "The rush is we have it on good authority that a third party is coming in, planning to take Takio out," Warrick said evenly. "We need to get the information we want first."

"No." Maria had gone rigid in his arms, and for a moment, Warrick didn't know what she was objecting to. She didn't make him wait long for the explanation. "No one's taking him out before I get to him. God owes me that."

"He does, does he?" Warrick glanced again at the

cross dangling at Maria's neck. It had to have been blessed by...someone, somewhere along the way. He wondered if Maria even knew it. "He has a way of making you regret requests like that."

"I won't regret it." Without another word, Maria pulled herself out of his embrace, their interview effectively over.

Almost, but not quite. Maria half turned away, then glanced back at him, her eyes so hard, Warrick was grateful he hadn't succumbed to the desire to drop his gaze to her ass, which, even in his peripheral view, was as impressive as the rest of her.

"Something else, Warrick," she said, leaning back close to him. "I'm happy to get you into the Guardia, stay by your side all the way to the Citadel, and do whatever it takes to convince everyone who's anyone that you're exactly who you say you are. But by God, if you take out Takio before I get my hands on him, I will make *you* regret it for the rest of your life."

She turned on her heel then and stepped free of the shower, not looking back as she stalked out of the room. And, damned or not, Warrick watched her the entire way.

CHAPTER SIX

Maria viciously toweled off in the locker room while Warrick wisely remained under the spray to give her a chance to cool down.

She wasn't an idiot. She knew he was going to try to take this op out from under her. In the time-honored way of the Feds stepping in to screw the pooch irredeemably, Warrick was going to try to grab Takio for himself. The reason why didn't matter. Fame, a vendetta for past wrongs, the war on drugs, she didn't care. She wasn't going to let him do it.

With a groan of exasperation, she stopped rubbing the towel over her skin quite so hard, giving up her attempt to wipe away the feel of the man. Was he really as big as she thought he was, or had she simply been jacked up on adrenaline? He'd felt every inch of six foot six, and his arms had seemed legit enormous as they'd wrapped around her, but…maybe she'd imagined that. How would she even know?

Unless she touched him again?

"Maria?"

"What?" she demanded, whirling on him. Her mouth went dry as he stepped out of the shower room with only one of Lou's ratty old towels halfway wrapped around his waist. She hadn't imagined any part of him, she decided. None of it.

"I didn't mean to startle you." He gestured to the lockers. "You happen to know the code to any of these? I didn't bring a change of clothes."

"Then you're screwed. Those clothes won't fit."

He frowned. "What do you mean?"

"Never mind." Rolling her eyes, she stoically went up to Jack's locker and banged the center of it once, hard. True to form, the door popped open, revealing a small pile of clothes. Jack had some definite quirks, but one of the more disarming ones was his OCD over his attire. She pulled out a pair of nylon track pants that had been loose on Jack, and a shirt that wasn't ripped to shreds. Jack favored boxer briefs, and there was a clean pair in the locker, which she handed over to Warrick.

She wondered if Jack had made it to Florida already. She hoped so. The man had his own demons, but he'd helped her when she needed it. That counted for a lot with her.

He'd also been way further down the path of being flipped than she'd even expected. He'd spilled everything—all of it—trusting her way more than anyone should, though she had a pattern of that in her life, so she took it in stride. As a result, Maria had known about his money stashed somewhere on the East Coast, and he told her what he'd done to get it. But what he offered her in addition to that information was pure gold. He'd been inside the first three Citadel towers hundreds of times over the last few years. He could describe the players, the cells, the security—all of it. He'd never been in Building D, though. All that Jack knew officially about that tower was that it was used mostly for storage and populated by civilians. But Maria wasn't buying it. More likely, Building D was where she'd find what she needed to nail Takio to the wall.

She simply needed her chance.

Warrick donned Jack's clothes with better success than Maria expected, but she didn't say anything else to him, and he returned the favor. They kept things surface and casual as they left the locker room and walked back through the main section of the gym. Charlie was dozing off at the front desk in front of his tablet, while Lou was up in the ring, sparring with a kid. Lou and his protégé nodded to them as they passed. Just another day at Lucy's, nothing to look at here.

They stepped out into the unusually balmy evening, the kind of night that reminded Maria of growing up on these streets. Warrick reached out for her hand, and after the briefest hesitation, she let him take it. When her fingers touched Warrick's rough palm, she sucked in a quick breath, immediately aware of him as a man in a way she'd simply never been with Jack. She'd have to watch that. Even if she was trying to cultivate the illusion of them hooking up, it wouldn't make sense to anyone if she was suddenly completely moony eyed over a complete stranger.

Yeah, that was exactly the reason why she needed to keep herself chill. For appearance's sake.

Get a grip, she ordered herself. It was simply the weirdness of Warrick's sudden appearance that was throwing her off. She still couldn't believe Stan was making her go through this charade, but she suspected he'd had little choice in the matter. When the Feds came in, local police were supposed to roll over and go paws up without so much as a whimper. And she was willing to be a good little soldier — up to a point.

"Pay attention." Warrick's low growl refocused her, and it was all she could do not to jerk away from the sudden menace in his voice. Instead, she kept her grip loose, her stride easy as they moved forward.

"What're you picking up?" She scanned the street, the neighborhood she knew so well, but she couldn't sense anything out of place. And this awareness, this paranoia, was also something different, something she'd not experienced with Jack. Not that Jack was completely clueless, but he walked around in a bubble when he was on these streets. The bubble of knowing that no one would take a shot at him, not here. Not when he was known as a lieutenant of the Guardia, protected by the gang's reputation as much as by the long-standing respect he'd more than earned over the years. Jack hadn't been a dick to anyone. He'd been a thug when he'd needed to be, he made his point early and often, but in between times, he more or less left you alone. He worked out at his gym, partied with his homies, and faked an interest in sex he no longer possessed.

She already missed him, to be honest. Warrick right now scared the crap out of her, on way too many levels.

"We've got a tail," Warrick said, not looking at her. "Eight men, medium height, medium build. Wearing street clothes, not dressed alike."

"Guardia?" Maria asked automatically. Cedo had told her to watch her back, but she didn't think it was from anyone from her own organization. But that left—

"Not Guardia," Warrick said. "Takio's people, most likely." He breathed out a tight sigh. "We gave them word through channels that the Red Spider was interested, but they shouldn't know I'm already here. Though it's possible."

Maria shot him a glance, trying to keep the concern from her voice. "Okayyy… So, what? They're making a move, keeping you close, checking you out?"

"Maybe." Warrick nodded, his gaze darting up and down the street, but his grin stayed on his face. Not a fake grin either. The guy was enjoying this. "No harm in them watching, as long as we have backup, which we do."

Maria arched her brows, and her gaze returned to the street. "Since when do we have backup?"

"Since several additional men, most likely Guardia, started showing up behind our tails. Though the way they're hanging back, I'm changing that assessment. Less backup, more a watch. They also don't know who I am, and that won't help us. We'll probably be on our own for this hit. I assume you're not carrying?"

She snorted. "That would be no."

"And is this the direction to your condo?"

"Condo would be an overstatement," Maria said. "But yeah. This is the way Jack and I always went home. And before you start with some rant about how we should've varied our habits, you got to understand that—"

"His comfort level was all part of your cover. I more than get it," Warrick said tersely. "And that's fine, as long as your cover hasn't been blown. Because I'm getting the sense that the guys from la Noche aren't just here to watch us."

"Yeah, I'm thinking it's not me who's the problem here," Maria shot back, and a hot, bright anger surged up in her. Anger at Stan, at the idea of risking her old cover that had worked so well, and at this guy, who thought he could waltz in here and take over everything without a whisper of warning. "*You're* the one who's screwing everything up."

But Warrick wasn't looking at her anymore. He was looking at the opening to Sycamore Park, which she and Jack had routinely cut through on their way to her apartment. Suddenly, the scrap of a park seemed dangerous, too quiet.

"We're going in, and then we're taking them down,"

Warrick said. "Nothing fancy."

She quirked him a look. Since when did anyone fight fancy in Compton? But her body was jacked now, arms loose, hands ready. She was —

The first of them came from the side, literally out of nowhere.

"Son of a *bitch*!"

To Warrick's surprise, Maria bellowed in real rage as the first demon leapt from the shadows behind an immense concrete monument in the middle of the park to send her sprawling, another one right there to punch her in the ribs. She twisted to the side, automatically protecting her body from further blows, and he waited the few seconds that seemed like hours as they assessed whether she'd fight back. She'd supposedly taken down a demon two nights ago now at the dance club. Holkeri was doing basic threat-level assessment to figure out what she was. Warrick had to let that happen; he knew he did.

But it didn't make it any easier.

There were only the two demons, though. The rest were humans, and they came forward immediately, focusing on Warrick. He parried their blows almost as an afterthought, trying to keep his eyes on Maria. He took out two of the men with uppercuts that would have made the real Jack proud, would serve to allow Warrick to preen when they did finally present themselves to the Guardia — the Guardia and Holkeri's filthy gang as well. But he could have dropped the humans in a heartbeat if he wanted.

He had bigger issues. The demonic duo all over Maria were spawn — base-level pestilence, stupid and vile. The offspring of demons coupling and recoupling with their own kind over the years, a strictly forbidden act...like most everything for demons. Only the original Fallen had remained blessed by God. Once those one-time angels descended to the rank of demon, however...they became an abomination. An afterthought.

Expendable.

But they still couldn't be killed by an ordinary human.

And sure enough, Maria surged back up a second later, fists flying, taking the first demon by surprise only by her speed. She wouldn't win this battle, couldn't win it, really, or Takio would send out even worse. But the fact that she was employing very human countermeasures — blocking and punching and kicking with speed and finesse but definitely without demonic capabilities — was enough, would be enough, would be —

The smaller demon bent low and charged Maria, catching her in the midsection and taking her to the ground. Warrick jolted as Maria's mind flashed to a memory that went beyond panic, beyond the here and now, her body suffused in real, paralyzing fear, not even for the Maria of the present moment but a Maria of the past, a ten-year-old girl who'd been helpless, horrified, afraid —

She swung out, and Warrick heard the sound of bones breaking.

That was it. His rage, never fully banked, rose to life in a furious rush, filling him in an instant. He couldn't kill the human assholes — they were attacking him, not Maria, and they weren't causing anyone any harm in the immediate vicinity — but to protect his summoner, he was technically allowed to do unto others some small measure of what they were trying to do unto him.

An eye for an eye.

He exploded into movement, striking hard and fast.

Two of the men were already on the ground. Powerful kicks bent their ribs, curled them over on themselves. Maybe there'd been a crunch in there; Warrick didn't know, didn't care. The remaining four weren't idiots. Instead of two attacking and two holding back to play cleanup, all four rushed Warrick. Catching the fastest, Warrick clocked the man with enough ferocity to take out the thug behind him as well, then swept the third with a kick to the abdomen that would put the man in the hospital, even if he didn't die. The last man now had blades in his hands, two blades, and he blinked in confusion at Warrick's hard, fast grin.

Every once in a while, fighting humans was fun.

But the blades were meant for offense, not defense, and the man wasn't special ops, just a street tough who liked to play with sharp pointy things. Warrick closed the gap with him, grabbing the man's left wrist hard enough to snap the small bones that made up the graceful extremity of his skeleton. More screaming as the blade dropped and the man fell back, then Warrick shoved him away so hard, he barely kept his feet. With a quick scan of his fellows, who were still moving, at least—the man fled.

Warrick bent swiftly and recovered the blade, then turned to Maria. All this had happened in less than five seconds, but those five seconds weren't something he could magically erase. Maria's legs were pumping furiously, her body twisting side to side as one of the demons fought to get a purchase on her—and Warrick couldn't—couldn't take them out. Not without putting Maria in even greater danger.

He flicked out his touch so briefly that the demon spawn didn't feel it. Not to incapacitate them, not to banish them—not yet.

But to know their names. Ganit and Furth. Ganit was on Maria. Furth was wheeling around to the side, howling. It was enough.

"Get off!" Maria surged up, her body bucking, and that gave Warrick his chance. He closed in on the two foul members of his brethren, and the one not on top of Maria turned toward him with a combination of rage and pain. Since she was still with him, Warrick's glamour held—the demons had no idea that he wasn't human. Unfortunately, however, that also meant he couldn't kill Furth, because no human should be able to do such a thing.

Instead, Warrick merely stepped nimbly aside as Furth rushed him, and realized the demon himself was not as prepared as he should be for this battle. He was drunk. Drunk and probably high, corrupted by the very beings he was made to corrupt.

He was also in legitimate pain, holding his arm awkwardly to his body. What was that about?

Furth wheeled around toward Warrick, who'd shifted position slightly as well, farther away from Ganit and Maria. The demon didn't seem to notice, instead surging toward Warrick with more speed. That was good—the idiot would be forced to wonder if he was more incapacitated than he realized, to allow a human to do…this.

Warrick slipped to the side again, already moving toward Maria and Ganit as Furth piled into the concrete monument, his momentum too wound up for him to stop. His howl was piercing enough to peel paint off any nearby cars, but Warrick had no more time for him.

He turned—finally—to Ganit.

Ganit wasn't drunk, but he also wasn't holding his own nearly as well against Maria as he should be. Warrick's mind clicked through the dangers of that as he did the only thing he could — he threw the knife at the demon. Not to kill him, though he could have, not to hurt him, though he wanted to, wanted it so badly, he could taste it. But the blade zipped across Ganit's line of vision, and the creature jerked back, the movement all Maria needed to buck her body hard and dislodge him even as Warrick launched himself at them both. He caught Ganit in the shoulder and pushed him clean away — straight into the wheeling body of Furth, who, on top of his incapacitated arm, was now bleeding from an impressive head wound. More blood stained the monument, far more of it black than red.

Ganit stopped as he banged off Furth, staring around in confusion. Evil might live on for generations, but intelligence did not. It was one of the more charming aspects of the youngest spawn of the ancients. Even their own ancestors despised them.

Warrick didn't wait around for them to figure things out. He pulled Maria up to a standing position — she was bloody, and she'd have a shiner for sure, but she was otherwise blessedly unhurt — and together, they ran.

CHAPTER SEVEN

"Keys, Maria." She heard Warrick's voice, but Maria was having a hard time following his words. Even though he'd reduced those words down to simple sentences that nearly all contained her name. She stared at him numbly, blinking. Why did she feel so bad? The Noche thug had clocked her, but she'd been hit before, and he wasn't a big guy. Plus, he'd reeked of weed and whiskey. She was also relatively sure she'd broken the guy's arm and that he hadn't broken anything on her. What had she missed?

"Keys," Warrick tried again, and she blinked at him. *Why is he – oh.*

She fumbled in her jeans pocket, pulled out a money clip and keys, then shoved both at Warrick. He took them, turning away as Maria looked around the hallway.

How had they gotten to her apartment? Her condo, as Warrick called it. She snickered. Condo. Even up north in her own patch, she didn't rate a building where anyone took care of shit for her. She rented one side of a duplex and counted herself lucky. At least that house looked like a house, with a yard and a garden behind it. On her salary, she ordinarily wouldn't have rated more than a concrete box unless she caved and agreed to have a roommate. And she'd tried that once already. Didn't turn out so well.

"C'mon, here you go." Warrick's hands were surprisingly gentle as he steered her through the doorway and into her cramped apartment. She stared at the stacks of magazines, the disarray, seeing it through someone else's eyes, and wondered why she didn't feel more self-conscious. She should feel more self-conscious. Even with Jack, she'd managed that.

"Jack never minded the clutter," Maria said abruptly, not knowing why.

Warrick chuckled. "I don't either. But you need to keep moving." He paused, glancing around. "There are no cameras, here. No bugs."

"Yeah, like you can check that fast." She swayed a bit, shaking her head carefully, as if it might roll off her neck. Which it might. She decided to take him at his word that they weren't being bugged. "But seriously, what happened back there, and why do I feel like I've been drugged? I've been hit before."

Warrick hissed a word she couldn't quite make out, then he grunted. "Of course you have. Your job. But this—this is different. Those guys were different. When guys like that hit a human it…affects them more."

Maria nodded, confused again. *Human?* To his credit, Warrick didn't stop gently moving her toward the sofa, never paused until he had her settled onto the cushions. The sofa was the best piece of furniture in the apartment, a Goodwill find that Jack had crashed on almost constantly over the past several weeks, when he wasn't bunking down with his Guardia friends.

Beside it now, Warrick seemed…way too big.

Her head started to pound. She blinked up to see Warrick in front of her, still as devastatingly gorgeous as she remembered.

"Take this," he said, and she peered at the two tiny

blue pills in his hand. "They're yours," he continued. "Bottle on the kitchen counter."

"Then I'll need more than two," she grumbled. Still, she took his offering and the glass of water he held out and swallowed the pills. She no sooner lowered the glass than Warrick was right there with a warm, damp cloth. She almost laughed at the expression on his face.

"Is it that bad?"

"It's bad enough," he growled, and she thought, and not for the first time, she realized, about how much everything Warrick said sounded like a growl.

"You know, I get the feeling you got a problem with anger issues," she said.

Warrick's bark of laughter was so abrupt, so startling, that Maria jumped, spilling her water on her jeans.

"Oh!" The sudden burst of cold was almost as alarming as Warrick's large hand palming a towel over the stain, a dry towel this time, the movement so fast, she couldn't process. She must have seriously had her clock cleaned for her not to—

"Sorry." Warrick's mouth was close to hers, too close, his worried eyes scanning her forehead, her cheeks, her mouth, as if the spilled water had caused far more damage than it could have, since it'd hit her lap, not her face.

"It—it's okay," Maria said shakily, aware that she was staring at the man's lips, but not so much caring at the moment. "I didn't mean to offend you."

The lips quirked into a rueful smile, the expression so unexpectedly beautiful that Maria hiccupped a breath. *What is my problem? People smile all the time!*

"You couldn't offend me," Warrick rumbled and eased back slightly, as if he too realized that he was leaning in too close. "We've got to talk about this before you pass out, though."

"This…" Unbidden, too many thoughts assaulted Maria, and none of them had anything to do with what she knew — *knew* — Warrick was talking about. He meant the attack in Sycamore Park, but all she really cared about was what had happened earlier: him standing in the shower with her, his arms wrapped around her body like he'd been doing it for a decade, her head resting on the broad plane of his chest. She wanted those arms around her again, she decided. She wanted her head on that chest.

No. That wasn't why either one of them was here.

Maria shook her head again, trying to ward the thoughts away, and winced as her brain seemed to slide around inside her skull. She had to focus.

She told Warrick what he wanted to know. "I recognized three of the guys on you from la Noche, but I couldn't tell you their names. I didn't get that close a look at them, more of a feeling."

"And the two men who targeted you?"

"No clue," she said. "They had to be Noche as well, but they weren't anyone I'd ever seen, definitely not anyone I'd seen talking to Jack. They zeroed right in on me, though. Probably someone connected to that Bonnie guy."

Warrick's gaze met hers. "Bonnie." He seemed to savor the word, roll it around his mouth, almost making its utterance a ritual.

That was…weird.

"Yeah, that's what they called the guy I…well, I didn't really, well…" She blew out a long breath. "Jack wasn't there for that, and I wasn't exactly clear with Stan, so you don't officially know this. And I'm only telling you because you need to know what really happened. It might get brought up."

"Got it," he said. "Go."

She nodded tightly, then launched in. "Two nights ago, I was supposed to kill whoever the Guardia asked me to. I had a plan worked out—I'm a pretty good shot. They don't know that. I know where to hit someone where they'll bleed a lot but not die, at least not if someone makes an even passable attempt at first aid. I was still pretty nervous, though. I didn't want to do the job, but with Jack picked up, it was that or do something less appealing."

It was Warrick who nodded now, his golden eyes almost sort of…glittering. She really had been hit hard, she decided. Next she knew, there'd be Disney bluebirds fluttering around his head.

"Okay, so I get to the back room, Cedo's there, he gives me the gun, the guys peel back, and there's one of the dancers, drugged out of her mind. Only I wasn't so much focused on her but on this Bonnie guy—I didn't know his name then."

Warrick spoke it again, and a shiver rolled down Maria's arms. She narrowed her eyes at him.

"You know him?"

He smiled, a dangerous expression crossing his face. "Only by reputation. And so instead of shooting the girl, you shot him."

"Well, that's kind of debatable. A gun went off. The trajectory made it my gun, but I would swear to the death it wasn't me who pulled the trigger. The more I think about it, the more I can't reconcile it, but that first shot…" She grimaced. "Anyway, the guy went down, and I fired two more shots for good measure."

"Because you didn't believe you'd shot the first time, and the gun needed to feel like it'd been fired for you to pass Cedo's test."

"Right. And then—that was that. The girl started screaming, half the room emptied, and the other half stood staring at the dude on the floor. Who was not right."

"Mm…" Warrick had lifted the towel again and pressed it against her head. It was still damp and surprisingly warm. It felt good. "Not right how?"

Maria let her eyes drift shut. "He bled out, which was bad enough. But it was, like, a lot of blood, and seriously messed up. Black and thick and kind of like liquid soot. Hell, it was hot enough to smoke, like it was on fire. I've never seen anything like it. And there was a lot more of it than there should have been, given where I'd shot him and how quickly he died. His heart should have stopped pumping that shit out—but it kept coming, a siphon of sludge."

"Cedo see this?"

"Yup. He was convinced Bonnie was high or something, that he was killed by the combination of the drug and the gunshot, not the gunshot alone. He kept saying there was no way I could've taken him out."

Warrick nodded. That answer seemed to satisfy him, so Maria continued. "He's the one who warned me about Takio potentially targeting me." She managed a wry grin and sighed wearily. "Score one for Cedo."

"Score one," Warrick agreed, though indignation flared through him, overheating his skin. If he didn't watch it, the warmth he was transferring to the damp towel would end up scalding Maria. But there was nothing she was telling him that he hadn't already known when he'd lifted that gun and aimed it at the demon staring stupidly at Maria, confident in his own invincibility. No human could kill a demon, or even seriously wound one. That was an incontrovertible truth. And unfortunately, Warrick hadn't been able to stick around to see the shock and confusion of the demon as it had fallen to the ground. Of course, neither had he been around to watch the reaction of this Cedo character.

He knew from Jack that Cedo wasn't someone to mess with. He also suspected he was almost certainly the second demon who'd been in the room along with the one Maria called Bonnie. Neither of them had picked up on Warrick's arrival or his departure. And apparently, though Bonnie had been dropped by the bullet from Maria's gun, Cedo had assumed that it wasn't the shot that'd killed Bonnie so much as the cocktail of drugs running through his system. Drugs that had been created by demons, after all, and so could potentially be deadly to other demon kind.

Would Holkeri think the same thing?

Maybe. But first Holkeri would want to rule out the work of another demon, which was why Ganit and Furth had been tapped to attack Maria. Any demon worth her salt would've been able to take out those two idiots. That Maria had only barely fended them off validated her humanity. Warrick hoped that her failure to defend herself more ably would be enough to divert the suspicion from her.

Another possibility for Maria being able to kill Bonnie was that she was somehow blessed by God. That didn't happen so often anymore, but it did happen, and she did wear a cross quite prominently. However, once again, Dopey One and Two had been able to take her down right in front of her big strong boyfriend. So the special-blessing theory was out.

That left option three, which was going to make Cedo cranky as well as Takio: that another demon had slipped in and done the deed. As complex as that scenario might seem, it happened often enough.

Demons delighted in nothing more than using mortals as a bluff or a shield to help them take each other out. The Syx might be the best at effecting glamour, but other demons also had access to that same ability. The older, cagier ones were damned good at using it.

Warrick tightened his jaw. Holkeri would be good at using it too, he suspected. He'd used it once before, after all, to strike at Warrick where he was the most vulnerable. Back before he'd gone by the name of Warrick at all.

"What are you thinking about?" Maria's sleepy voice brought him back.

"Takio." He grunted. *Holkeri*. This wouldn't be the first time they'd crossed paths since the breaking of the world. But it would be the last, he resolved.

"What about him?"

Warrick looked over to catch her watching him, her eyes filled with fatigue but not with pain anymore, her face somehow more beautiful even as her skin turned yellow and dark, angry strips of red pooled beneath her eyes. She would ordinarily have an impressive black eye to show off to Cedo's thugs and make Takio's dogs preen, but Warrick wasn't about to let that happen. He would wait until she drifted to sleep, and then — then he would heal her.

Even demons retained the barest whispers of abilities from the Beneficent Father. The beloved creations of such a powerful being could fall only so far…at least those, like Warrick, who still proved useful despite their condemnation.

Knowing Maria was waiting for an answer, Warrick shrugged. "He's proud. He'll want to send a message."

Maria grimaced. "I kind of thought that was the point of attacking us in the park."

"That's a start, definitely. But rather than taking your beating like you were supposed to, you held your own. You fought back."

"I fought back because I had you. My Red Spider buyer, Captain Big Shot. You fought like you were on fire, and once those idiots scrape themselves off the ground, they'll be reporting what happened. We could both be targeted for that."

He nodded. "Which is why I need to know *your* specific interest in Takio and this Noche gang."

She straightened carefully, but he knew her well enough already to know her next words would be lies. "I don't have any interest outside my assignment," she said stiffly. "I was sent down here from Sylmar because I have local history, and I wouldn't look too out of place in the old neighborhood."

"That may explain why you were chosen, but it doesn't explain why you *wanted* to be chosen."

"I told you. It's my job."

"There's more to it than that. You have to volunteer to go undercover, and the pay isn't that much better when you factor in all the extra hours you're actually working."

"Maybe I—"

"*Maria.*" Warrick didn't intend for his voice to sound so desperate, so pleading, but the combination did the trick. Maria stopped in the middle of her banal explanation and stared at him, really stared at him.

"Please," Warrick said. "I don't mean to pry. I truly don't. I'm sure your reasons are every bit as valid as my own for taking Takio down. But I have to know them to understand them. If I don't, something might happen while we're inside the Citadel, something that doesn't mean anything to you but is a direct outcome of whatever it is that brought you to Takio's door. He's— he's been around the block long enough to be able to uncover anyone's secrets. You better believe he's going to be working to uncover yours if he can. Especially if that secret is linked to him."

For a long minute, Maria stared at Warrick, then she looked away, her lips pressed together. And kept lying to him.

"I got nothing against Takio that a hundred other people from this neighborhood don't," she said. "He's been in this community a long time, and he's a bad guy. I shouldn't have to need any other reason to want to take him down."

Warrick exhaled. He'd been so close—so close to getting her to cave. Had she picked up on that, seen through his attempt? It didn't matter. Because she was warded with the cross around her neck, a cross he couldn't even touch without his fingers blistering, he was stuck. Until she gave the information to him voluntarily, he would have to wait.

Wait…and keep a constant guard.

CHAPTER EIGHT

"Pretty impressive fighting, Maria. I didn't know you had it in you."

Cedo sat at one of the empty booths in the roped-off VIP section of the strip club, where he usually held command performances so that he and his men could watch the women on stage. If it made whoever he was meeting with distracted or, even better, uncomfortable, so much the better.

"I didn't either." Maria shrugged, keeping her eyes on the lieutenant, not on the dancers. "It's not something I hope to repeat anytime soon."

It was the afternoon after the fight, and her face still felt like day-old raw meat. Maria had been called on what passed for a red carpet, but at least they were all sitting — including Warrick. She'd expected the courtesy for a buyer, but if Cedo had left her standing, she would have been seriously concerned. Still, there was no denying the way the lieutenant was eyeing her, his gaze straying to the vee of her T-shirt way more than it usually did, especially given that Warrick was sitting right there.

With a big show of accepting Warrick's story that he was a buyer interested in checking out la Noche's wares, Cedo hadn't given Warrick more than a cursory quiz.

Warrick's responses had been to the point, unconcerned. Maria suspected there'd been an intense background check on Warrick before Cedo had summoned her to bring him back, but the lieutenant now seemed completely relaxed.

What was it with Warrick and his canned charisma?

The Fed wasn't Maria's problem, though. Cedo was. Cedo, who was still staring at her like she was some kind of jigsaw puzzle that was missing a few pieces.

She decided to go on the offensive. "Is there something I did wrong?" she asked, letting her panic show in her face enough to demonstrate her respect for the lieutenant, his position in the gang. "Should I, um…" She swallowed. "Should I have let them take me down in the park?"

"What? No." Her relief was real as Cedo rejected that assessment out of hand. "No. La Noche appreciates strength. They sent, what, eight guys after the two of you? Eight," he repeated, eyeing Warrick. For his part, Warrick lounged back in his chair like a cat with all the cream. He'd already given his accounting of the fight, and he'd been pretty accurate too. It'd made him come off like a badass, and it hadn't surprised Cedo. Yet the lieutenant sharpened his focus to Maria, interested anew. And once again, his gaze shot briefly to her neckline before returning to meet hers.

"Eight men, and you handled them. Even you, who only picked up boxing when you started hanging with Jack. Broke the one guy's arm and everything." Cedo seemed to consider that. "You did good, though. You didn't try to beat up the assholes, you tried to stay alive, defend yourself, and get them off you. Which is what you should do. What anyone in your position should do. Let them see you are defending, not striking, but that you won't give up."

Maria nodded, but it was as if Cedo wasn't talking

to her exactly, but repeating a mantra that had been drilled into him at some point, sort of a litany of self-defense. She glanced toward Warrick, but he was peering intently at Cedo too. Taking the opportunity that the moment of Cedo's distraction provided, she lifted her hand to her chest, tugged up her collar. Her fingers strayed over Cara's delicate necklace, and she stilled for a half second before continuing the brush of her fingers to push back her long hair.

Then she dropped her hand back to her lap, lacing her fingers together tightly. Was that Cedo's problem? Cara's necklace? Had he been ogling her breasts, or was his focus more on the tiny gold cross? They never talked about faith in the Guardia, ever. In private moments, she had with Jack once or twice, but Jack was at a crossroads in his life. Crossroads were excellent locations to have conversations about faith.

Still, surely her cross didn't make the leader of the Guardia uncomfortable. She'd been wearing it constantly for five months, and he'd never made a single comment about it. Why the sudden focus?

Her mental clamor was cut short as a man walked up to Cedo, then leaned down to murmur something in his ear. Cedo's sudden smile was electric.

"Excellent," he announced, lifting his tequila to Warrick. "Takio says you check out. He wants to see the two of you. Tomorrow."

That made both Warrick and Maria sit up straighter. "The two of us?" she asked, unable to help her surge of excitement. "Why?"

Fortunately, Cedo took her eagerness for panic. "Apparently, you've impressed him, that's all," he said, then nodded to Warrick. "And of course, he's more than happy to entertain a buyer for his brand-new...*product*. We'll send a driver along to protect you as well, at least as far as the front gates."

"Will he protect us as well as the guys you had on us yesterday protected us?" Warrick's words were delivered in a dark rumble, though once again, Cedo didn't seem to take offense. "Because they weren't all that useful."

"They weren't supposed to be useful to you," Cedo said, leaning back in his chair. "They were supposed to watch."

"Well, that part, they had down."

"And lucky for you, your account corroborates theirs," he said. He pointed his finger like a gun at Warrick, and Maria felt the first stab of uneasiness. There were undercurrents here that she couldn't quite tease out. Cedo didn't seem mad at them, exactly, but he did seem keyed up. On edge.

"What is it that Takio's, um, products do?" Maria asked, if only to break the tension. "Do you know?"

Cedo's gaze flashed back to her. "Million-dollar question—multiple millions, as it happens, buddy, so I hope you're prepared," he said, including Warrick in his response. He smiled, and another jolt of panic skittered through Maria. The guy was definitely on edge. "Truth is, though, we've been trying to get the goods on this mix for the last month without success. We know Takio's made some kind of breakthrough with the newest combination he's been testing—testing because we've gotten him what he needs, I might add—but we don't know the details. We've got a couple of ideas, but we also have to protect ourselves. We're a family here."

Beside her, Warrick snorted derisively—too derisively. Cedo narrowed his eyes at him. "You got a problem with that, brother?"

"I've got no problem with family," Warrick said, his words clipped. "But family doesn't let family get the shit kicked out of them. You let Maria here get attacked. I

95

still want to know why."

"Aw, give that a rest, man," Cedo said, sounding genuinely surprised — and even more relaxed in a weird way. He waved at Maria. "She was barely scratched, actually ended up looking a lot better than I expected she would, based on the hits the guys said she took."

"Hits they could've done something about," Warrick countered.

Cedo waved off the suggestion. "They were under strict orders not to intervene. I don't want Takio getting any ideas about how dangerous the Guardia is. Let him focus on selling his wares to you," he said, pointing to Warrick. "While Maria here sees as much as she can and reports back. Because depending on what she brings back, maybe you don't need to work only with Takio. We do have all the raw supplies, after all. Everything he's got comes through us. That could be worthwhile, yeah?"

Maria's brows went up. That was...bold. Cedo actually sounded like he was open to cutting a side deal with Warrick, the kind of deal that would immediately get him killed if Takio knew about it.

More intriguingly, Warrick seemed on the same wavelength. He leaned forward slightly, holding Cedo's gaze.

"What is it, Cedo? What is it you think we'll find?" Warrick's voice was low, tight. Like he already knew what the lieutenant was going to say. Which was a good thing, because Maria didn't.

Cedo also leaned forward conspiratorially, almost eager to please, and once again, Maria wondered how Warrick had that kind of effect on the men around him. Was he affecting her too, somehow? Was the attraction she felt for him real...or some kind of mind trick?

The lieutenant's next words refocused her, as he

gave up all pretense of vague generalities. "Rumor has it that la Noche is about to corner the market on technoceuticals."

Maria straightened, able to credibly feign ignorance despite the fact that she'd heard that word more in the last few days than she had in the last three years combined. "Technoceuticals?" she said, making a face. "Tell me that is not as sci-fi nutball as that sounds."

Cedo's smile was grim, but he didn't take his eyes off Warrick. "It might be sci-fi, but it ain't nutball, not by a long shot. The drugs have been pouring into la Noche's warehouses, getting stockpiled for distribution. But nothing—not a single vial—has leaked out. Especially not this new mix Takio is working on. We have no idea what kind of drugs these are, what the effects are, what the fallout will be. We don't know who Takio is going to be targeting, and if this is happening only in LA or if it's cropping up all over the country. And the fact that we don't know this shit is getting on my nerves, frankly. That's not how you treat your lieutenants, and we deserve to be in on this."

Warrick was sitting back now, watching Cedo intently. "You think he—what? Is setting you up for a fall?"

"Man, I don't know what to think." For the first time, Cedo seemed less angry and more legit worried. "But it sure as hell looks like that could be the case."

Warrick scowled as Cedo focused more on the problem that Takio—Holkeri—presented, and less on Maria. He didn't miss the way the lieutenant had been staring down her chest, as if the demon had never been that close to a good set of breasts. But that was bullshit. Cedo had been alive for every bit as long as Warrick had. He'd fallen, he'd sinned, he'd been damned...but here he was, making his living off the backs of humans, a strict violation of everything they both had once stood for. Warrick didn't know Cedo personally from the days of the great Flood, but he knew the type.

Cedo shot another glance at Maria's neckline, and Warrick finally got it. The cross. He didn't know where Maria had gotten the thing, but the same way he had wondered, he suspected Cedo was also trying to decide if there was some special divine intercession that Maria had merited to make her less susceptible to the demons Takio had sent after her. Where Takio no doubt seemed to be taking the possibility as a threat, however, Cedo was clearly viewing it as an opportunity.

He got to the meat of that opportunity a moment later. "Takio's going to be all up in your grill, Maria. I hope you got a good stomach, because he ain't the prettiest thing to ever crawl out of the Citadel. He looks like road rash on a good day, and on a bad day..." He grimaced. "You won't be able to look at him straight on. Not if you're not prepared for it.

A surge of grim pleasure shot through Warrick, though he knew he should be bigger than that. Knew it and didn't care. That he'd screwed up Holkeri enough over the years to damage his ability to project a true glamour to another demon, even a far less powerful one like Cedo...pleased him more than it should.

Maria paled a little at Cedo's words. They'd never gotten a good description of Takio, even from eye witnesses. The man changed his appearance like most people changed shirts. "What happened to him? I know he tends to avoid cameras...but that's all I know."

Cedo shrugged. "You'd avoid 'em too, if you looked like him. As to why, there's been a ton of theories. That he was caught in some kind of acid fire, that he got up close and personal to an explosion, even that he disfigured himself. On purpose."

Warrick's lips twisted into a hard smile. The truth was far simpler than that. Holkeri had been one of God's most precious Fallen. When he'd first been banished to the other side of the veil, Warrick had been tapped to do the honors. And Warrick had had his own axe to grind. He'd only newly been minted as a demon, after all…and he'd been condemned because of Holkeri.

Warrick had taken his payment of rage for that debasement out of the demon's skin.

The fact that some meat sack of a human kept opening the door to let Holkeri back in simply proved how stupid God's children could be.

Cedo continued, his eyes fixed on Maria. "What's important, though, is that you're eventually going to have to look at him, and it'd be better if you didn't flinch."

Maria shrugged. "I won't flinch."

"Good," Cedo said. "Because while he's sizing you up, I need *you* to size up the room he's sitting in, and I'm going to need it as accurate as you can remember it."

"Like, his office?" Maria frowned.

"His office, his bedroom, his playpen, I don't really care about the room itself. Most likely, it'll be in Building D, from our intel. But what you have to find is some of this newest tech drug. He'll have it out on display, to show it off to Warrick here. You score some of it yourself, it's gold."

Maria nodded, her lips pursing as she considered Cedo's words. "What do you want us to do with the drug once we get it? They're not going to let us walk out of there with it stuffed in our pockets."

"You got that right. Our intel is that they do a search of everyone leaving the place—but not a thorough one. And not an internal scope or MRI of any kind."

She wrinkled her forehead. "An internal scope?"

"Like I said, they're thorough, but they're not *that* thorough. You swallow some of those pills, especially if you can take them out of a larger vial to do it, they won't think to check."

"Whoa, whoa, whoa," Maria said, holding her hands up. Warrick knew better than to raise an objection. Jack had been part of the Guardia for nearly two decades. He knew how they worked. And what he knew, what he could remember, Warrick now knew too.

"I'm no drug mule," Maria said, turning, almost wild-eyed, to Warrick for support. She was too panicked suddenly. Too nervous. He could read it in her eyes. Another flash of memory burst briefly into her mind, a pretty, dark-haired girl bleeding in Maria's arms.

Now Warrick needed Maria to play it cool, though. "It's an easy enough process," he said. "I've done it."

She curled her lip, looking genuinely disgusted. "You've *done* it?"

"Sure. You put the pills in a larger case, swallow it, move through security. As long as you don't need to take much…"

"You won't," Cedo said. He held up a shrink-wrapped plastic oval, then tossed it to Maria.

She held it like it might bite her. "You can't be serious," she protested. "What if it's an injectable—or a powder?"

"Nope," Cedo said definitively. "Takio likes pills. Easier to keep track of, easier to measure, easier to transport. You get out of there with the drugs, and you get them to me—aces. I don't care how you do it. But it needs to be you, not him," he said, jerking his thumb at Warrick. "Takio is nervous around you, but taking some piece-of-shit buyer apart bit by bit to find some missing drugs ain't going to be a problem for him."

Warrick snorted internally, but Maria looked genuinely concerned. "Cedo…"

"Maria. Don't break my heart here, yeah?" Cedo's words had taken on a placating tone, but there was no denying the steel in his voice. "You knew when you joined the Guardia, hell, when you fell in with Jack, that sometimes family requires that you make sacrifices. That you do things maybe you wouldn't ordinarily do for the betterment of the family overall."

"Yeah, I got that. Like that part when you left me to fend for myself rather than sending your guys to help me out. That's some serious family shit right there."

"We were watching you, Takio was watching you, but Takio was also watching us," Cedo said. "We passed the test. So did you. He's going to feel better about us, and he should. We've given him nothing but our utmost loyalty, and we want to make sure we're not getting screwed in the process. If he's planning a payday with these new drugs, the Feds are going to be all over us, and while we're willing to deal with that, there better be a payout. That's all."

"If you say so," Maria muttered.

A bell chimed in the depths of the club, and the lights came on, a swirling kaleidoscope of color. Cedo's face burst into a smile. "Ah! Excellent," he said. "Tonight, we'll dance, we'll drink, we'll celebrate," he said. "Takio is sending more of his lieutenants to us, no doubt to keep an eye on us—us and you. So we'll do him one better and throw him a party."

Maria had gone still again. "Why is he sending his guys? He still has his doubts?"

"The man has survived as long as he has because of those doubts," Cedo said, nodding. "The Guardia has survived as long as it has because we have doubts too. But we have something better, something I'm not sure Takio fully understands. We have family."

Beside him, Maria stared stonily at the Guardia lieutenant. "I think your idea of family needs a little bit of an adjustment," she said. But while her words were bitter, they were also resigned. She would do whatever was asked of her, Warrick knew. Up to and including ingesting illegal substances if she couldn't come up with any other way to smuggle them out. She knew the long-term advantage of this. Her team at the LAPD would have to make sure that she was intercepted before she got three feet outside the Citadel, but they could arrange that—if it was even necessary. He had a feeling it wouldn't be.

All he needed was to get inside Holkeri's lair, and a lot of things would be taken care of quite differently than either Cedo or Holkeri could imagine.

Cedo, however, was happily watching a waitress set several bottles of chilled tequila in ice buckets on his table.

"*Excelente*!" Cedo grinned. "Tomorrow, you fight for the Guardia. But tonight, we dance and we drink. Most of all, we enjoy the life we have been given, yes?"

Warrick smiled at him, all teeth. He'd enjoy sending Cedo to his reward when the time came. He'd enjoy it a great deal.

CHAPTER NINE

Maria leaned heavily on Warrick's shoulder, grateful that at least some of her drunkenness was feigned. But she hadn't been able to completely get out of the constant rounds of tequila that Cedo and the rest of the Guardia lieutenants had been forcing her way.

Warrick seemed completely unimpaired, though he'd done his level best, at least as far as she could tell, to drink everyone under the table. How was it possible for him to consume that much liquor and still require her to remind him to stumble as they weaved their way home?

And the reminder had been necessary, she thought. Throughout the night and even as they'd escaped back into the finally cool December evening, with the incessant hum of Christmas music in the air, Maria had felt like there'd been eyes on her — on them both. Watching, assessing, judging.

Warrick had carried off his role beautifully. He had laughed when it'd been called for, been remote and intense when anyone got too familiar. And he'd never left Maria's side for longer than a few minutes. It was becoming all too easy to imagine that the two of them had already started a passionate affair, never mind that they'd just met.

It became even easier every time she touched him.

They'd had to do that several times over the course of the evening, Warrick casually slinging his arm over her shoulders, Maria reaching out to touch his hand. They'd even kissed a couple of times, fortunately able to keep everything light and easy, but she hadn't missed the increased focus of Cedo and the same shifty-eyed lieutenant she'd first seen in the back room of the strip club the night Bonnie died. Why would they care so much if she and Warrick were a legit item unless they doubted one of their stories?

Warrick, for his part, seemed completely at ease with the scrutiny, though of course, she hadn't specifically pointed it out to him. She hadn't said anything to him that she wasn't completely okay with being overheard, and even now, as they finally made their way up to her apartment, she couldn't shake the feeling that they were being watched.

"Drunker," Warrick murmured beside her, and she complied immediately, leaning so heavily on his arm that when her feet gave way beneath her, she merely grabbed hold. Warrick laughed, the sound bright and almost buoyant, the laugh of a happy drunk. He'd gotten that right too.

"Oh, c'mon!" Maria squealed as Warrick reached out to steady her, setting her down on her feet again as if she was a rag doll. "Maybe I wanted you to carry me."

If it'd been Jack, he would have shot back a laughing response, but Warrick didn't hesitate. He turned and, with one quick motion, scooped her up in his arms like she didn't weigh anything more than a bag of groceries.

"Warrick!" she spluttered, and he grinned down at her.

"You're heavier than you look," he teased.

"Hey!" As she pounded her hand on his chest, he

laughed again, and then they were at her door and pushing inside.

Out of force of long habit, Maria swept the room with her gaze, every careful pile of magazines and old mail, every exposed wall socket and light switch plate. She'd made the place almost completely cameraproof — at least for conventional units. She'd plugged bright pink covers into all the exposed wall sockets and switched out the light switch plates for the same garish pink; she had lamps that were all one piece, with LED lights; she had absolutely no knickknacks, books, or other objects that could hide a camera. Her tablet was out but looked untouched, and the papers on the coffee table were stacked in exactly the same way she'd left them, but on the kitchen counter…

She forced herself not to pause. The tissue box. It was empty, of course — had been for days. Only now, it was no longer upright, but on its side, its opening facing the room, with a clear view of the entire space. They hadn't left it that way — she knew they hadn't. Despite the apparent clutter in the room, she was completely OCD about her apartment, had even taken pictures in the beginning of how it looked when she left it and when she came back, to make sure nothing was changed. Whether there was a camera tucked inside the tissue box or not, didn't even matter anymore.

Someone had been in her apartment.

All at once, Maria was intensely glad for Warrick's presence, for the way he held her so tight and in such an unusual position, so that no one would think it strange that she shrank against him, her eyes darting around the room. "It looks so different from this height," she offered, ending on a hiccup. She looked up to Warrick, prayed he would see the intensity in her eyes. "Put me down?"

"Not unless you kiss me first." He grinned, cuddling

her close. Obligingly, she stretched her head up toward him, their lips meeting hungrily.

She spoke her fear against them. "Someone was in here."

Warrick went still for a brief second, then kissed her again, more thoroughly this time. "Agreed," he murmured at the end. He shifted, and she eased down his body, her mind moving at breakneck speed. Had someone come into her apartment while they were at the party, knowing where they'd be — and installed cameras — or at least bugs? Why? Because of her, or Warrick?

Had to be Warrick, she decided as he stepped away from her. Or maybe how quickly they'd apparently hooked up. Clearly, someone wasn't buying his capital C charisma. And even worse, she couldn't look for the damned things, not and tip off the watchers. But she absolutely *knew* that someone had been in her apartment. For that reason alone, she needed to continue to act the part she and Warrick had carefully set up.

"I cannot even believe you don't have beer in here."

Maria glanced up, realized Warrick was now standing with his head inside the fridge, both hands rooting around inside. She frowned in real confusion. "Are you drunker than I think you are?"

She moved toward him, barely remembering to act drunk herself, but Warrick did little more than shuffle out of the way so she could squeeze by him and pull out the bottle of beer. Warrick swiped for it, missed, and half collapsed on her, his head dropping down near hers to hiss in her ear. "One camera that I've picked up so far. Two bugs. Tissue box, microwave, door hinge."

Picked up? Did he have some sort of tracker — was that what he'd been doing when she thought he was fumbling around in the fridge, looking at his tech?

"Hey!" Maria yelped with as much surprise as she could muster, legitimately struggling as Warrick's full weight came down on her. The beer bottle went crashing to the floor, and Warrick spouted off a slurred expletive. Then she got him upright—too upright. He nearly toppled over backward until he seemed to get his bearings.

"Okay. Okay, honey. I got you, sweetheart." Maria started giggling between each word, because Warrick's eyes were wide, almost panicked. Had he never tried to act drunk before, or was this simply part of the charade? Because he was doing a damned fine job of it. "We're going to get you to the couch—the couch, okay? You'll do better on the couch." And she would do better on the couch, especially if they were supposed to end up all over each other for the benefit of someone watching them. Having Warrick stretched out in bed with her invited possibilities she couldn't quite wrap her head around.

"Couch," Warrick agreed solemnly, and then he started laughing too, his big shoulders shaking, his breath coming in rushing gasps.

"Hold on, hold on there, be careful, big guy, breathe in, breathe out...slow it down." Maria kept up the patter as she guided Warrick to the couch, settling him down on it. "You all right here for a minute while I clean up the beer?"

"Get me a beer?" he asked, then dissolved into honest-to-God giggling. For a moment, Maria could only stare at him. Then she straightened.

She smiled. "Of course. I'll be right back."

As she turned, tossing the words over her shoulder, the reality of what was going on here crashed back home. *Oh my God.* Warrick had said there were cameras and bugs in the room—but how on Earth could he know that? He hadn't even really looked.

Had to be a tracker. Some sort of high tech…something, that was way above her pay grade.

"Hey, you need me to help you—"

"No! No, I'm good. You stay there." Maria hustled into the kitchen and threw towels over the broken beer bottle, sopping up most of the liquid as she did. The towels were from Goodwill, and she had no interest in fishing the glass out of them, so they went in the trash. When she turned around, she looked out through the kitchen cutout—Warrick was up again, poking at his phone.

"Um, honey?" she asked.

"Got it!" He grinned as Ella Fitzgerald's unmistakably warbling voice suddenly filled the apartment. Maria blinked. He was playing mood music? Or…oh. Maybe his phone held the tech he needed. That made a lot more sense.

Maria dived into the fridge for two beers, popping off the caps. She kicked the fridge closed as she came around the corner, then paused as she scanned the room. No Warrick.

Then he appeared from her bedroom.

"Hey, babe." The voice was rough, gravelly, the body muscled and tight, and the clothes—

"Um, you suddenly get too hot?" Maria managed, setting down the beers on the coffee table as Warrick strolled back into the room. Now he was wearing nothing but a pair of pajama pants slung low on his hips, and his hipbones suddenly fascinated Maria far more than anything in her life. His body looked made for pajamas, she decided. Pajamas and—

Stop it, she ordered herself. She looked up as Warrick reached her, letting him pull her into first a hug, and then a slow dance around the cramped apartment to Ella Fitzgerald's beautiful melody.

"You good?" he asked over her head.

"Oh, I'm good," she sighed against him, the adrenaline dropping away all in a rush. Maybe they could sit back down on the couch, cuddle for a while, fall asleep. That could work. She was so unbelievably exhausted, and the tequila she had consumed was legitimately starting to hit her. If they could sleep, truly relax, forget about the cameras, Takio's thugs, her own unruly reactions to Warrick's presence...that would be good. That would—

"Fantastic," Warrick murmured. "Because I think you're overdressed."

Warrick didn't know why Maria was so stressed all of a sudden. She'd been fine in the kitchen, getting him to the couch. She had to know this was only going to go so far. He wasn't actually going to have sex with her on the couch, especially now that they had an audience. But suddenly she jumped whenever he shifted, and her eyes as they looked back at him were panicked, unsure.

But he hadn't been lying to her. There were two cameras in the small living room, another in the bedroom. Human tech had come a long way since he'd first walked the earth, but one of the advantages of being a demon, was—you knew when you were being watched.

And they were absolutely being watched. By whom, he didn't know. Chances were, however, the goons doing the surveillance were expecting him and Maria to behave a certain way, or alarm bells would start ringing.

Maria apparently thought the same way. "I'll—uh—go change."

"Not necessary," Warrick said, and it really wasn't.

When it came to adorning the female body, he'd never seen the need for clothing. Jewelry—yes. But flimsy lingerie or materials with soft fuzzy yarns? None of that was good. Less was far better.

"Let me help you with this," he breathed. He eased Maria back onto the couch, offering her a smile when she lifted a hand to her head, shaking it as if she was a little tipsy. She *was* a little tipsy, he realized belatedly. She was also genuinely nervous. They'd already seen each other naked, so he doubted it was because of him. Had to be the cameras. Even though she was undercover—and she had a rock-solid body—Maria couldn't be completely chill having unknown somebodies watching her strip down.

Come to think of it, he wasn't completely chill with that either.

"You gotta trust me, babe," he said with a leering grin as her gaze snapped to his. He kept his gaze hard and steady though, trying to communicate more than his words could convey. *You are safe. You are protected.* "I totally got you."

Finally, Maria's mouth eased into a smile. "You do, huh?" she teased. "Seems to me like you were the one who just dropped your favorite beer all over my floor."

"But look here, there's another one," he said, lofting one of the beers from the coffee table. "It's like magic."

"Magic, huh?" she repeated, rolling her eyes. But her manner was smoother now, easier, as she—finally—relaxed. "I can work with magic."

For a moment, Warrick wondered what Maria would think if she really understood the truth about him. He wasn't magic, not exactly…but he was something she'd never experienced before, something she arguably should never encounter. He was a demon, the lowest scourge of God's angelic realms…and yet, as

110

a one-time angel, there were still things he could do, things he could teach Maria. That had been the initial command of the Fallen, after all—to teach. To show. Though the angels who had remained in God's bright embrace had never wanted to believe it, God *hadn't* initially condemned the Fallen for simply wishing to bridge the gap between humanity and the heavens. He'd let them fall, after all.

And then He'd given them their charge to share their knowledge.

It was only when they'd failed that charge that they were damned.

But here, with Maria in his arms, Warrick remembered what it had been like before...when he *had* been worthy of love, of hope. It truly had been magic, for all that he couldn't share that full truth with Maria.

But he could share this moment with her, right now. And that was more than he deserved.

"I'm glad to hear it," Warrick murmured, leaning up to kiss her soft lips. Maria might still smell like sky despite all the hours in the club, but she tasted like tequila. He'd barely registered the impact of the heady drink when he'd been in the bar, but on her lips, it became far more intoxicating. She kissed him, tentatively at first, then more deeply, then reached for his head, pulling him close as she kissed a trail toward his ears.

"We need to put on a show," she whispered urgently.

"I know."

As she shifted back, Warrick's grin turned more intent. "Speaking of magic...I think it's time we made your clothes disappear."

"Warrick!" Maria's surprised reply was stifled by a giggle as he reached for her shirt, pulling it over her head in one smooth movement. Her breasts fell easily in her lacy bra, and he left them enclosed in the soft fabric for a minute longer, instead going for her jeans.

"I'm going to freeze," she protested, but only halfheartedly, as Warrick slipped down the zipper of her jeans and peeled the warm fabric down and away from her waist. The skin of this part of her body still fascinated him, its smooth surface and untouched by the weathering sun, the deep rich tan of her arms and lower legs nowhere in evidence here. He'd seen human bodies for millennia, every size, shape, and skin color. He'd also seen his share of tan lines, but once again, there was something about the feature on Maria's body that transcended anything he'd ever seen before. She was simply — perfect.

"Yes," he breathed as he pulled her jeans over her narrow hips, down her muscled legs. She'd already kicked off her sandals, so in short order, the jeans lay crumpled on the floor, while Maria watched him with a smile on her face that was less goofy relaxation and more ready-for-anything determination.

He didn't know what made him do it, then. Even as his head dipped down, his lips parting, he could hear Maria gasp above him as she realized his intent. But if he was honest with himself, he wasn't only doing this for the camera. That was what he would say later, what he might even convince himself of, but all he really wanted to do in this moment was tilt his head forward this last remaining inch and drag his lips across the soft black fabric of her lacy underwear, the section that made a delicate vee in the apex of her thighs. He inhaled the mingling scents of skin and musk and cocoa butter, and almost thought he'd pass out. Instead, he fisted his hands to either side of Maria's hips and held himself perfectly still, tracing a line gently — so gently — along that scrap of cloth until she sighed heavily and stretched out beneath him.

"Warrick," she practically moaned, and whether it was for the camera or not, he honestly didn't give a damn anymore. He closed his teeth around the thin string that arched over her hipbone, pulling the fabric taut. Maria hissed, her head now resting against the cushions of the couch, her hands lifting and her fingers tangling in his hair. She shivered as he licked his way over the sensitive curve of her hipbone, along the soft curve of her belly. Though it was everything he could do not to pull her panties free entirely, that wasn't the script here, and he knew it. He had no interest in anyone seeing the perfection of Maria's body the way he had in the shower room. In fact, he wasn't sure if he could handle anyone other than him ever seeing that again.

Which was ludicrous. And yet...

Warrick pushed himself higher as a keening need built up within him, the blood that drained out of his head into points south not helping his discernment. But then his face was level once more with Maria's beautiful breasts, her long legs clamped to his sides as he paused another moment to study the symmetry of her form. The soft mounds of her breasts shifted easily under his touch, the nipples pebbling as he drifted his mouth over yet another swath of delicate fabric.

His mouth opened with a guttural growl, and he took a taut, dusky nipple into his mouth, tugging gently as Maria arched beneath him. He hadn't touched a woman this way, so intimate, so intently, in longer than he could remember, but his body certainly remembered what could, should, *must* come next. Heat swamped him, practically radiating from her, and Maria purred, her legs sliding up over his hips and crossing behind him, locking her tight.

Warrick's eyes almost crossed.

He leaned up farther, rocking into her, and Maria

sighed as he shifted his body higher. Now he was even with the sensually graceful curve of her neck, and he drifted his mouth along it, resting a long moment on her fluttering heartbeat, reveling in the knowledge that he was doing this to her, that he was causing her pulse to jump, her body to relax and open to him, her skin to warm. Her hands had fallen away from his head, and she lay on the couch now without an ounce of the panic, the real fear he'd felt in her moments before.

And he'd done this. With his mouth, his touch, his skin against hers.

Him. No one but him.

Warrick edged up yet farther, pressing against Maria's body, feeling the long, slow, languorous breathing as she sank beneath his weight.

"This is good," he murmured against her neck, certain that the camera couldn't pick up his voice. "Really good, no one would —"

Warrick lifted his head to gaze into her eyes. He froze for a second, then grinned.

Maria was out cold.

CHAPTER TEN

"This place is one of the worst hellholes I've ever seen," Warrick muttered beside Maria. She couldn't agree more.

The Citadel, as it was known to the locals, was officially Holly Hills Apartments, four towering apartment complexes of easily twenty floors each that hunched together in a perpetually dirty gray section of Compton. The sun never seemed to break through the haze of mist and smog over this stretch of blocks, and the place was eerily quiet. There was no clamor of birds or crying of babies or even screech of cars. Even the wind blew with caution around the Citadel, determined not to draw attention to itself.

When it had first been built in the 1970s, Holly Hills had been positioned as a means of escape, a luxury high-rise for residents looking to literally move up in the world. But nothing remained of either the luxury or the hope that must have attended those early promotional campaigns. Now the flat stone walls squared off in defiance like the affront to society they were, and though the apartments were full, no one admitted to living inside the Citadel. Nor did anyone bother the residents with pesky little things like census forms or tax documents.

It was an island of silence in a city teeming with noise.

Warrick and Maria had been driven by one of Cedo's stooges, who'd let them off a good four blocks from the Citadel, the unofficial beginning of la Noche's turf. No one emerged to stop them as they made their way casually down the street, but Maria had never felt more naked without her gun. Still, the first thing that would happen was that they'd be searched. Roughly and without dignity. It was one of the major reasons she'd opted for loose pants and a thin T-shirt atop her thick-soled running shoes, and for once, she hadn't tried to conceal anything in the rubber soles of those shoes. She was in no mood to play around here. She had a job to do. Several of them.

She slanted a glance to Warrick. She'd woken up with his arms wrapped around her, both of them still clothed to some extent, though she couldn't fully remember how she'd gotten stripped down to her underwear. She was pretty damned sure she'd cry with frustration if she ever got a peek at the camera feed that had been trained on them the whole night, but she and Warrick had remained cognizant of their audience throughout their prep for the meeting with Takio at the Citadel. Now, finally, out of range of the camera operator, Cedo's driver, and anyone from la Noche, this was their last real chance for conversation.

And all she wanted to do was find out what they'd done the night before.

Warrick, however, seemed to be on a totally different wavelength. "Top of mind," he said abruptly. "What do you know that Jack didn't?"

The question was abrupt, but Maria rolled with it. Warrick had been almost eerily in tune with Jack's knowledge, had shared with her things Jack hadn't told her about the interior of the Buildings B and C of the Citadel, but there was still more information to share. There always was.

"No women in the open areas," she said, and Warrick glanced at her. "I noticed it the first time through, and then the second. By the third, I saw a few, but they walked only with the men. La Noche doesn't have women anywhere that matters. The apartments, sure. But not in the lower portions of the building, and not in the courtyard. So if you get bagged and then uncovered, and suddenly you're seeing women, you're probably up high, somewhere in the residences."

He nodded. "And how well do they know you? Beyond their attack on you the other night?"

"They don't," she insisted. "I've been racking my brain over it, and I've got nothing. The only thing that they have on me is that I shot Bonnie, and that was a fluke as much as anything."

The next question came quickly, rapid-fire. "Why do you want to take la Noche down, Maria?"

She scowled at him, refusing to be tripped up. "It's my job."

"It's more than your job. There's something else driving you—again, it would help me to know what it is." Warrick's words were quiet, polite, but that didn't change their urgency. And for some reason, walking in the gritty sunshine where she didn't have to meet his gaze, it was easier to share the truth. At least part of the truth.

She sighed. "La Noche's been a part of this neighborhood for a long time, since before I was born. But Takio came in when I was still a kid, and things...changed. We all knew it, even though this wasn't really our patch. Different people showing up, spreading out into the community. They didn't stay inside the Citadel then. They started roughing up some of the other gangs — well, we thought it was roughing up. Turned out it was more like recruiting. Guardia didn't last long. The others fell soon after that. Once they did…" She shrugged. "Things got quiet again. At least to me. I was a kid. A little kid. Nobody much worries about a five-year-old or even a ten-year-old girl. But pretty fifteen-year-old girls? A little harder to miss. Especially when they live their lives loud and fierce and unafraid. My cousin Cara was one of those girls. First, she had the world on a string — money, swagger. Then she started talking back to her mama, even got a tattoo, and Cara had never been like that. It wasn't her way." Maria pursed her lips. "I think that was when she started wearing the cross pendant, ironically enough. Maybe something her mama gave her. But…it didn't work. Eventually, she dropped out of school, though she told her mama she was staying with a friend and still going to class. Her mama was a nurse — she was grateful someone was looking out for Cara, I think. Or maybe she didn't want to know."

Maria sighed. "It got worse, slowly but surely. She was gone for a few days at a time, one time a week. When she got back, she got even quieter. Then she got sick a lot. Then one day, she threw up, and it wasn't only food."

"She was a mule," Warrick said.

"She made me promise not to tell, and of course, I didn't. But someone did. I started following her to her drops, trying to…I don't know. Protect her. Keep her safe. As if I could do anything as a ten-year-old kid."

"She was killed?"

"She…" Maria swallowed. She'd gone over it so many times in her mind. Cara had been convinced that the men she'd called *Los Diablos* knew she thought they were evil, that she could see them differently, but Maria had always discounted that. She was convinced that Cara had been killed for a far more practical reason.

Now she sighed. "She'd been playing a dangerous game with the pills she'd been carrying. There was always some loss that was expected, but her loss percentages were too high. Someone in la Noche knew it, warned her. She didn't care. They never laid a hand on her—she swore they didn't, but she kept pushing it. She figured if she could pool enough of the pills...sell them to the right person...she'd get out."

Maria shook her head, surprised she could still put one foot in front of the other as she saw that night again, harsh and horrible before her eyes. "I'd been watching her, I always watched her, but then..." She pursed her lips. "I saw something in the shadows around her. Something that scared me. And by the time I looked again, Maria was surrounded by Takio's men. They— they had knives. Knives that flashed in, pulled out. So fast...too fast. They gutted her before I could get to her, and I—I didn't see what they pulled out. But she was still so beautiful, lying there, covered in blood, her hand red and shiny, and then there was this—this little gold cross she always wore."

Maria could no longer see the sidewalk in front of her, only Cara. Beautiful, broken Cara and her shiny, bloodstained cross. "She wanted me to ask God to come and save her that night. Said she couldn't do it herself, that she was no longer worthy. She even gave me the words, a kind of prayer. But what would God do? She was breathing her last, the police were coming, I could hear the sirens, and I didn't want to share her with anyone, not in that moment. I especially didn't want to share her with a God who could let such a thing happen to her."

She blinked, and Cara was gone. The night was gone. There was only concrete and dirt and the Citadel growing ever closer. She lifted her hand to set Cara's necklace swinging. "Some things don't change all that much in fifteen years. Some do."

Warrick nodded. "You think anyone there remembers you from that night?"

"Oh, maybe." She shrugged. "But even if they did, they wouldn't care. A whole lot of girls that grew up in the neighborhood got pulled into the gangs one way or another. Some even created their own small families as sort of a support organization, all of it following the money trail of la Noche. When you have nothing to begin with, you begin to take chances that maybe you wouldn't take in another scenario."

"A lot of girls die, though, in places like this," Warrick said, surprising her. "You changed your life over Cara's death. Why?"

"Honestly?" Maria lifted her hand to her chain again. "Because Cara had something I didn't. Not the money, not the popularity, not the beauty — though she had all that for sure. But she had faith, you know? Faith in God. I never once had that — still don't. It wasn't like I had it and lost it like some people. It was never even an option for me. Whereas she seemed like she inherited it." She shook her head, grimacing. "I couldn't save her when I should have. So instead, I decided to save others. Or help protect them, anyway."

Warrick opened his mouth as if to say something, then shut it with an audible snap. They walked along for another two minutes, only slowing their steps when the Citadel hove into view. Slowing but not stopping. There was a man standing at the "Holly Hills: A Luxury Community" sign. He didn't look like the apartment's rental manager.

"Gun," Warrick said drily.

"I picked up on that." The man held not a pistol, but

a rifle that would look equally at home on a big-game hunting safari or in an eastern European war theater. He didn't move until Warrick and Maria were right up on him.

"Welcome, friends," he said, his face expressionless. "Your meeting is with Mr. Soldaro. He's looking forward to meeting you." His gaze flicked to Warrick. "Both of you."

The inflection in the man's voice was off, and Maria tensed. The doorman was too smug, too excited. She'd seen that kind of feral excitement in Pablo right before a score—or before Cedo had decided to put someone in his place. What was going on here?

Stick to the plan. They needed to find any indication of drug manufacturing or trafficking. Maybe, if they were really lucky, they could pocket a pill or two while they were at it. Then Takio would be routed out of this hellhole, and Maria would have the satisfaction of seeing him taken down. It'd be enough. It was all she was going to get, so it would have to be enough.

"Then let's go," she said.

Both of you.

To Warrick, the phrase carried an unmistakable emphasis. Unmistakable and bad. He watched the windows of the blank-faced building in front of him. At first, he could see nothing in the empty glass, but as they drew closer, it started. A flutter of a curtain, the peeling back of a blind. The first of the apartment complexes, the one fronting the parking lot, was occupied. With what, he wasn't sure. If it were him, however, that's where he'd put his guard base. You didn't want anyone signaling the cops from an upper-story window; you wanted to present a solid front.

Not that cops ventured this close to the Citadel anyway.

The flunky doorman—regrettably human, as it turned out, but well on his way to darker destinations—led them into the front doors of the building, which was apparently Building A, buzzing through using a keypad that looked surprisingly modern. Warrick could tell Maria noticed that detail too. Inside, the place smelled like urine and decay, but was cleaner to the eye than he expected. Someone apparently came in and picked up after the worst of the demons. And there were definitely demons here. The guard station had once been a receptionist desk for the area, as if the original designers of this complex had envisioned office space being rented out in the base of the main building. Now two demons stared up at them as they approached, barely managing to keep hold of their glamour. The doorman didn't stop as their trio walked by, but Warrick reached out with the slightest flick of a touch, gathering the demons' names. If there was a confrontation—and he was almost sure that was what Holkeri was setting up—the more foot soldiers he could take out with a simple command, the better.

Nobody spoke, but as they moved through the building, Warrick tried to hear the sounds of living above them. The front apartment was teeming with demons, now all of them watching and waiting. There was a legion in this building alone. Probably most of Holkeri's force.

Warrick's eyes had started to burn from the feral stench that only another demon could truly sense, when they broke free of the building and into the courtyard, a barren, treeless space that had once been something of a park. Now it was a stark tan patch of dirt, bisected with walkways that were unnecessary now that there wasn't any grass. No trees, no bushes. Instead, the courtyard served as a makeshift parking lot for white-paneled, windowless vans—easily two dozen of them. They had no markings on the side except for a small scattering of official-looking numbers and letters on the one driver's side door that he could see, and though they were older, they were clean. Nondescript. No one would notice them or remember them after they went by.

"We've got an audience," Maria muttered, and Warrick's gaze lifted to the buildings to either side of them. Sure enough, these windows weren't empty. Faces filled them, both at the height of adults and, more chillingly, children, all of them staring out at the newcomers.

"Two hundred families live at Holly Hills." The doorman suddenly spoke up in front of him, and Warrick glanced toward him, touching his mind with the gentleness of a whisper. The man's name was Nico Martin, twenty-five years old, Takio's highest-ranking human…which wasn't saying much. "Each of these families owes their livelihood to la Noche and their lives to Mr. Takio. They'll do anything for him."

The human was nearly vibrating with excitement. Warrick suspected he was talking out of turn, but that didn't make what he was saying any less true. Unlike Maria, the doorman wasn't warded against him, which was how Warrick could discern his name.

But Takio would know that a demon could read Nico's mind, of course. And if he at all suspected that a member of the Syx had tracked him down, let alone Warrick…

Both of you.

His cover might not have been blown, but clearly, Takio suspected something. He was putting up walls for Warrick to knock down.

"How long have you been here?" Maria asked as if

123

she didn't expect to get an answer, which proved to be the right approach. Nico looked back with a contemptuous sneer, clearly not intending to reply. But Warrick got the impression that they didn't get too many visitors at the Citadel. And a lack of visitors meant a lack of the opportunity to show off.

He was right. The doorman grunted as they crossed the midpoint of the courtyard, all the while keeping his rifle up across his chest in ready position. "I'm one of Takio's most trusted lieutenants," he said, his stride lengthening as he spoke, pride evident in every muscle. "My mother lived in apartment 330C when Takio moved in and routed out the slumlord that was systematically raping and killing his way through all the residents too poor to go anywhere else. Takio saved my mother. Saved me. Gave us work. Food. Money to spend. Promised the same if we wanted to bring friends, other families in, to fill up the empty rooms. We did. That was fifteen years ago."

Maria stiffened beside him, and Warrick didn't need to read her mind to guess why — fifteen years ago, Takio had moved into the neighborhood. Fifteen years ago, Maria's cousin Cara had died.

"Now Takio is the most powerful general in all of LA, and la Noche is feared throughout the city. He rewards loyalty and service with safety and power. He runs the other gangs. He runs the government, the police. No one does anything without Takio's permission."

Warrick nodded, searching his memory for Jack's intel on the place.

Except, despite what Maria believed, Jack had very specific experience beyond the first building. First off, once he'd been parted from Maria, he'd had his head hooded every time he'd left the building — Building A —

and it remained hooded until after they'd entered the second building, whatever that building might be. He'd been turned several times, losing all sense of which building he may be in. Eventually, he was able to recognize Buildings B and C, but he knew D only as some sort of lab storage area — tables, shelves, plastic, pills. Lots of pills. He'd never seen anything in production, however. He'd only been there to pick up product and transfer money.

"They put me in there last time," she said, gesturing to the building to the left. "No explanation. Just stuck me there and left."

Nico nodded. "Building B. That's the quarters for the unmarried women. They stay there to keep safe from the guards. Takio is very strict about that."

She shrugged. "I didn't see any women. It was nothing more an empty lobby, with guards at the door."

"You wouldn't have seen them," the doorman said. "You see them, that means you're not coming back out." He grinned then, and it was an uncomfortable look on him. "Not until Takio says you are. And he's a tough man to convince."

This was a human, Warrick struggled to remind himself. A child of God. As such, he was off-limits to Warrick.

To Warrick, but not to Maria. And from the set of her jaw, she was more than ready to take the guy out.

"Good to know," Maria said softly, her gaze fixed on the upper floors of Building B. Sure enough, the few figures he saw in the windows were all women. They ducked away as soon as they noticed him looking at them. Prisoners, almost definitely. Probably being trained in whatever services the gang most needed. He thought of Maria's cousin Cara. Before her murder, she hadn't yet moved into the Citadel, but she'd been being groomed for it. Promised the world in return for her faithful service…and even at fifteen years old, she'd smelled a rat…and maybe seen it too, if what Maria was saying was true. She just couldn't get away from it in time.

Children of God, Warrick reminded himself again.

They finally crossed the last of the courtyard, where the fourth building waited for them. Beneath the extended porch, more guards shifted in the shadows. This building, the one Jack was sure held the lab, as he'd called it, was the most important. Behind it lay a parking lot and access road, and then what looked like bombed-out office buildings, the same as existed on the other sides of the Citadel. A moat of destruction serving as an additional layer of security.

The doors of Building D opened with a metallic hiss, and Warrick's brows went up. Decidedly high-tech for a 1970s apartment complex. Beside him, Maria tensed. She'd noticed it too.

As they walked into this last building, though, Warrick could see that Takio's particular flair for décor remained. The place was an empty concrete box, devoid of furniture, anything on the walls, or even people.

They went through a second set of doors, the sound of them sliding open reverberating off the walls. There was definitely something different about Building D, Warrick decided.

"Mr. Soldaro asks that you go to the basement," the doorman said. "I'm afraid the elevators are out. You'll take the stairs."

"You, not we?" Maria rounded on him. "Where will you be?"

"Mr. Soldaro was impressed with your abilities to defend yourselves the other night. He requires you to impress him further before he is willing to see you."

Nico stepped back through the doors, which hissed

126

shut. "I'll be here to escort you to Mr. Soldaro, on your feet or in a bag," he said through an intercom. He grinned, then, his eyes gleaming with an unholy light. "I hope you enjoy your stay."

A trap, Warrick realized. *Of course.*

Warrick heard the howling before Maria did, but then again, Maria's ears weren't as finely tuned as a demon's were.

"We go down," he said, pushing her ahead of him. And they took off in a run for the basement access as a horde burst out of the far doors.

CHAPTER ELEVEN

"Down, down!" Warrick shouted, and Maria didn't need any convincing. She'd caught only the barest glimpse of the men pounding into the lobby, their eyes wide, their hands outstretched, like zombies hyped up on crack. But the one thing she noticed in a hurry — none of them had guns. Takio had unleashed a horror of doped-up crackheads and set them on kill — but their only weapons were knives.

And as she and Warrick rounded stairwell after stairwell, the first scream of the men above her reverberating down the concrete column, she began to rethink that idea too. Had they been carrying anything in truth, or had she imagined that?

"Move it!" Warrick shot ahead of her and snaked his arm out, half lifting Maria off her feet as he pounded down three more flights in the time it took her to gasp out a protest. Then they were through the basement doors and into a well-lit space filled with shelves, tables, and packing materials. There were stairs and a service elevator at the far end, the latter fronted by stainless steel doors.

Other than the plastic and trash, it was empty.

What's more, it looked like it'd been empty for a long time.

"Shut down," Warrick said, with far less bitterness than Maria felt. "Takio is cleaning house."

"Then what's the point of these guys?" She gestured angrily at the howling. "What purpose could it possibly serve?"

"He's...cleaning house," Warrick said again, more thoughtfully. His eyes suddenly widened as understanding seemed to strike him. *Well, good for him.* One of them should know what was going on.

Maria glanced again toward the service elevator, but something caught her eye in the shadows. Moving...something was moving along the right side of the basement, crouching behind the tables.

"Listen to me." Warrick turned suddenly, rounding on her. "What I'm about to do, what you're about to see — it's not going to make sense. It can't make sense. It's not supposed to."

She scowled at him, taking an experimental sniff of the air. "You mean I'm going to be hallucinating?"

His eyes flared. "Sure. We'll go with that for now. Bottom line, though, do what I say and stay the hell out of sight."

"I know how to fight, Warrick," Maria retorted, her hand stealing to her necklace. "Even without a gun."

"You don't know how to fight this." As if to punctuate his words, an enraged bellow sounded from the stairway — and everything happened at once.

Maria's hand clenched around her gold cross, jerking it, and she felt the chain suddenly grow slack in her hand. She'd snapped the delicate strand of gold. At the same time, the basement door slammed open with enough force that it banged off the wall, then stayed that way, its hinges broken. Maria fell back several steps, nearly regaining her feet, then slipped in something on

129

the concrete and fell hard on her ass.

Warrick turned away from her and roared something incomprehensible as the mob rushed to greet him.

"Maria?"

The voice was so soft, so vulnerable, that Maria figured she must have misheard it. She struggled to stand again, slipped, then, with a curse, planted her hands on the floor and stared down into the murk.

Then the coppery, too-sweet smell hit her. Blood.

She wrenched her hands up and stared at them, revolted as she scrambled up and stared in the harsh light of the basement. Her hands were coated with the viscous red substance, only it was too fresh — too new. Someone would have had to have been gutted even as they'd been running down the stairs for so much blood, so warm, to still be —

Was this a hallucination? Was it already starting?

"Maria?"

The voice was there again, whispering, plaintive, but Maria wiped her hands furiously on her jeans, turning back toward the chaos. In the center of the room, Warrick was brawling like a man possessed. He held two wicked-looking knives in his hands — no, she thought with horror, gaping as her eyes focused. Not knives — claws. Claws that, swear to God, looked like they were still attached to the animal paws that sprouted them. Where in the world had he gotten —

She looked more closely at his attackers. There were dozens of them, and more coming through the basement door even as she watched. But with each new wave, she began to notice differences. At first, the men looked like your garden-variety commandos, dressed in fatigues and tight microfiber shirts, as built and ruthless looking as Warrick, but on a smaller scale. After them, however, the men grew…sloppier, was all she could think to describe it.

She stared in growing horror. No, not sloppier. More slippery. Their faces shifting, their limbs moving disjointedly, their run more a broken lope than the efficient dash of soldiers. Their hands were suddenly too long, their faces too, mouths hanging open and slavering tongues lashing out, tasting the air. And with all of it, the screaming grew more intense, until Warrick looked like he was surrounded by a roiling sea of creatures who were more animal than man. *Oh my God.* This had to be a hallucination, she decided. Because these creatures looked *exactly* like Bonnie had…right before he died.

"War—" she began, then choked off the word immediately as her own name was shouted out.

"*Maria!*" The voice had now climbed to a quavering scream that broke through the shouts of the beasts in the center of the room, becoming its own mournful wail. Maria turned, slipping again in the blood, but there was no one standing there. She stared down in horror at her feet, her white shoes now caked in red up to the laces.

How could there be this much blood?

As she brought up her head again, she saw something, the lurch of a body dragging itself out of the light, back into the shadows behind one of the rows of tables. The tip of a shiny patent leather Mary Jane.

Maria froze in place, her mouth going wide in a scream she couldn't utter. She thought she heard crying. Was that crying?

"Who—who is it?" she managed, though her throat was so dry, she could barely force the words out. "Are you bleeding?"

She winced at the stupidity of the words, the moment of grim humor shaking her out of her reverie. "I'm right here. I'm coming around the corner, okay?

Don't throw anything at me. I'm here to help you."

"Help." The words sounded broken, forlorn, and eerily familiar. Keeping her eyes trained on the patent leather toe, Maria stepped carefully around the worst of the blood, blood that still stood in a stark, deep crimson pool, shiny and wet. There was too much of it, too fresh, for Maria to wrap her head around it. And then there was that shoe, the toe gleaming shiny and pristine despite the gore surrounding it.

She wiped her hand again on her jeans, then lifted it to her neck, absently touching the cross that hung there—then frowned, remembering too late. The delicate necklace was no longer around her neck.

She couldn't stop now, however. She rounded the table…

And fell back.

"Maria." Cara lay on the floor in front of her, holding her stomach, blood pooling out around her as she stared, her mouth open, her eyes wide and impossibly vacant as they fixed on Maria. "Why didn't you protect me?"

Warrick felt the rage billowing up inside him, furious and hot. With Maria safely away, hidden behind one of the rows of tables, he could let his glamour slip and take full advantage of his abilities. His mind raced forward, ripping through each of the horde that opposed him—all of them expendable demon spawn, he noted grimly.

Holkeri was seriously cleaning house.

Warrick counted off their names with furious speed, a roll call of the damned. Some he dispatched immediately; others loped out of his reach to attack again from another direction. And all of them screamed in a jabbering fury, their minds broken — far too broken, even for demons.

They'd been broken on purpose, he realized. Was that how Holkeri had managed to avoid detection so long? He'd used his own kind for his foul drug experiments?

It made a certain sort of sense. Demons were expressly forbidden to harm the children of God, but that didn't mean everyone listened. There were simply too many of them, both humans ripe for exploitation and demons who viewed them as little more than cattle. But Holkeri had already run afoul of God's punishment once. He knew the price he was paying with every human life that he and his minions took. So who better to turn to for his drug trials than creatures so despicable that they didn't even have a vengeful god to rely upon?

Still, it was abundantly clear that Holkeri's experiments had proven to be enormous failures, if this crew of spawn was any indication. Unless Holkeri had been *trying* to come up with a way to destroy his own kind as gruesomely as possible.

There was a sudden slash from the side, and Warrick lashed out with his improvised weapon of a broken demon's claw. His defensive blow struck home, and a geyser of blood issued forth, coating the walls and ceiling. It was a killing blow, as evidenced by the soot that came up with it. But there was no denying that this blood had been tainted long before the touch of death marred it.

He tasted the drug that still pumped through the demon's system, breathed it in, and hissed as he felt the immediate and visceral impact on his demonic body.

Of course.

Holkeri hadn't chosen the least of their kind only because they were handy stooges, bound to follow the higher caste—but by their very nature the demon spawn had been part of the test. The drug that was coursing through their systems felt like a homecoming to Warrick, a taste of the life essence that had once driven him—not now, not anymore. But back when he'd first set foot on the wondrous creation of earth, first felt the sun on his skin, the breeze lifting his hair—he'd felt this essence, this hope. To be a Fallen had not been the curse that others had imagined. It had been a *revelation*.

A revelation his kind had not been ready for. And perhaps never would be.

But Holkeri clearly didn't think that way. Because this drug...this drug that Holkeri was cooking in the basement of Building D was the very essence of what it had meant to be one of God's chosen. As if, impossible as it was to imagine, he could be turned from a demon back into an angel...maybe not in the eyes of God, but by every other barometer: strength, mental faculties, speed, psychic abilities.

No wonder the archangel wanted Holkeri's creation destroyed...even if the earliest incarnations of the drug had had the exact opposite effect on the spawn who'd been Holkeri's test subjects.

Warrick stiffened as a new, far more insidious thought skittered across his mind: maybe the drug had failed *because* Holkeri had used it on spawn. Spawn were two steps removed from being a Fallen. What if that was merely one step too many, and when a demon sampled this drug...

He hissed out a breath. A drug that could roll back the scourge of condemnation—returning demons to their state of Fallen—would change *everything*. Particularly given how many demons now roamed the earth. Suddenly, there would be a race of superbeings once more on the planet. They would be taller, stronger, faster, smarter, more beautiful — *better*. And a Fallen at full strength was virtually unkillable, except by another angel. Worse, there could potentially be scores of them, enough that they would not merely need to teach and guide humans, as God had originally intended…they could, with very little effort, *rule* humans.

As if spurred by his own thoughts, a new wave of demons lurched into the basement, these showing far less physical damage than the first batch — but whose eyes were all glaring crystal white, their mouths dropped open as they unleashed terrible howls of pain.

So, that answered that. Demons had fared better than spawn physically — but not mentally. At least, not with this iteration of the drug. Had Holkeri been holding these unfortunate creatures bound in this building in order to watch them? And, more importantly, had he expected Warrick to clean up his mess for him, or merely to serve as collateral damage, one of two humans who'd gotten too close to his operation?

Warrick thought he heard a scream far across the room now, where he'd left Maria. How had he moved so deep into the bowels of this basement assembly room? And what else was Holkeri developing besides the demon-transformation drug? Because surely that wasn't something he planned on releasing to the general public. It was one thing for a demon to aspire to become a Fallen…but humans would have no way of handling the bodily changes, the mortification of the flesh, that such a change would require.

Then again, Warrick had walked among mortals long enough, to know that they most wanted that which they expressly could not have. What would happen if an ordinary human took such a drug as this? What would they be capable of?

"Syx!"

135

Warrick riveted his attention back to the demon directly in front of him, a hulking beast that, unlike his fellows, did not even bother with the glamour that would have allowed him to look almost human. Instead, he towered above Warrick, his arms hanging down, his heavy claws knuckling the concrete floor. His weight back on his heavy haunches, legs folded beneath him in preparation to pounce.

Warrick stared at him, confused. This creature was not riven with drugs, or at least not the same drugs that were coursing through his fellows. Instead, his mind had been broken, shattered over and over again, then fused back together in the most brutal way possible, until there was nothing of the beautiful creature of God that had once been allowed to live and love and walk this earth, no longer part of the vaunted pantheon of the Father but not yet the cursed scourge that so many of them were destined to become. This creature still possessed a shred of understanding that he was the pinnacle of grace, for all that he bore the appearance of the vilest spawn. How —

And then Warrick knew. This was a Fallen before him. A Fallen who somehow had been convinced it was already a demon.

The wretch before him seemed to register Warrick's recognition, because it launched itself at him in a burst of fury and pain. Warrick unleashed his own pent-up rage to counter it. Together, they spun, the two of them caught up in a vortex of fire. The Fallen took Warrick's fire and added his own, and Warrick tasted the Fallen's sin that he'd committed but had never been judged for, the sin Holkeri in his strength had managed to entrap him with. Holkeri had held the Fallen in his thrall until the one-time angel's mind had been so deeply destroyed and his once-angelic body so hideously damaged that he could not call out for justice that would not be his, could only exist in a sort of half-life, drained of his essence, his power, until he became the thing he reviled most, the abomination of the demon without even glamour to stand between himself and the creatures he loathed.

Warrick screamed with the pain of a millennia of suffering, and ended the Fallen's torment.

Maria fell to her knees as the roar of the battle swept over her, then began crawling toward Cara's beautiful, broken body.

"Cara, sweetheart. It's me. I'm here."

"Why didn't you call to God for help?" Cara moaned again, huddling over on herself. "I trusted you — needed you — "

Maria fought the sob as her mind struggled to understand what she was seeing. Of course this couldn't be Cara. Cara had died fifteen years ago, had been only fifteen at the time. The teenaged girl on the dirty floor in the basement wasn't Cara. She couldn't be. Even if she had the same long, dark, glossy hair, the same enormous dark eyes and full, lush lips. Even if she had her voice which was as sweet as Cara's was.

Even if she'd been gutted in exactly the same way.

"Who did this to you?" Maria asked, desperate not to spook the girl any more than she had to. This wasn't Cara, it was another victim, another young girl, another sick product of the same twisted mind that had created the drugs that Cara had smuggled in her own body in order to belong, in order to excel.

"Maria, why — "

"Shhh, honey, shhh…" Maria edged forward another inch, something worrying at her mind. She wildly scanned this pocket of the room, but she could see no one else in these shadows. There was only her and this fragile, broken girl. Had Cara been so small, in truth? Maria couldn't remember. To her, Cara had been her beautiful older cousin, lithe and mysterious and always in motion, always filled with life, with joy, with laughter.

Until she grew quiet.

Until she started disappearing, her bright light all too quickly dimming.

Until she died one warm night in Maria's arms, her blood spilling out into a wide, shiny pool.

"You should have called," Cara said again plaintively.

And that was it, Maria thought. That was the problem. She *had* to be hallucinating. Because nobody knew that story. She'd been alone with Cara, or virtually alone, surrounded by lights and sirens and screaming people. But no one had come to comfort or render aid to the two huddled girls at the edge of the parking lot. No one had even seen them until it was far too late.

Maria paused in her crawl, rooted in place, and Cara's eyes opened again, tears standing on her thick lashes. "Hold me, and tell me it's going to be okay," she whimpered, and Maria's heart nearly burst all over again.

"I will, sweetheart, I—"

"Don't move, Maria."

Warrick's voice cracked into the sudden silence with such command that Maria froze again, crouching as if she expected him to rain down blows upon her head. Opposite her, Cara's eyes flew wide with fear, the same fear that Maria had seen in them all those years ago, when she could have helped, could have called, could have done *something* to protect her beautiful cousin.

138

Could have, and didn't.

But she could now.

"I've got you, sweetheart," Maria cajoled. "C'mon, look at me."

"Maria, no. What you're looking at is not human. If it touches you, it will kill you." Something was different about Warrick's voice this time, but she didn't have time for him, didn't have time for anything but the child who was lying in a pool of blood in front of her. This wasn't Cara, she knew that, but she was still a child in need. A child who'd been fed the lines that only Cara would know, only her beautiful, free-spirited cousin, who—

"Help me," Cara said, her eyes wide and filled with so much pain, so much beauty. Maria felt the tug of that impossible pain, that harrowing beauty, and she leaned forward, holding out her hand even as Cara, slowly, so slowly, peeled back her fingers from her midsection and shifted forward—

"*No.*"

Maria was shoved aside so quickly, she went face-first into the bloody mess on the floor, the bulk of Warrick's body shooting by her with a speed she wouldn't have thought possible. In a flash, he was at the girl's side, but as Maria watched, instead of scooping her up to transport her to safety, he reached out and gripped the girl's neck and yanked her to her feet.

"Warrick!" Maria gasped, but she couldn't seem to make her legs work, couldn't scramble to her feet as the girl who looked so much like Cara flailed and beat her hands feebly against Warrick's powerful forearm. But even as she watched, the girl's legs kicked and writhed and…and elongated, the thighs growing thick and gnarled, the knees bony, the long calves jutting back to accommodate enormous paws. The girl's hands also twisted against Warrick's arm, growing long, vicious-looking talons as above his gripping fingers, the face contorted, lengthening and sprouting a snout and teeth and blackened eyes.

"No!" it cried, and it was still Cara's voice that howled, still her last anguished plea, until Warrick roared something else back at it, words Maria couldn't understand, and suddenly, the creature in his grasp exploded into sooty, wet spray, coating the walls around them, Warrick, herself. With something that sounded like a curse, Warrick thrust the remains of the creature away from him as Maria finally managed to struggle to her feet and whirl around, her full circle bringing her back to Warrick all too soon.

"Where…" she gasped, barely able to speak. "Where did they all go?"

The room was completely devoid of life except for the two of them standing there—but that wasn't to say it was empty. A thick layer of black goo dripped off nearly every surface. The tables and chairs, the cabinets, the shelves, the overhead light fixtures. Even the walls were coated in streams of the stuff. She turned to Warrick, taking in his eyes—definitely glowing, not a trick of the light—and his bleak face. "What just happened?" she finally managed.

Warrick's golden-amber eyes dimmed. He blinked as if coming out of a fugue.

"We'll get to that," he growled. "First—you dropped this. Put it back on, and double-check the latch."

He handed Maria her cross, swinging from its golden chain, the chain's ends soldered back together again. As she took it, she couldn't help but notice that the skin of Warrick's fingers had been burned white.

CHAPTER TWELVE

With a professionalism that surprised Warrick, Maria insisted on searching the basement for any evidence of an illegal drug operation beyond the obvious packaging paraphernalia—no easy feat considering the wealth of black sludge that coated every open surface. More importantly, she'd accepted his decision not to discuss what she'd seen. She'd rehooked her cousin's necklace around her neck, nodded, and announced their need to search.

Predictably, they'd turned up nothing.

Maria seemed less satisfied with this outcome than Warrick, though. "There's always a stash—always," she grumbled, peering around the room. "Even if it's a legit stash by the counters, an overage to bring counts up to snuff in case of a systems snafu."

"Well, a legitimate stash would have been emptied when they left."

"Fair," she said, but she didn't look convinced. "I'm not saying that I know these people perfectly, but I've been around the Guardia long enough to know that wherever there's an opportunity, there's theft. Not on a grand scale, not that anyone would notice, but we're talking millions of pills being pushed here. Accidents happen, shit hits the floor, and these people are addicts. There's no way they ran a completely tight operation here. Other than the doors, there's nothing state-of-the-art about this place."

"Which begs the question, why here?" Warrick nodded. "Proximity to suppliers?"

"Or proximity to the target market. Whoever Takio was planning on selling the drugs to."

Warrick grimaced, but now was not the time to explain to Maria how wrong she was. Now was also not a time to think about how many demons he'd just banished back beyond the veil. He'd lost count after about eighty.

"We can't go back up the way we came," she said, squinting at the basement door. "They've got to have cameras on us."

"They did," Warrick grunted, gesturing at the ones he'd picked out in the room—four of them, now all coated with thick, black blood. "I don't think they're very helpful right now, but you're right, they'll be coming down to assess the damage, and soon."

Warrick had about hit his limit on dead bodies, even bodies that weren't technically human. Besides, they had a bigger issue. They had to get out.

Still...it had been an epic battle. One that no one would believe he and Maria had survived as two ordinary humans.

He scanned the shadows of the room, noting the service elevators and doorways. "Have you ever been down here?"

"That would be negative," Maria said. "I've been in A and B, that's it. I don't know that Jack ever got down this far either."

"He did," Warrick said, feeling the steel in Maria's gaze as she turned it on him. "He was not as clean a player in all this as he wanted you to believe, Maria. That's reasonable, of course. He liked you. He admired you."

"And I was his ticket out," Maria said wryly. "If I knew he'd truly been in the thick of things with the drug operation, that would've made it more difficult for me to cut the deal that I did that got him out and off to Florida to be with his sister."

"Or to be with his money in some harbor town where no one recognized him after the surgery he plans," Warrick corrected her.

Maria blinked, then smiled wearily. "Fine. At least tell me he wasn't directly involved with the selling or trafficking of these hallucinogens, or whatever these are," she muttered. "Or selling and trafficking anything else, for that matter."

"He wasn't," Warrick said, glad to be able to confirm the truth on that point. "Jack was a product of his environment and his appetites, but he tried to maintain some code of honor even in the midst of all that."

"Good. So, what was he doing down—"

"Wait." Warrick straightened, their momentary foray into Jack's better qualities triggering something in his fragmented memories that he'd originally overlooked. Glee. Something about this place had made Jack happy, and the man hadn't been an idiot. Though he'd been in the assembly room only a few times, he'd seen the pharmaceutical gold that was being packaged there. If he'd known it was only a temporary setup, what would he have done?

Slowly, Warrick pivoted, scanning the room. "Anybody coming or going from the building was subject to a full body search and the digital scan. He couldn't have secreted the pills out of the compound without ingesting them."

Maria snorted. "That really wasn't Jack's style."

"Agreed. When he was down here, it was strictly to get pills and make deliveries for Takio. Closely monitored deliveries. No way could he have taken anything out of here without being noticed." Warrick went over to the service elevator.

"Don't hit that," Maria warned. "They'll be down here in a flash if they think the fighting's over."

"There's a stairwell back here," Warrick said. Sure enough, over to the right was an exit door that led to a second flight of stone steps. It was unmanned, of course, since the operation had left the building.

That still amazed him. All those demons roaming the upper halls, and Holkeri had simply—left them there? Failed experiments to elevate the spawn or to return actual demons to their exalted former state? The creatures he'd banished had been mentally torn apart, crazed with pain and need. But they were not God's favored children.

Did Holkeri think he could get away with his acts because of that?

"Warrick." Maria was peering at the nook at the base of the stairs. "These are sign-in and sign-out cards. Seriously old school. We have them at Lucy's. One of the things Jack always got a kick out of. If he'd noticed this here…"

Warrick jolted, another fragment of memory coming back to him. "He noticed," he said. The hanging file was well out of the spray from the fight in the center of the room, and the cards still stuck out of the slots—but there was an opening at the top, big enough for a clipboard.

She stood on her tiptoes, trying to feel around the opening. "I can't reach."

Warrick moved to where she was standing, reached inside. It took only a moment for him to brush across the telltale shape of the capsule. Five of them. No one would think Jack was the one who'd tossed them here—they wouldn't know who'd done that deed, would have shrugged and returned them to the main supply or, more likely, pocketed the stash for themselves. All Jack had needed to do was wait.

Warrick pulled the pills free and handed three of them to Maria. She stared at him as he glanced back to the card holder.

"This was nearly a year ago," he murmured, going over in his mind what Jack's shattered memory had brought him. "He forgot he'd stashed the pills, maybe was high when he'd done it, which is why they'd left him alone in the first place."

"They knew he wasn't going to get out of here with anything." Maria nodded. She looked down at her outfit and frowned. "There is nothing on me that's not stuck together," she said. "You good with carrying these?"

Wordlessly, he took the three pills, adding them to the two more that he'd palmed. Maria would get her three—plenty for her to analyze. The archangel could take them from her at any time, should he decide to do so. Meanwhile, Warrick would have two to deliver to Michael himself. If these pills represented some new drug that Holkeri was trying to use to turn back the curse of demonism...

It couldn't be possible, could it?

A shout sounded deep in the building, then a clatter of feet on the staircase they'd first descended, at the far end of the room.

"Time to go," Warrick said, pulling Maria with him. They pressed into the rear stairwell, and he was about to race up the stairs when Maria stopped him.

"Wait!" she said. "They'll know that's where we're going—we don't have any other choice. They'll block off the exit with their radios. We should stay here."

He skewered her with a look. "We stay here, and

145

your life is in greater danger than before. You summoned me, and I came to protect you. The new threat will be one I cannot let stand. I will be forced to kill the rest of them."

"Um…I *summoned* you?"

Warrick grimaced. That had been more than he'd wanted to say. "This really isn't the time—" he began, his words cut off by the scatter of gunfire peppering the far stairwell. Clearly Nico and his team wanted to make sure Warrick and Maria weren't trying to come up the way they'd come down.

Apparently, Maria agreed. "Okay!" She nodded vigorously. "We'll try these stairs."

Warrick grinned. "I thought you might agree."

They piled up the back stairs even as the sound of shouting grew louder in the basement behind them. Eventually, they came to a door that was locked and padlocked—but only locked and padlocked, Warrick decided. There were no electrical wires attached to it. The elevator door he'd noted below was wired, yes, but not this access portal. Which meant it was usually heavily guarded.

But that wasn't his problem today. Still riding high on the adrenaline spike of banishing so many demons at once, he reached out and ripped the door off its hinges.

"Jesus!"

Maria hesitated only a moment as Warrick tossed the door to the side, then gamely ran through as he gestured at her almost angrily to precede him. They raced into a large room that had once apparently served as the building's attached garage—not for the residents, though, but for commercial equipment. The service elevator had a bay here, and there were three large garage doors for truck deliveries.

"You know those are going to be attached to some sort of alarm system," she said.

Warrick didn't seem to hear her. He passed her and kept on running, reaching the door a full five strides before she did. She thought for sure he was going to punch through that one too, but he pressed his hand flat against the door instead, his shoulders convulsing.

"What is it?" Maria demanded, looking back over her shoulder. "They're coming up fast, exploring all the exits. They're going to see the shattered door."

"That might not have been us," Warrick said, still exploring the door with his fingers — not even exploring it, but more like testing it for weakness, his hands splayed on the flat surface as if he had some sort of electronic stud finder embedded in his fingertips. "There's a full contingent of demons that's been let loose here. It will be easy to lay any damage at their feet. That's exactly what Nico will do. It's what I'd do."

"Who?" And *wait*, demons?

"The doorman." Warrick's gaze shifted to Maria again, and he frowned, but he was clearly still distracted. *Did he really just say demons?*

Warrick reached out and put one hand on her shoulder, the other one against her face. He stared at her intently. "You're still bleeding."

"Head wound. They're bleeders." She shrugged, though in truth, she did feel light-headed — whether that had to do with the fight, the horror back in that lab room, their mad dash up the stairs...or the fact that Warrick had put a name to the creatures who'd attacked them. Not a hallucination, but...demons. Honest-to-God demons.

No...no, that couldn't be possible.

She shoved the thought away. "You need to focus,

Warrick. The moment they realize we're not down there, they're going to come running for us up these back stairs. We need to be gone."

"No," Warrick said. "We need to wait until they pass by us. Then we can follow them."

"But—"

"Shh. Keep your hands on my skin—my arms. My waist. Don't look at any of them as they pass us. You don't have to shut your eyes, but keep your head down." He pulled Maria close behind a stack of pallets, wrapping his arms around her as the footsteps hit the stairs they'd just climbed. There was a rush of outrage and confusion as the door that Warrick had ripped off its hinges was discovered, and then a knot of armed guards poured through the doorway onto the oversized loading dock.

"Search!" ordered the doorman—Nico, Warrick had called him—as two of the men ran forward and checked the garage doors.

"Locked, sir!" they cried.

Others fanned out in a wide arc, one of them passing within five feet of Maria and Warrick—he never glanced their way once, though their hiding place was hardly ideal. Still, with Warrick's arms wrapped around her, it was as if she didn't exist. As if neither of them existed—as if they were both invisible.

You summoned me, and I protected you.

The full contingent of demons.

What she'd seen in Bonnie...Cedo's eyes...the creatures in the basement. Those were real, not hallucinations.

The devil men, her cousin Cara had called them. *Los Diablos.*

"Open it," the doorman barked, startling Maria back to the present. She watched through slitted eyes as, obligingly, one of his men pounded something on the keypad, and the clanking assembly of the garage door moved up, revealing the dingy gray sky beyond. Maria caught sight of a parking lot, a few cars that had seen better days, and the street beyond. Still clutching her to him, Warrick moved then, and she didn't need to be told to stay close. Moving soundlessly, they followed the others out the door and into the open air.

"No sign of them, sir."

"There should be bodies," Nico said. "Takio said there would be bodies. At least the woman's."

Maria's eyes narrowed, but she didn't resist when Warrick lifted her into a fireman's hold, settling her onto his shoulder. She grabbed his shirt and pulled it free of his camo pants, then laid her hands along his back. If she needed skin-to-skin contact to keep this charade going, she was more than happy to do it.

A phone trilled, and Nico cursed, gesturing to the man to answer.

The man still hesitated. "What should we report?"

"We report what we saw. Nobody made it out of there alive. If Takio wants to see the bodies, tell him we'll bring them to Morpheus once we clean them up. If he tells us not to bother, we're good. If he wants them, we keep looking."

The man nodded, clearly better trained than Maria was, since she was already poking the doorman's plan full of holes. Nobody put two people through a crucible like that and didn't want to see the results.

Nico's direct report seemed to be making the same realization, wincing as a strident voice came over the line—a female voice, Maria realized. So not Takio, but someone close to him. Someone apparently pissed off.

The man hung up. "He wants the bodies, and he wants them yesterday. He also wants samples of the residue brought for analysis."

"Fuck," Nico said. "We find the bodies, then."

The man fidgeted. "And if we don't?"

"Then we get two bodies that are close. Surely we have enough people in this complex that finding a man and a woman who fit the description won't be that hard. Kill them, cut them up, and serve them up in pieces."

Despite herself, Maria nearly choked. *What?*

Her mind raced through the possibilities. If she were responsible, even indirectly, for the death of a man and a woman from the Citadel's poverty-stricken slums, she would never forgive herself. And the couple would have to be hacked to pieces convincingly enough that it could be proven that was the way they'd died—cut up while they were alive. She definitely couldn't live with that.

Warrick clamped his hand on her thighs, but his body heat had kicked up another five notches. He'd heard Nico as well. Good.

Another scream howled from inside the building, and the men turned, rifles up.

"Goddammit." Nico growled. "We can't fucking deal with them and get the bodies. You two—go round up likely candidates. You saw them, tall woman, taller man, shouldn't be hard to find. As long as the fucking animals are loose in the zoo, we're not going to find anything. And we don't have enough tranqs in the world to keep them quiet for long."

Another scream, and several more men ran—or more like fled from the building, the last one waving wildly as the garage door crashed shut—and suddenly, Maria got it. The high-tech doors, the barricaded staircases. Takio wasn't trying to keep people out...he was trying to keep his lab rats in. Lab rats that even now had been driven to the point of hysteria with so many of their brethren dead beneath them. Their minds might have been fractured, but their vital urge toward self-preservation had to be clicking in…whatever the hell they were.

Demons.

They couldn't let those things escape any more than they could let Nico kill two innocent victims. Surely Warrick had to see that. Surely there was something that could be done.

Beneath her, Warrick breathed two quiet words she could barely make out. "Stefan," he whispered. "Raum."

CHAPTER THIRTEEN

After mentally communicating what was needed at the Citadel, Warrick didn't wait for the other members of the Syx to show up. They would triangulate on the coordinates of the call, drop into the loading parking lot of the Citadel building, and figure out from the screams where best to go. When he'd sent the summons out to them, his directives were clear enough: make a big noise.

As to the human sacrifices...

He grimaced. Humans could do what they wanted to humans. That was the game. But this one wouldn't play out exactly as planned, given the C-4 he'd suggested Stefan and Raum bring with them. They wouldn't blow up the building—but they would blow off its doors. Then they'd take care of the rest of the demons as they poured through the opening. Child's play, considering how deranged the demons inside Building D were at this point. After that, they could keep Nico and whoever else was on his team from doing any damage to anyone until more humans landed on the scene.

Warrick moved around the corner with Maria, dropping her lightly to the ground. As she stepped back from him, her eyes were wild, panicked.

"Warrick, we can't let Nico kill those people," she hissed.

"He won't. But we have to move."

"No! I'm serious!" Maria growled in frustration as he took off, tugging her along inexorably with him. He'd done this often enough, he knew the clearance protocols. The faster they got away, the —

Boom!

The explosion was so intense, the surge of heat so great that he and Maria went flying, the two of them breaking contact as their bodies were flung across the parking lot and hard up against the chain-link fence. Warrick immediately rolled to his feet, but Maria lay in a crumpled heap, out cold. He crouched and checked her vitals, grimacing in relief as he picked her up again. She was his to care for, and she'd nearly been killed twice so far on his watch.

Holkeri was going to pay.

He turned as she stirred against his chest, could almost feel her lids flickering open. "What — fire?"

"Emergency vehicles will be dispatched, even to this hellhole," he said grimly. "Nico will have his hands too full to find anyone to kill and dismember — especially if he's given to understand that some of the test subjects were set free specifically to hunt him down."

"But — what?"

Maria swooned again, causing Warrick to frown down at her. As her head lolled to the side, he saw the massive gash on her temple and exploded with a flood of curses he hadn't used since the fall of Atlantis. Humans were so frail!

Without any other recourse, he held Maria close and started walking down the street. He couldn't heal her in broad daylight, not and still protect her. But he couldn't let her bleed out on the street either. He needed somewhere private.

An EMT vehicle careened around the corner, clearly heading for the Citadel, and Warrick angled Maria away, remembering too late he'd dropped their glamour of invisibility. The van passed him at high speed, then Warrick turned in surprise as he heard it slam the brakes, the cherry-red vehicle flipping a U-turn in the middle of the street and racing back toward him. Warrick leapt back as the van nearly ran up on the curb, then the driver stopped it and jumped out, running around the back of the van to open its rear doors.

"I don't need—" Warrick began, then recognized the bright blue, laughing eyes of the driver.

"Get in!" Finn shouted as he flung the doors open. "Go, go! Get in!"

Warrick climbed into the van, surprised to see a bunk already outfitted for a patient as Finn slammed the doors behind him. He dropped Maria onto the bed, strapped her in. She still didn't move as Finn hauled open the driver's side door again, then vaulted into the seat.

"Since when do you know how to drive a van?" Warrick demanded.

"The Lord works in mysterious ways, my brother!" Finn howled, and they shot off down the street, sirens and lights still going. "You got a destination?"

"Hollywood Boulevard." Warrick's lexicon of LA locations was limited to Jack's memories, but the nightclub Morpheus had made an appearance in a few of the more booze-soaked entries in the man's mind. And Nico had mentioned it too. He pulled open one of the drawers in the van's shelving, hauled out antiseptic pads. "How'd you know where to find me? I made the summons from ground zero."

"And Stefan and Raum were happy to oblige you, bang-bangs and all. God, I love having access to actual materials when we get called. I got tapped by Death."

"Death?" Warrick looked up from where he was wiping the worst of the blood away from Maria's head. Fortunately, only a little of it seemed to be hers, the rest of it the spray from the demon he'd iced too near to her. "What's her interest?"

"Apparently, all things Syx are her interest right now," Finn said as Warrick returned his attention to Maria. He laid his hand alongside her head, palm to temple, and closed his eyes briefly, whispering the words of healing that had been among the many gifts bestowed upon the Fallen. Even with all they had suffered and everything that had been stripped from them, the Syx could still do a great deal with and for humans. Maria's skin began to knit together as Finn continued.

"Between our impressive job on the beaches of Aca-*pul*-co and the one-man Spawnageddon you pulled off at the Citadel, Death is angling for a fast track to get us turned legit. Michael isn't having any of it, but she's piling on with the whole Day of the Demon the world just endured. Reports are coming in, and they are not good, my brother. Most of the horde that was released are still getting their feet under them, so we've got half the crew that's confused as shit and half that's ready to party — hold on!"

The vehicle lurched to the right, and Warrick threw himself over Maria, but her straps did their job of holding her tight in her bunk. When he peeled himself away from her, he nodded, satisfied. She was still out, but she was breathing normally once more. He touched his finger to her neck. Her pulse was strong, too strong almost, her heart pounding the blood through her arteries. Did humans' adrenaline elevate even while they were unconscious? He didn't know, and he didn't care. Maria was all right. A quick search of the rest of her body confirmed she had no other injuries except a swollen ankle and a banged-up knee, and he continued his murmured prayers as he worked over each area.

"Whereabouts on Hollywood?" Finn asked over the sirens. "We got maybe another twenty minutes."

"Club called Morpheus. I don't know anything about it. We'll need a room too — somewhere close."

"Good thing we have the power of a worldwide information superhighway at our fingertips," Finn said, and despite his breakneck speed and the fact that he was driving predominantly with the horn, he yanked out his phone. Within another minute, he was dialing a number.

"Well, hello, Pinnacle Hotel, I'm going to need a reservation — yes, those are sirens. This EMT vehicle is right on top of me." Finn continued his rat-a-tat conversation as Warrick eased back, finally taking a moment to attend to his own injuries. The personal glamour that demons had been gifted with in the earthly plane were the same they'd assumed as Fallen, but it damaged much more easily, revealing the abomination beneath if demons weren't careful. He pulled his shirt off and winced as he laid his hand over his bruised ribs. Another whispered prayer, and he could take a deep breath again. He used the antiseptic pads to wipe away the blood from his face and torso, wincing slightly as the sharp astringent bit into his broken skin. With another swipe, that was set to rights too.

"You're all set," Finn called back. Warrick looked up in time to take a duffel in the chest. "And you both stink like tar. Do something about that, okay?"

"Where are these — forget it, I don't want to know." Warrick dumped the clothes out on a counter, then quickly peeled out of his pants and boots, replacing them with a similar outfit in much higher quality material. "Morpheus isn't a luxury club?"

"It's a total luxury club, so luxe it's casual, my man. But you can pick up fancier gear for tonight." As Finn talked, Warrick filled his pockets with the weapons his fellow Syx had thoughtfully included as well. Ceramic throwing stars, wooden stunners, miniature knives that looked like car keys. "According to Death, if that's where Holkeri is holed up, you're going to have a bitch of a time separating him from the herd. And you're going to have to pull a lower profile than you did at ol' Holly Hills."

"Noted."

Warrick turned back to Maria...and found her staring straight at him.

Maria tried to sit up, only to discover she was strapped to the bunk. Before she could react, however, Warrick was right there, popping the latches of her straps and standing back as she swung her feet to the floor and straightened.

"Who are you, specifically and exactly?" Her question was sharp, but at least Warrick had the grace to look abashed as the motormouth driver whistled low in the front of the vehicle. "And who the hell is he?"

"Finn—"

"I got this, Finn," Warrick growled, effectively shutting up the younger man.

Almost. "Shutting up!" Finn agreed. He bent over the wheel, giving the road in front of him his full attention.

Maria didn't take her eyes off Warrick. He'd saved her life once already, twice, possibly, if you counted the attack in Sycamore Park. But had he also intervened a third time?

You summoned me, and I protected you.

"Who are you?" she asked again. "Or should I be asking *what* are you?"

"Ohhh, burn." The words were only barely audible coming from the front of the van, but Maria heard them nevertheless.

Warrick's jaw tightened in a grimace, but he didn't shrink from Maria's gaze. "You tell me," he said, gesturing at her neck. "You summoned me."

Reflexively, Maria's hand leapt up to the cross she hung there, but the first answer that sprang to mind didn't feel at all correct. "You're not an angel."

His smile was rueful. "Not for a very long time."

Something in his words caught her. She hadn't read the Bible in decades, but she had read it before. Once. When she was a kid. And Cara had believed in it wholeheartedly, of course. The Bible, the church on the corner, the cross around her neck she'd gotten from some aunt or another. All things that Cara believed in, none of which had saved her when it mattered. "But you were once?"

Warrick nodded. He drew breath to speak, and Maria raised a hand. "In English, please. I don't know my um, biblical history or whatever, all that well."

A small smile eased across Warrick's face, making him look impossibly weary. But he continued. "The short version is—I was an angel. I fell, becoming a Nephilim. And then I sinned through an act of rage, harming humans in the process. For that sin, I was damned. After that, I agreed to protect God's children against those of my kind whose sins were even worse than my own. I became a protector, an enforcer able to be summoned by those in need."

"That was you who shot Bonnie," Maria said, her fingers still gripping the cross around her neck. "You showed up behind me because I said Cara's — oh my God!" Sudden realization struck her, and she shrank back on the bed, hitting the cold siding of the emergency vehicle. "Cara's prayer. She was right, you would have come if I'd had the courage to say it for her — someone would have come!"

"*No.*"

Warrick's words were so forceful that Maria jerked, her hand dropping reflexively from the amulet to grip the edge of the bed.

"The cross around your neck is powerful, Maria. It's a ward, more so than most religious jewelry, and it keeps me from knowing your thoughts. But when you lost it in the basement at the Citadel, I could touch your mind. Your memories. You *believed* you were seeing Cara on the floor there, so that night was fresh in your mind. Cara gave you the cross too late, Maria. The prayer. She was already too close to death before she asked you to make that plea." Warrick sighed. "It happens all too often."

Maria blinked hard, the tears welling in her eyes, but mastered herself to glare at Warrick. "You can read my *thoughts*?"

"Not anymore," he said, gesturing to the cross. "Do you know where it came from?"

"I…" She frowned, looking down at the necklace. "I don't. Cara wore it nearly all the time. I never asked her where it came from." She glanced back up at him. "But you heard me when I used her prayer earlier this week. And you came."

"I did," Warrick agreed. "I — Finn — everyone on my team is bound to answer the call of a human confronting a demon. I answered yours when you were taking aim at Bonnie. You wouldn't — couldn't have killed him. It's not for God's children to murder the damned."

"The first shot," she muttered. She'd been right. She

hadn't shot her gun—Warrick had. "That's why Cedo was so surprised, because..." She blinked. "Wait. Bonnie is...was a demon. And Cedo and that—that other guy who seemed to know what was going on when I...we shot Bonnie, he was too?" What was that man's name? She realized she didn't know. Cedo had never called him by name.

Warrick merely stared at her. He didn't have to answer. She already knew the truth. "Um, how many of you *are* there?"

A rolling voice came from the front of the van, in perfect game-show style. "Ladies and gentlemen, it's the question of the hour!"

Warrick's jaw tightened so hard, she was surprised he didn't crack his teeth into pieces. "There's no way of knowing exact numbers. But demons have walked the earth since the first fall, at the dawn of humanity. Recently—very recently—their numbers have significantly increased."

"And your job is to kill them."

"To banish them," he corrected.

Her eyebrows shot up. "Like, to hell?"

"To wherever they can't do harm to the children of God." Warrick said the words without a hint of self-consciousness, but Maria's mind had already rabbited to her next realization.

"So those things in the basement were totally demons—all of them?" she asked, unable to keep the horror out of her voice. "That thing that looked like Cara?"

"Glamour is one of the oldest abilities of both the Fallen and demons," Warrick said. He turned to the pile of clothes, then tossed several items to her. "We're nearly at the club where Takio is holed up."

"Not Takio, no," Maria said as she grabbed the

clothes. There was something else she was going to say, something else she wanted to ask, but this took precedence. "Finn called him something else. Holkeri? Holkeri. Something like that. That's why you're here. You know him."

Warrick nodded. "I know him. He's one of the oldest of our kind, and the most ruthless. I have banished him before. The fact that he returns to live among man, with all he has done, is a testament to his strength. But strength can take you only so far. Humanity has a way of wearying even the most discerning souls, and demons have never been known as discerning."

"Mmph." Maria struggled to pull off her T-shirt and sports bra, then replaced it with clothing that made her pause.

"Um, Moncler? Seriously?"

At Warrick's blank look, Maria held out her T-shirt. "This shirt. It's like three hundred dollars or something. I saw the brand in a Nordstrom's once."

"Then it will suit our needs," he said. "Takio—we'll call him Takio—is holed up in Morpheus. It's a club—"

"I know what it is," she said. "It's high-end but likes to act low-key. Right." She yanked up the underwear and new pair of jeans, not trusting herself to check the brand of either. Sliding off the bench, though, she paused. Looked down.

"My ankle," she said flatly, then her hand went to her head. Her scalp felt smooth and cool to the touch. "And come to think of it—my head. How is it… I know I cracked it. Hard."

Warrick's eyes flared with a heat Maria couldn't quite understand, but that drilled straight through her, sending her own heat boiling through her veins.

"You are mine to protect," he said simply. "I healed you."

Warrick couldn't deny the surge of emotions that nearly swamped him—lust, certainly, seeing Maria's beautiful body, a body he'd held and healed. An ownership he couldn't allow. Pride in the way she was looking at him now. Desire.

Ruthlessly, he shoved all that to the side and focused on the matter at hand. "We have rooms at the hotel beneath the nightclub. We'll enter privately," he said, recalling Finn's conversation as they'd driven. "Do whatever reconnaissance we can. You'll need to check in with Stan?"

"Probably." Maria blew out a breath. She finished pulling on her ankle boots, and ran her hands through her hair a second time, then a third. With Warrick's touch, no one would even know she'd been attacked by the horde or blasted across a parking lot. He quelled another absurd swell of pride. He had a job to do here, and he would do it. Then she would return to her world, and he would return to his calling.

He nodded. "We have these as well," he said, holding up the small plastic bag he'd found in the EMT vehicle's storage drawers, now containing pills. Three of them. Maria's eyes lit up as he tossed the bag to her. "You can get them to him, but only if it's a discreet pickup. As far as Takio knows, we're both dead."

"We got a confirmation on that dead, by the way," Finn chimed in from the driver's seat. "Once they iced the rest of the horde at the Citadel, Stefan produced a couple of bodies burned beyond recognition."

Maria blanched, but Warrick waved away her concern as Finn kept talking. "The head goon was happy to buy it, took pictures, and sent them on his phone, then Stefan distracted him long enough that he couldn't bag the bodies before the poh-lice showed up. Bodies that weren't actually there, natch, so nothing to bag. All the glamour, none of the goop. But bottom line, you're in the clear for at least a couple of days. We got the head goon, Nico, in handcuffs for reasons not even he's sure of, and half the police force is descending on the Citadel as we speak. Not saying it's going to much help the people who are left, but...

"It'll be better," Maria said, almost like a mantra. "It's got to be better."

"It can't hardly be worse," Finn agreed.

Warrick handed Maria a phone, and she punched in a number, turning away. He moved up to Finn's side as they rocketed through the streets, though Finn no longer had the sirens going.

"I'm going to miss those sirens," Finn sighed.

"Any other directives I'm missing from Michael?" Warrick asked, his voice low. He wasn't used to working this closely with the archangel, and he wasn't a fan. He was pretty certain the archangel wasn't either.

"That would be negative," Finn said, his voice instantly turning serious. They had fought together since before the Atlantean war. Though Finn was the youngest among them, he was Warrick's closest ally. Warrick had seen what had caused Finn's fall into disgrace, had seen the anguish that the demon now covered with his quick comebacks and ready wit.

Now Finn slowed the vehicle yet more, turning off the main drag. "Michael hasn't said a word since he shuffled you out here, hasn't tapped any of us for a meet and greet either. Maybe he's still trying to sort out how many demons have made landfall, but I think he's keeping his own counsel. He's got an elite group of enforcers to play with, and it's up to him how to use us." Finn grimaced. "It's also not such a bad thing that we're so much in demand, I'm thinking. Kind of cuts down on his desire to ship us back to our bolt-hole."

Warrick's growl started low in his throat. "He can't keep us from answering when we're called."

"No," agreed Finn. "But he can replace us, according to Raum. As long as we're damned, he holds all the cards." He slanted Warrick a look. "Raum might maybe have mentioned what Holkeri was trying to do in his little basement love nest. He get anywhere close to the goal on that?"

Warrick sighed, remembering the barest hint he'd gotten of his long-lost state of grace. "Let's just say I think the archangel will be glad to have this drug out of circulation."

Finn snorted. "Oh, I bet he will."

"Warrick?"

He turned to see Maria standing uncertainly behind him. She held up the phone. "Stan still thinks you're DEA, because that's who's breathing down his neck. He wants to check in with your superiors, coordinate response."

Warrick winced, lifting his hand to pinch the bridge of his nose. "Tell him that only the minimum number of operatives should be on-site. That I'll have my guy contact him, and he shouldn't act before that."

"You're going to have someone call him?" she asked, her disbelief obvious.

"Of course not." Warrick scowled. "If he needs a name, say I'm with...I don't know." He searched his mind for the last government office he'd allied himself with. "Office of Strategic Services."

Maria blinked. "Office of—"

"Whoa, whoa, whoa, no." Beside him, Finn barked a laugh. "Do *not* tell him that. Tell whoever Stan is that Warrick's so deep undercover that he will not be recognized by the DEA no matter what, and that Stan's

164

got to play it cool."

"Right."

Maria turned back to her phone, and Finn took another right, bouncing back onto Hollywood Boulevard. "Target is up on the right. I'm going to go back to their medical/special guest services loading dock. They know we're coming."

"Thanks," Warrick said.

"Anytime." Finn said. He stopped at a light and looked up to Warrick. Maria's voice still murmured in the background. "The rest of the Syx aren't going to be able to go in there, I'm thinking. Michael's setting this up so it's your party."

"I know." Warrick gripped Finn's shoulder. "I'll see you on the other side."

Finn turned into the bright façade of the Pinnacle Hotel. "That you will, my brother. That you will."

CHAPTER FOURTEEN

Maria grabbed the key card from Warrick and moved toward the elevator, wondering if anyone in the hotel would recognize him. Takio might know her, but with her long black hair and Latina features, Maria was relatively inconspicuous in LA. She could blend.

Warrick could blend too, only not at all for normal reasons. At six foot six, he definitely stood out in this town of actors and musicians, so she figured he'd at a minimum present himself as shorter. But would he go for boring too? Was that even an option for a six-thousand-year-old demon killer?

She snorted. She still wasn't sure how the glamour thing worked. If someone took Warrick's picture, then what? It came through only as a blur? That might have worked in the early 1900s, but nobody would believe today's cameras screwed up every shot.

Early 1900s. And the way Warrick spoke, in that deep, resonant rumble, it seemed like he was a lot older. Like thousands of years older. He'd mentioned that he'd fallen, even used the term Nephilim. Did angels still fall in today's day and age? Or had that been a one-time party that had gotten out of hand?

It made her head hurt to think about it. And it made her heart ache to realize how foolish she'd been for doubting Cara's faith. Maybe if she'd believed in her older cousin, had acted immediately that night…even if Cara couldn't have been saved, perhaps some of the members of la Noche would have been taken out by one of the Syx, and so many *other* lives would have been spared.

So many questions Maria would never know the answer to…so much guilt she'd have to carry with her, a debt she'd spend her life trying to repay.

Maria grimaced as the elevator climbed all the way to what the hotel called the Emperor's level. Not quite the penthouse, but not jammed in with the great unwashed either. Probably cost thousands of dollars a night, but hey. The funds weren't coming out of her budget, and not the Feds' budget either, since Warrick was no more an operative than Santa Claus was. So who was paying for it? Could Warrick also make illusionary money that actually worked?

The elevator chimed, came to a stop, then opened onto an elegant spill of pale, plush carpeting that led to a series of doors along a luxuriously appointed hallway. Maria moved down the corridor until she found her and Warrick's assigned room, then stepped inside, bemused as she executed a cursory search of the opulent interior.

The place was bigger than her apartment—even the one back in Sylmar—with a complete seating area, kitchenette with dining nook, and enormous king bedroom. The bedroom alone was worth the price of admission, whatever that admission price had been, and…

She rounded the corner into the artfully designed bathroom—and stared. There was no tub in the Pinnacle's Emperor's suite. Instead, a shower opened up with no doors and fully six spigots sticking out from the wall, exactly like Lucy's locker room shower yet totally not, with the inlaid stone floor and walls, the fact that the spigots were arranged in a vertical and not horizontal pattern, the low lighting, the heavy spa robe hanging invitingly on the shower hook over an honest-to-God puffy satin hanger, the luxurious towels...

Before she could stop herself, Maria started pulling off her expensive new clothes, laying them carefully on the granite counter of the sink—T-shirt, Dolce & Gabbana jeans...*Dolce & Gabbana!* Bra, underwear, boots, socks. She stared at the small, expensive pile, missing her gun. She wasn't in the barrio anymore, after all. She didn't have to pretend she wasn't a cop. As soon as she was done with her shower, she was going to get back on the phone with Stan and ask for her weapon. He owed her details about where they'd meet for the pill pickup anyway, and she needed something tangible besides Warrick to defend her from whatever goons Takio had around him in this place.

Takio. Her lips twisted as she considered the guy. She'd still never met him, she realized. He'd sent his agents into her world three different times, and she'd been witness to the death and damage they'd rained down around her, and she'd never even seen the Big Bad himself, had nothing to go on but sketchy photos and Cedo's and Jack's vague descriptions.

Were those photos, those descriptions so terrible because he was a...

She snorted. Try as she might, she couldn't use the words, not even in her own mind. No matter what she'd seen in the Citadel's basement, what she'd seen Warrick do, the idea of demons coexisting so closely with her own world was—impossible. She was willing to believe the hallucination idea more easily than the idea that there were real demons walking the streets.

Maria's glance strayed back to the shower. She was safe for the moment, anyway. Safe...and in desperate need of any shower that rocked six showerheads.

She padded across the cool tiled floor and into the shower space. She could reach the faucets while avoiding the main thrust of the sprays, and she quickly turned the knobs until a waterfall was unleashed against the terra-cotta-and-cream-patterned enclosure. A quick reconnaissance of the bathroom yielded all the fancy soaps and shower products a girl could need, and she dumped them onto one of the three—three!— different ledges in the shower, then quickly stepped under the spray.

"*Oh...*"

Maria placed her hands on the walls of the bath, willing the heat, the pressure of the water to pound her into oblivion. She had enjoyed her fair share of showers—and Lucy's water pressure was a minor miracle in and of itself—but she knew for a fact that never in her life had she experienced bliss like this. If this was how the other half lived, she might be needing an upgrade.

As she picked up one bottle, then another, however, her mind quickly moved on from its paroxysms over the shower and back to the problem at hand. They still needed to take down the drug lord Takio nee Holkeri. Maria still needed to wrap her mind around the reality of demons walking the earth...now more than ever before, apparently. And she would very quickly need to reconcile herself that this op was well and truly busted. For a good reason—they were about to get their man. But that meant more than Maria returning to her small apartment in Sylmar, her work on the force, her life.

Because she really didn't have a life. She'd spent the last fifteen years building her strength, accumulating all the information she could about Takio and his lieutenants. She'd finished high school, taken enough college courses to enter the police academy in good standing, become a cop. And she'd been a good cop. Not a great one, but a good one. Good enough to get the undercover job when it came up, good enough to be dropped back into her old neighborhood with no one the wiser, good enough to flip Jack with a speed and efficiency that had impressed her handler and surprised herself.

But all that was done, she thought, as she tilted her face up to take the full brunt of the spray. All that was…

Maria heard the door open to the hotel room like a crack across her senses. Immediately, she whipped her hair back, cleared the soap from her eyes and hands, and slipped out of the shower, missing her gun more than ever. There wasn't anything sharper in the bathroom than a nail file, but she picked that up and slipped it between her fingers. Not great, but at least it was something.

No one spoke; no one called out. Surely Warrick would have called out, right? Had they covered that in demon covert ops training?

Rolling her eyes, she considered her options. If the new arrival was Warrick, which it almost certainly had to be, she was safe, she was protected. If it wasn't Warrick, she was screwed.

She clamped her teeth around the hilt of the nail file as she pulled the robe off its hook, quickly lashing the thick terry cloth garment around her. Then she returned the file to her hand and walked to the open door of the bathroom, grateful she'd left it ajar. She bent low. If a bad guy was looking for movement, he'd be expecting it at head height. She glanced out quickly, pulled back, and straightened.

Okay, it was definitely Warrick out there. She stepped out from the doorway but still hesitated, content to simply watch him for a moment. He was standing with his back to her, his attention riveted fully on the view over downtown LA, his entire body looking taut enough to spontaneously combust. Marie realized that she hadn't truly looked at him again since the attack at the Citadel. Now she indulged in the luxury of it. Warrick's long, thick frame was poured into a black T-shirt and expensive draping trousers that hugged every curve and dip of his broad back and tight backside. The material stretched over his heavy thighs in a way that unaccountably made Maria's mouth water.

This is a demon, she reminded herself. *I'm seeing what he wants me to see.*

But...didn't there have to be some truth at Warrick's core, to even present an appearance that resonated so strongly with her? It wasn't his body that she was reacting to—at least not entirely. It was his dedication, his drive, his fierce need to protect. And then there was how he treated her...

He *had* legitimately reacted to her, she found herself thinking unexpectedly, first in the shower at Lucy's, and then again last night on the couch in her apartment. She hadn't imagined that. And right now, staring at him, a longing stole over her that started out as simple desire and quickly grew into a need strong enough, she almost staggered. It went beyond the quick gratification of sex, though that was certainly there, and well into the simple craving of another person's touch. Of Warrick's touch. A man who'd fought beside her, a man who'd protected her. A man...or something like a man...who'd come when she'd needed him most.

Maria had spent most of her life walled off from any sort of relationship, even the most fleeting. But she didn't want a relationship, she told herself. She merely wanted—that touch.

And she knew, at least at a minimum, that Warrick would be willing to touch her. To hold her. Wouldn't he?

Maria swallowed. What was she going to do now?

What the hell am I going to do now?

Warrick stared out the window with the intensity born of six thousand years of training and focus, but he was almost laughably inadequate to the task. He needed to get his bearings, needed to adjust his body to accept the fact that Maria was standing alone in a fall of overheated water, wet and naked and—

Stop that.

The moment he'd entered the suite, he'd stopped cold, surveying the space quickly to reassure himself it was uncompromised. It was, save for the fact that water was running full tilt in the next room, and Maria had been nowhere in sight—though the scent of sky was everywhere in the hotel suite and even now wafted out on billows of steam from the bathroom. It didn't take an expert to figure out that she was taking a shower.

Otherwise, she hadn't left so much as a footprint in the main area of the suite. Warrick had dropped his purchases on the small dining table, quickly searched the living room and bedroom. No one there. No one really could be there, not this quickly. He'd walked into the clothing boutique and made his selections with a speed and entitlement the store attendants seemed used to, and he'd contacted Finn to get him the other supplies he'd need now that he'd seen the layout of the hotel. He'd even poked his head into the nightclub, ignoring the cordoned-off ropes and hurrying waitstaff preparing for the night's shift. It was a long way from the strip club in Compton, but perhaps not so different in the end.

Now he needed to make sure Maria was ready for the night ahead, make sure he was, for that matter. But he hadn't expected to return to his hotel room and be faced with—

"Warrick?" At Maria's voice, Warrick turned, bracing himself for the sight of her naked. Instead, it was actually worse: She stood wrapped in a white fluffy-looking robe, her hair swept back, every inch of exposed skin rosy with steam. Her eyes were wide and almost pleading in a way that deeply unsettled him.

"What is it?" he asked, instantly alarmed. Maria flushed, bit her lip, and gestured back to the shower, which was still blasting. He didn't miss the fact that tucked into her hand was a pathetically small nail file. She'd been scared, he realized. He'd scared her.

"Would you—would you mind standing guard? In there?" she asked, the question sounding so obvious, so straightforward, he found himself agreeing without fully working through the details.

"Of course."

Maria swiveled back toward the bathroom and, a second later, disappeared, and Warrick drew in a long, tortured breath. He could do this. Of course he could do this. Maria was a human in need of protection, and he'd been assigned as her protector. Whatever she required, however she required it, he was honor bound to give. If she asked for anything that he felt he couldn't give, of course, he could deny her...but denying a well-intentioned human any request was counter to everything he had been created and forged for.

And she was taking a shower. He could handle a woman taking a shower.

Resolutely, Warrick stomped up toward the bathroom, stepping into its dimly lit interior. The way it was set up, he couldn't see Maria from his position by the door, but the robe she had been wearing had been tossed onto the counter along with her clothes — along with the nail file, he noticed.

He stood for a moment, unsure. He could hear her in the shower, he didn't need to have eyes on her to protect her, and his heightened awareness covered the full length and breadth of the hotel suite. If anyone tried to get in, he'd know it. He didn't need to see —

"Warrick." His name floated out to him so softly on the heavy mist, he wasn't sure Maria had even said it aloud, but he could no more resist its pull than he could stop breathing the air of this plane. He moved without thinking to the edge of the shower, then stepped around the corner.

His blood roared to life, the needs, the passions of his physical form nearly swamping him.

Maria stood facing him, her body bared to the cascading stream of water. No, not stream — *streams*, jets shooting out from above her but also to either side, blanketing her in a cascade of sensual, wet heat. She stared at him with huge eyes, her stance at once beckoning and vulnerable, her need so crystal sharp, it seemed to cut him like a hook, piercing him, then drawing him closer to her, every step an exquisite mix of pain and pleasure.

"Join me," she whispered. "Please."

The command was real, absolute, and impossible to ignore. Warrick stripped almost without consciously realizing it, shucking his shoes and socks, shirt, pants and briefs, then moved again toward her. He didn't stop until he was a bare inch from her body, his hold on his own form as ruthless as he could make it, though there was no denying his reaction to her. He couldn't seem to stand within five feet of the woman without going hard and ready, but this — this was so much worse.

Maria lifted her palms and placed them flat on his

chest, her attention apparently mesmerized by his presence so close to her. She splayed her fingers wide, skimming the hard planes of his pecs, drifting her fingertips over the flat nipples. He grimaced. This, he could withstand. This, he could endure, this —

Maria sighed, the sound of such pure feminine contentment that Warrick's sight began to fracture. As a Fallen, he had been reborn to meet the needs of mortals, the needs — and the desires. But he had long ago conditioned himself against those needs. He served in other ways. He gave of himself differently.

Now, however, his entire body burned for her to ask of him what he was nearly turning himself inside out to give. He couldn't — wouldn't force her. The idea was anathema to him. But he also couldn't — wouldn't deny her. And not because of how he was made, but…because he wanted to. For the first time in millennia, a human would whisper for him to protect, to defend, to give, and he would do it with every ounce of his being, not out of obligation, but out of his own base, carnal need.

But she had to ask.

"Thank you," Maria said, the words so quiet that Warrick nearly lost them in the rush of his own blood in his ears, the spray of the water. But as she slid her hands down his chest, circling his hips to rest on his ass, he swallowed. He wanted the woman so badly, it had become a physical presence between them, a presence compromised further as her fingers left his hips and found his hands — hands which were hanging uselessly at his side.

She lifted those hands, and he watched in almost stunned fascination as she pressed them to her breasts.

The moment Warrick felt the soft, heavy weight of her breasts in his palms, he exhaled a ragged breath, surprised to realize he'd not allowed even the flow of oxygen to interrupt that moment. He palmed Maria's breasts, squeezing them gently, and she gave a soft, strangled moan of her own, her eyelids fluttering shut. She swayed toward him, her lips parted, and as she lifted herself up on her tiptoes, he bent down, his hold firming on her breasts as he brushed her lips with his. She tasted exactly like he remembered, a mixture of salty and sweet, blood and heat and sky, and Warrick felt his own need redoubling. She leaned into him, her hands dropping once more to cup his ass, and he hissed against her mouth.

Maria didn't stop, didn't slow the steady palpating rhythm of her palms, but she pulled back enough to stare at him, her eyes wide and hot, her skin glistening with the spray of hot water. The movement of her leaning back tilted her hips forward, and Warrick gritted his teeth as she pressed his erection into the sensual curve of her belly, her core radiating heat.

"Do you want…this?" she asked, pulling him in close to her. It wasn't the question of a seductress. It was honest and straightforward and unflinching, and Warrick's response was barely more than a gasp.

"I want it," he managed. "But I'm a demon, Maria."

"I know what you are."

He winced. She didn't. She couldn't, not really. And yet he wasn't strong enough to show her the truth…was definitely not strong enough to deny her.

"Then you should know you are in complete— control," he said, gritting his teeth as another surge of desire shot through him. "You can ask anything of me, and I will give freely—not that you can compel me, no." He moaned, seeing the flicker of worry that skated across her eyes while her hands continued to roam along his back, his buttocks, his thighs. "It's simply that you…drive. The process. That it is your choice first."

She chuckled, the sound one of such feminine power that he would never tire of hearing of it. "Then let me be as clear as I possibly can," Maria said, stepping back from Warrick far enough that her hand could reach between them, her fingers encircling his thick shaft. She squeezed, hard, and he hissed a strangled breath. "I don't care that you're a demon. I see *you*. I want *you*. And if you're willing, I'd like you to make love to me, Warrick, wherever, however, and doing whatever you want."

I see you. She didn't, he knew. She didn't, and yet...

Warrick paused another precious second more, his gaze searching hers almost desperately, his pulse pounding, his cock in her hand seeming to swell yet further in response to her slow, rhythmic squeeze —

Then he grabbed her.

Chapter Fifteen

Maria had never felt so close to playing with fire as she did this moment — and she'd never felt so alive either. As Warrick lunged at her, she stepped into his embrace, reveling in his strength as he wrapped his arms around her, lifting her high and pressing her hard against the shower wall. His mouth claimed hers with the intensity of a brand, his weight supporting her as she pressed back into him, wanting him closer, so much closer, wanting to feel every part of him against her skin.

She lifted her hands and tangled them in his hair, causing him to growl against her, a feral, almost primal groan of demanding need. A moment later, he wrenched away, blindly staring around the shower, then swung her to the facing wall where he could push her flat while she still stood, brace her and slide down her body, his mouth teasing, tasting…tormenting.

"Warrick," Maria moaned as his mouth found the hardened peak of her breast, the responding cry of her own need melting the last vestige of her restraint. Once again, she twisted her fingers in his hair as he closed his mouth around her, gently tightening his teeth and then sucking hard enough that Maria's back arched in reflexive response. One of her hands fell to his shoulder, but Warrick wasn't finished, turning his attention to her other breast as his right hand lifted to palm the first, squeezing and kneading, the twin spikes of sensation making Maria gasp. How long had it been since anyone had touched her, let alone spurred her to such heights of exquisite sensation? How long had it been since she'd allowed anyone so close, so intimately close?

As if Warrick could hear her thoughts, he sighed against her, his body shivering despite the heat surrounding him. And then, so quickly Maria felt she was being carried along on a dream, his mouth dropped farther to skate along her waist, her hips, arcing toward the part of her that was practically throbbing in panicked desire. *Will he stop, will he continue? What do I really want? Is he really going to* —

"Warrick!" Maria gasped, her eyes snapping open as the first touch of his tongue slipped along the most intimate part of her body, laving the sensitive folds. She gripped his shoulders, but she might as well have been trying to move a mountain. She heard—felt him whisper words of reassurance against her, and though she had no idea what he was saying, his hands on her hips steadied her, his mouth shifted to her inner thigh, letting her catch her breath, letting her heart rate drop, letting her —

Just that quickly, Warrick returned, and Maria's need flared even more hotly as he danced his tongue along the tight nub of nerves that was now on high alert. She didn't want to break, didn't want to tumble so quickly into the flood of orgasm, but he seemed to read her body like a map. Her every shift, every tremor, taught him something new, and every subsequent touch made Maria's breath hiccup, her heart stutter.

"Please," she moaned, and once again, she didn't know what she was asking for, until Warrick's hand slid from her hip to ease over her thigh, sliding up between her legs. Then, as he licked her with a long, intimate stroke, she felt the pressure of a finger at her entrance. With another sensual flick of his tongue, he slipped the finger into her. Then a second one. And then as his tongue circled and flicked, he —

"Oh..." Maria couldn't breathe, could barely think as she tumbled over the abyss, the orgasm that had been building suddenly shooting her up and over the edge in a burst of crazed sensation. She convulsed against him as he pulled her away from the wall and wrapped a powerful arm around her body, steadying her on her feet even as her legs threatened to give way.

"I've got you, I've got you," he gritted out, speaking with so much conviction that Maria had no choice but to believe him. When she finally recovered her breath, however, she realized he had not withdrawn from her, and even as the initial paroxysms of her orgasm receded, he moved his fingers subtly, sensually, and she was building anew, building and then racing as his mouth dropped once more to the vee between her legs, his lips moving to speak words she had no hope of hearing against her frail flesh. Blood raced out of her head so quickly, she couldn't think, couldn't reason, could only feel as the second wave crested higher and higher — and then it didn't so much as break as explode into oblivion, shattering her as well into a hundred thousand crystals of white-hot light.

She sagged forward, leaning heavily on Warrick as he stood in one fluid motion, his warm arms cuddling her close. "Beautiful," he murmured against her hair, and Maria didn't know whether she should laugh or cry, the onslaught of her emotions too fraught, too fragile for her to fully understand. Her spasms of need gradually relaxed into more gentle trembling, but Warrick's embrace never loosened, his arms steady around her as she leaned into his strength, his certainty.

Finally, she lifted her head, and his mouth was right there, meeting her more than halfway and somehow sending a new sensual thrill through her as his lips met hers. It suddenly felt so—*right*, standing here, with a man she'd barely met, in a room she hadn't known existed—

Not a man, her mind urged her to remember. A demon. *A demon!* That seemed like it should be bad...very bad. And yet, Warrick had come when she'd summoned him, had protected her time and time again. And all the fears she knew she should be having were distant...so distant while his arms were holding her close, his mouth was pressed against hers, his heart was thundering in time with her own as the evidence of Warrick's own need pressed against the soft sensitive skin of her abs.

She reached for him, certain her intentions were plain, and Warrick slid his mouth alongside hers, consuming her with a fiery trail of kisses as he dragged his lips to her cheeks, her brow, her temple. He reached the edge of her ear and breathed out harshly, his whispered words sounding choked. "I—I cannot harm you with disease or illness. But I..." He swallowed, his body bucking hard against hers. "No demon is sterile, no matter how forsaken."

"It's okay—it's okay. I'm covered." Maria could hardly wrap her head around having this conversation. She'd barely had sex with a man in years, yet here she was with a perfect stranger. What was she doing?

She didn't know, and right now, she didn't care. She was on birth control, had been since she'd been a teenager, never willing to trust that she would make the right decision when the time came, and definitely sure that she didn't want to trust a man to tell the truth about something so important, even a worthy man. "I'm—you don't have to worry about that. You won't make me pregnant."

Warrick narrowed his eyes at her but accepted her answer. It seemed he could do nothing other than accept it, his jaw set tight, his eyes hard with desire. Maria shifted, and his body bucked again. He straightened, still holding her. She nodded, and he lifted her again, leaning her against the wall as her legs settled naturally around his hips. They were perfectly proportioned, she thought, their bodies fitting together as if they had been made for each other.

Warrick sought Maria's gaze, his eyes wild, but she used the advantage of her leverage to adjust her body until his shaft was poised at her entrance, her body practically dissolving into a flood of heat. She tilted her hips forward, inviting him inside her, but he stood rock still, not even his fingers twitching, as if he would break her, as if he would surely do her harm.

"I want this," she said again, her gaze never leaving his. And then, when he still didn't make a move, she slid him deep inside her.

Warrick couldn't breathe. Didn't want to breathe. Didn't want to do anything but hold Maria close and preserve this moment for another eternity. The pressure of her tight channel around him was the most exquisite torture he'd endured in centuries upon centuries of finely tuned pain, and he reveled in it, his body convulsing as she contracted around his cock. Positioned the way she was, her legs resting on his hipbones, her ankles crossed behind his back, he could thrust himself so deeply inside her that he was seated all the way to the hilt. And she took him too, welcomed him into her body and hummed with purely female satisfaction—which in turn only made his cock swell further with his own desire.

She was going to kill him, he knew, and he was more than happy to have found this way to die.

"Maria," he murmured again, only the word sounded different to his ears, too short, too abrupt, and when he pulled his head away to look at her, her eyes met his with a dreamy, unfocused look, as if she hadn't fully heard him either, but she didn't care. All he could do was focus on the way she felt as he slid deep into her, then pulled out, her core pulsing with molten fire. He could carry on like this for hours, he thought, and then Maria's eyes cleared, her smile tipped into a satisfied smile, her skin warmed at the intensity of his stare.

"You like it?" she murmured.

"Like it…" Warrick understood the words, but he couldn't quite grasp their meaning as she shifted and writhed over him, her body suddenly mobile. Her hips rotated, then began pumping in slow, rhythmic thrusts, and Warrick suddenly went from peacefully riding the wave of sensation to being caught up in a hurricane. His breath caught, his legs went rigid, and his grip firmed on Maria's hips.

"Careful," he muttered.

"I don't want to be careful," she said, and the frank honesty of her reply somehow managed to jack him up further. "I want to ride you as long as you can stand it, and then I want to feel you come inside me, Warrick. Can you do that?"

Warrick's gaze narrowed to a pinprick. Had she really just said that, or had he imagined it? But as if to punctuate her request, Maria's hips began to grind into him again, her hands sliding down his waist to rest on the curve of his ass, pulling him into her in time to his own thrusts. The pressure in his cock grew impossibly heavy, and his breath now came in shuddering, explosive breaths. She laughed then, the sound low and hungry and female, calling to the very basest point of Warrick's nature — and to its highest point too. He couldn't wrap his head around that at this exact moment, but that didn't change the fundamental nature of its truth. Maria wanted him — all of him, pouring into her completely. He could understand that, consider it dispassionately, distance himself from it —

They continued like that, his need ratcheting up, cresting then ebbing then building anew, as their bodies twined together, their faces touching, their lips, their foreheads, their hands. Then, when he'd thought he could take anything she could give and still maintain control, Maria leaned forward, her body arching into his, straining both his cock and his control as she placed her head against his temple, her hot, sweet breath fanning against his ear.

"Come inside me, Warrick," she ordered.

He could no more deny her than he could deny his own next breath, and with a rumbling growl, Warrick slapped his hands hard on Maria's hips, lifting her high as he thrust into her, pulsing once — twice — and staggering under the wave of satisfaction as Maria cried out in surprise, her own body jerking with telltale force as Warrick finally tumbled over the edge and into the oblivion of orgasm.

His sight went white again, but this time not because of the pain, the agony of a horrific memory buried deep in his past, but for the visceral rapture of the present, the heady rush of release so powerful, it nearly made him roar. It was only the last shred of awareness about where he was and with who that forced him to remember himself long enough to keep his essential nature from shining through.

As it was, though, he half careened against the facing wall of the shower, his body still pulsing inside Maria's as his mind gradually cleared. He eased her free again, helped her find her feet, but he wouldn't—couldn't let go of her. They stood under the shower for a long time, their breathing gradually slowing, their bodies loose and lax under the falling water of the shower. The water that was still steaming hot, sizzling as it struck him and turning instantly to steam, Warrick realized.

Maria realized it too. Her eyes grew wide as she watched the tiny rivulets disappear into smoke. "Are you doing that on purpose?"

Warrick grunted, a genuine smile stretching his lips as he cradled Maria close. He bent his head and brushed a kiss over her head, wondering at the events of the last forty-eight hours. Too much had changed too quickly for him not to be at least somewhat wary...but wary of what, or who? He had thought his heart hardened long ago against any temptation a human could offer, yet here he was, standing naked and sated and unable to conjure up even the slightest remorse for the act.

They rocked together then, timing seeming to vanish for this precious moment, everything seeming to vanish outside the water's spray.

"So..." Maria said in his arms, her voice light, teasing. "This demon thing. Beyond showing up when I need you, and the extra special healing powers, is there anything I should know?"

"Know?" Warrick repeated. "What do you mean?"

"Like, can you conjure up a pizza?"

He blinked. "A what?"

"A pizza? Or, say, a calzone. I could really go for a calzone right now. No?" She leaned her head back against him, lifting her gaze. "What about supernatural speed? I think you've got the whole strength thing down, but—I need to make sure I know all your superpowers."

He couldn't help himself, he laughed, and she laughed too. It seemed so—natural, he realized. As if he'd been born and lived all his life to stand here in this space with this human woman, as if this had been part of the plan all along.

As if he had been created only for her.

"I've never taken stock of my abilities," he said, truthfully. "I've only done what was asked of me, what was needed."

"Well then, we'll have to draw up a list." She rose up on her toes, kissed him. And for a long, blissful moment, he simply kissed her back, unable to keep from sighing when she finally pulled away.

"You good?" Maria asked the question warily, no doubt sensing Warrick's thoughts—sensing them but not able to penetrate them, not in the way he could do with humans...any humans except those who'd taken care to ward themselves. And Maria still wore the cross around her neck, he noticed. He wasn't even sure she was aware she did.

"I'm good," he rumbled. He reached out and turned off the faucets, then guided Maria out of the shower. He reluctantly let her go. To give his hands and arms suddenly aching for the loss of her something to do, he grabbed up a fistful of towels and shoved them at her.

She chuckled, taking the pile, then handing half of them back. "Unless you're planning to evaporate all that water on you from the inside out, you need these too."

They toweled off, and she once more wrapped herself in the bathrobe, while Warrick opted for the towel wrapped around his hips. He eyed his clothing, dropped in a heap on the bathroom floor, but the thought of anything next to his skin except for Maria was too much to bear. She was at the counter, opening a bottle of water when he emerged. The sight of her there, damp and clean and wrapped not only in a bathrobe but in the smug aftermath of physical pleasure, jacked him up again. He was grateful for the towel that he'd settled around himself as he paused, watching her from a safe distance as she padded toward the sitting room. He still didn't move as she sank onto the couch, instead pulling in long, slow breaths, exhaling with equal steadiness.

What was wrong with him?

Maria flipped a long coil of wet hair over one shoulder, glancing back his way.

"We should probably discuss next steps," she said, and he breathed out a tight sigh of relief. Yes, next steps. Next steps he could handle, next steps were good. Next steps involved something other than tackling Maria to the floor, taking her again and again, until neither of them could speak, could talk.

Next...steps.

Gritting his teeth, Warrick picked up his own bottle of water and stared blindly at the back wall as he tried once, twice, to unscrew the cap. He finally succeeded and took a long swig, the cold rush of fluid instantly warming to match his internal body temperature. If there was an open flame around, he'd probably set the whole room on fire, he thought grimly. Granted, it had been thousands of years since he'd lain with a woman...but it had never been like this. Ever. He wasn't even sure what *this* was.

"Warrick?"

"Right," he said, wheeling away from the counter and moving toward the small flight of stairs that led down to the hotel suite's sunken living space. It was beautiful in the setting sun, the warm spill of sunlight making the most of the western-oriented windows, and he glanced up to that fiery splendor for one more second before stealing himself to confront Maria.

Then he finally turned —

And froze.

"Maria."

She wasn't wearing the robe anymore. Instead, it was spread out beneath her, a makeshift blanket against the cushions of the couch, her long, lean, muscled body stretched out and on display, the creamy expanse of her skin now flushed pink from the crown of her head to her toes. Her breasts swelled, the nipples pebbled tight in the cool air, and her eyes were hot as they tracked him across the room.

"What are you doing?" he gasped.

She shrugged one shoulder in a sensual roll, lifting her breasts again and presenting them for Warrick's ravenous gaze.

"It appears I'm not quite finished wanting you," she said, her cheeks flushing deep red even as she spoke the words. "I can't — I know we should focus, I know there's so much for us to do to prepare, to plan, but all I can think of is how much I want your arms wrapped around me, how much I want you inside me again."

Warrick remained impossibly still for another second more, drinking in the sight of her — her long, gorgeous hair, her clear eyes, her lush lips and strong jaw. The strength that radiated from her bones and the pain mapped out on her skin in a thousand little scars — the deep core of heat that billowed out from her, surrounding him in its sensual embrace.

"Maria." He breathed out her name like it was a benediction. Which, for him, it was.

She lifted her arms, and he slid into them.

Chapter Sixteen

Hours later, the sun long since set deep over the western skyline, Maria turned in Warrick's arms. They were back on the couch, wrapped in a comforter from the bedroom. Warrick's frame stretched over the length of the couch, sinking into the deep-set cushions, and she lay tangled on top of him.

"So how is this going to go tonight?" she asked. "According to Stan, it's been elevated way beyond LAPD, and in a hurry. He assumes he has you to thank for that."

"Who will be on-site?" The question was only mildly curious. Apparently, Warrick was used to working around others.

"DEA, from what he's saying, a few LAPD plainclothes to keep up the illusion it's a joint operation. And me, of course."

He rumbled unhappily. "You shouldn't be a part of it at all."

Maria's brows shot up, and she sat up on the couch, staring at him. "Excuse me?"

Warrick opened one heavy-lidded eye, but the gaze that confronted her was anything but. He had been sleeping deeply not a minute before. Now he was hyperfocused.

"Your presence had purpose in getting us into the Citadel, catching Takio off guard. It doesn't now. He believes you will be there, yes, but I suspect that now that he's sure I'm in play, he'd come to Morpheus anyway. The world has changed, but it won't change for him until I'm no longer a threat."

"He thinks he can take you out."

Warrick nodded. "I could very easily walk into Morpheus this night alone and take care of him myself, without putting you in harm's way."

Maria opened her mouth, closed it. As much as she wanted to deny that truth, she'd seen what Warrick had done in the basement at the Citadel apartment building. He'd taken out an entire crew of screaming monsters, while she'd been trapped on the floor, mesmerized by merely one of them. She had a healthy opinion of her skills and abilities, but she wasn't an idiot. Warrick didn't need her.

However, when he didn't say anything more, she narrowed her eyes. "And yet you're not telling me to stand down."

"I can't order you to do anything," he said gruffly. "But in truth, you are more than simply a human who has summoned me. You're…an enigma. An enigma Takio can't resist. An enigma under my protection, which makes the temptation all the sweeter."

She sat up farther, pulling the comforter around her as Warrick sat up too.

"In other words, I'm no longer your ticket in to see the guy," she said wryly. "I've been promoted to actual bait."

Warrick nodded. "Takio is aware of you, aware that you hurt one of his own. But only a demon can kill another demon—and, in truth, only a demon can do real harm to one."

"Which is why you needed to take that shot at the strip club. The one that killed Bonnie."

His eyes glowed a deep golden amber as he watched her, and she frowned. "But...but wait a minute," she said. "You said only a demon could harm a demon. What do you mean by harm?"

"I mean most humans can't do more than scratch the surface of a demon's skin. The smarter members of my kind know enough to feign significant injury in an altercation with humans, so their unique characteristics are not noticed. But not all my brethren are smart." He smiled grimly. "In fact, a far greater number of them are exactly the opposite. They enjoy their vaunted status among the children of God. They revel in it. As such, they draw attention to themselves."

"They don't fake their injuries."

"They do not."

"Which means those...those guys in Sycamore Park." She swallowed. "Those were demons?"

"Technically, they were spawn." At her confused glance, he regarded her more intently. "I told you I could make you pregnant. All my kind can. When a demon or one of the Fallen mates with a human, the resulting offspring is considered a half-breed."

"Well, that term's super PC of you." Maria made a face, but Warrick kept going.

"When a demon mates with another demon, however, their offspring is spawn. They, thank God, are sterile. They're considered the lowest caste of demon."

"Yet another round of sensitivity training is necessary, I can see."

"Trust me, spawn don't deserve your pity. When you hear the stories of demonic possession, the harrying of the true believers, the visitation of plagues—those are spawn. Demons can at least remember what it was like to be a child of God. Spawn cannot. They're used most often as the foot soldiers and mercenaries of their demon overlords, because they not only don't have an issue with harming humans, they take unique pleasure in it."

"So you're saying those guys who attacked me were spawn."

"Without question. And most of the creatures at the Citadel that were loosed on us were spawn as well."

"So if they're just spawn, me breaking that dude's arm was not all that big a deal."

"On the contrary," Warrick said, his eyes glittering. "Spawn are still demons. They still carry the strength, the resilience of their forebears. You should not have been able to move them an inch, as hard as they were trying. Yet you not only moved them, you injured them."

"Okayyy…" Maria said. "And you want to tell me why that's possible?"

"Honestly, I have no idea," Warrick said. He gestured to her neck. "I suspect it has something to do with your ward."

"My wha — oh," Maria said, lifting her hand to pull her cross away from her neck. "But it's nothing special, I don't think. I don't even know where Cara got it."

Warrick shrugged. "Perhaps, but that doesn't change the fact that it carries with it a greater weight. Because of your belief, because of Cara's — I don't know. But I'll tell you this. If I'm mildly curious about a human with the strength to even slightly harm a demon, you better believe that Takio will be fascinated…especially once he realizes you're still alive. And that's also part of why you're being put into the line of fire tonight, though if God were truly merciful, you wouldn't be."

"Wait, what do you mean? Of course God is merciful."

Warrick gave a soft, rueful laugh. "God is merciful to His children, ever and always. The love He bears for you knows no bounds."

"Yeah, but…" She frowned. "He doesn't have any mercy left over for you?"

Warrick's eyes were impossible to read as he stared back at her. "Before, I would have said no. He let us live even as He condemned us, which some would count as mercy — but not all. I have always counted it as justice, the justice we deserved. But now…"

Warrick sighed again, leaning down to brush his lips over her brow. "Now I have met you, Maria Santos. And that is more mercy than any creation could ask for, no matter his place in the heavens."

"Oh…" Maria's breath seemed to stall in her throat, and she could only stare, eyes widening as Warrick stood. She was momentarily distracted by his naked beauty as she watched him pace across the sitting room. He jogged the short flight up the stairs, then disappeared into the bathroom. A second later, she heard the shower go on, and she smiled, shaking her head. After herself, she'd never seen anyone appreciate a shower as much as Warrick.

"How much harm can I do to demons, then, exactly?" she shouted, but there was no response from the bathroom. Warrick wasn't technically ignoring her direct question, but he was acting like he didn't hear it. Since they'd already taken three showers together in the intervening few hours, however, Maria didn't feel like going under the blast again. Instead, she retrieved her clothes and pulled them on, glad her hair was already dry — even if it was a knotted tangle. She moved back into the main part of the room, working through the worst knots, when the door buzzed.

"Finn," Warrick supplied from the bathroom. "He won't come in. Get what he has and tell him to leave."

Frowning, Maria obligingly moved toward the door, peering through the spyhole to see the young, handsome Finn standing outside. He held up a bag, grinning, his eyes sparking with an electric-blue glow.

"Room service," he announced, and she opened the door.

He didn't make a move to enter. "Your weapons, Miss Santos," he offered, executing a short bow and handing the brightly colored bag to her.

She frowned as she took it. It had a picture of the Eiffel Tower and a hot air balloon on it. "Warrick said you can't come in?"

"Not my circus, not my monkeys." Finn shook his head. "Warrick has to fight this battle alone. Well, alone with you," he said with a wink.

"But you brought us here."

"Transpo is allowed." He grinned. "The rules are a little complicated, but that's to be expected for a six-thousand-year-old process. Trust me, you'll get used to it."

"So, you're a demon too."

"Of course." He saluted smartly. "Now, tell Warrick to get this through his head. He's gonna be facing an eerily familiar situation upstairs in Morpheus, and all the players are almost set. We got humans, we got demons, we got spawn, we don't have a Fallen yet, but that's about the only group not at the party, and since that setup's a particular fav of Holkeri's, Warrick needs to be smart."

Maria nodded. "Anything I need to know?"

"Definitely, but now is so not the time for me to tell you. But after this gig goes down tonight, look me up and I'll give you an earful." He leaned forward almost conspiratorially. "And since you're wondering, my vote is with that ward you're wearing, you can totally mess up a demon, as in—"

"Finn!" Warrick's bellow was loud enough to shake the walls, and Maria jerked her gaze toward the bathroom. By the time she glanced back to the doorway, Finn was gone.

She let the door shut as Warrick stamped out of the bathroom, the towel once more slung around his hips. It was honestly the best look she'd ever seen him in, but she didn't have time for sightseeing now.

"Seriously? I can mess up a demon?" Maria asked. "That's allowed?"

"Bag," Warrick growled, but he kept coming. She opened the bag and pulled out six throwing knives and a gun. She handed the knives and the gun to Warrick, watching as he scrutinized them, momentarily distracted by the beauty of the weapons.

"How did he get these past security?" Maria asked, her brows going up as she glanced back into the bag.

"Came in from the roof," Warrick said, as if that was explanation enough. She removed her gun next, and a box of ammo, then rolled up the bag.

She looked up to see Warrick frowning at her. "What?"

"Do you want to try to harm me, Maria?" he asked. "To test the strength of your ward?"

"What? No," she said emphatically. "There has to be another way than that."

He quirked his lips. "You'd rather try your luck with a demon in the field of battle? One who doesn't care so much about killing a human?"

"Well, that doesn't seem like so much of a good idea either."

"No, it doesn't." He pointed to her necklace. "I don't know where Cara got that, and I'm grateful for whatever protection it gives you, but remember—it didn't save her on its own. So I think we're far better off assuming it's not going to save you on its own, either."

"Well, it brought you to me, didn't it? When it mattered?"

Warrick opened his mouth, shut it. Then he sighed. "Yes," he admitted. "I guess it did."

"Then that's enough of a superpower for me."

Warrick leaned down, brushed Maria's forehead with his lips. "You must take better care of yourself, Maria Santos," he murmured. "You must."

"I will," she murmured. "Promise."

Warrick grimaced as he took Maria's declaration, an oath she couldn't truthfully give. He might not be able to read her mind directly, but even he knew that.

He also knew there was more, so much more that she craved to know, to understand. The questions clamored so obviously behind her eyes, he was surprised he couldn't already hear them.

She didn't wait long to give them voice.

"So, Finn mentioned there would be spawn, demons, and maybe even a Fallen on hand tonight."

Warrick nodded. "Possibly. Holkeri is a very ancient demon, and we already encountered one Fallen in his thrall. It's possible that he has captured more."

"Right. And…I mean, I know you said you were a demon, but that's what you really are, right? Fallen?

"No," he said quietly. "I was once, but it has been a long, long time since I was an angel of God."

"Yeah, but so…" She swallowed, clearly struggling with what she wanted to ask next. But he owed answers to her now. She had brought him more solace in her touch than he thought he'd ever experience again in this lifetime, and she was his to protect. Even—especially—

from himself.

"You want to know my sin," he said. "To know how I stepped out of the light of God's grace and into the darkness."

Maria winced. She opened her mouth to protest, but he shook his head. "It's your right to know," he said simply. He turned toward the skyline, the lights of the city burning bright.

"Mine isn't a story that's all that surprising or unusual. All the more reason I should have seen the test coming, prepared myself against it. The world was cycling ever rapidly toward real war. The humans had finally seen the truth of the gods they'd allowed to walk among them. Creatures of power and ability that put them on a level above all others."

"Wait, gods?" Maria frowned. "I thought you believed in the one true God."

"I believe in the God of Creation, yes." He nodded. "I believe in the God of all gods, Master of all Masters, the Unmoved Mover. And I believe there are many stories about that God, many paths to His truth. When you have lived as long as I have, it is easy to gain that perspective. And by the time the war on the lesser gods drew near, those lesser gods had enflamed themselves and their followers to a fever pitch. All these supposed deities were set against the children of God, particularly those children who had developed their own human abilities to nearly godlike strength, sorceresses and magicians alike who drew their abilities not from beings outside themselves, but from their own inner strength."

"Okay…" Warrick could tell Maria was trying to hold on to her belief, but her perspective was limited by the very nature of her one short life.

"As the conflict drew near, it wasn't only the gods who sought to develop a following, to elevate themselves in the eyes of the humans so that they wouldn't be banished beyond the veil between the worlds. It was members of the demon horde as well. One of those eager to build such a following was Holkeri." He turned back. "Takio, now. I hadn't realized he'd already stepped out of the light and into the darkness, that his descent had transformed him into a demon. At the time, I still believed him an equal. A friend."

"A friend," Maria echoed. She stared at him, eyes huge, but Warrick was too caught up in his own memories to soften his tone.

"A friend," he said again. "And as such, he lured me into a false belief. He taught me to trust him, tempted me to believe him when all my senses argued against it. All my beliefs in my own discernment were held hostage to my desire to count him as my comrade, not my enemy. And by the time I realized his duplicity, it was too late. He took something from me that, in my blindness and rage, I didn't see was simply part of a trap, part of a means for him to show his strength to those who followed him. When I reacted in rage, I sought only to kill—to hurt—to damage beyond compare not only my hated enemy but all with whom he surrounded himself. And Holkeri had prepared well."

"He'd surrounded himself with people," Maria guessed. "Humans."

"Humans," Warrick agreed. "Humans I could not help but destroy in my blind desire to get to Holkeri. And as such, he trapped me in the net of my own rage, and that rage was my undoing. I was transformed into a demon that very night."

"And Holkeri?"

"I made another choice that night, in my agony, twisting in the flames of righteous retribution. I became an enforcer. Not content to walk the earth as a scavenger, I consented to banishment beyond the veil — able to be called out by those who needed protection, needed vengeance, needed a sword of God to strike down their enemies." His lips twisted. "It didn't take long for me to be called out to strike Holkeri. I wasn't successful, but neither was I entirely unsuccessful. And I had many more opportunities, many times thereafter."

"Many times…" Maria's eyes widened. "You've been called out more than once to take him out?"

"Oh, I have. But he is a demon who responds to every summons by the humans who would pull him back into this plane. And so, inevitably, I am the one called to remove him once more. My sin is rage, and I have been forced to pay for that sin, all too many times." Warrick smiled darkly. "Then again…So has he."

CHAPTER SEVENTEEN

Maria entered the nightclub without incident, flashing her ID to the hostess and nodding coolly as her name generated a thousand-kilowatt smile. As far as the staff at Morpheus was concerned, she was the biggest deal in the club tonight. She was escorted to a primo VIP table with views of the dance floor as well as the stunning Los Angeles skyline, now lit up — literally — like a Christmas tree. Morpheus itself had adopted the holiday theme, the blue-and-purple lighting accentuating the glittering strings of lights that hung in fringes from the ceiling, towering artificial trees that stood like snow-ghost sentinels in cordoned-off outposts around the room. The trees did an admirable job of adding to the ambiance without blocking the view, and like everywhere else in LA, Morpheus was mostly about the view.

A magnum of champagne was waiting for her at the table, already chilled in an enormous bucket. The moment she sat down, a waitress wearing a tiny but impeccably tailored white dress moved up to her. The woman pulled out the bottle and poured it, giving Maria a knowing smile.

"This is one of our best vintages," she crooned, her voice somehow audible over the thumping music.

She paused to allow Maria to take a taste, and Maria

nodded with approval. Yep, pure sparkling water. Warrick was taking no chances with her. Her gun was discreetly tucked into her handbag, which was a glittering confection of sequins and silver. Though Maria wore the expected little black dress, unlike most of the women decked out in pencil skirts and slim-cut sheaths, she was wearing a minidress with a widely flaring skirt over micro shorts. Her boots came all the way up to her kneecaps and were remarkably sturdy for all that they were high, the heel relatively functional. Those heels would also make a mean weapon, should it come to that.

Maria glanced around the crowded room. She certainly hoped it didn't come to that.

Warrick was nowhere to be seen, but about everyone else in the club was doing their level best to be noticed. She couldn't even pick out the DEA operatives, so score one for whoever was dressing them tonight. Maria sipped her sparkling water, eyeing all the beautiful people. It was the closest she had ever gotten to such a concentration of wealth and fame and power in one place. The actors and actresses were outnumbered by the celebutantes, but those showed up in ever-increasing numbers as the minutes past the hour ticked away. Every other VIP table was filled except for a few in the far corner, probably the second-most-prized real estate after her own table. A bouncer the size of Mount Atlas stood near her, discouraging anyone from approaching. Though, given she was one woman at a table meant for six or eight, it didn't take long for her to start drawing stares.

Maria squared her shoulders. She wasn't the prettiest woman in the room. She definitely wasn't the richest or the most popular. And at this distance, no one could see the scars that lined her skin, certainly not the scars she carried inside her. But everyone around her looked at her as if she belonged at that table, as if she were somehow more special than they would have ever expected if they'd seen her on the street. Some of the women looked at her with envy, some with irritation, some with simple curiosity. The gazes of the men were easier to discern.

It was one of the most bizarre experiences of her life.

"If you're going to wear that cross with any authority, you're pretty much going to need to get used to it."

Maria looked up, expecting to see Warrick. Instead, the woman who stood beside her looked like she'd been hewn out of marble. She was tall, though not as tall as Maria, and her body was all sharp angles. Her shock of white hair was cropped close to her head on one side, tufting longer on the other into spikes, and her body was encased in a scuffed leather jacket, leather pants, and shit-kicker boots.

"Blue!" someone yelled across the floor, and from the way the woman's lips twisted, Maria got the impression that she was the one being addressed.

Still, no one was supposed to approach her this night except...

Maria frowned. "Um, you can't possibly be Warrick."

"You're right." The woman snorted, leaning down toward her. "I'm known as Blue here, as much of a fixture as the chairs and tables for the moment. But Warrick knows me as well, and not by the name Blue. Since you're wearing that cross, however, you're part of his path. I want to make sure you're up to the task."

"I can't help you with that." Maria looked across the room. "It's not mine."

Blue glanced down at her, swirling her drink in her glass. Maria suspected she hadn't taken so much as a sip of the clear liquid. "Isn't it, though?" Blue asked, and there was the faintest Irish lilt to her voice, an inflection Maria hadn't caught at first. "You're wearing it, aren't you?"

"Only because it's original owner can't." Maria's lips twisted. "She died a long time ago."

"A bright light, burned out too quickly..." Blue mused, and Maria shot her a hard glance.

"I'm sorry, you said you were a friend of Warrick's?"

The woman gave her a wry smirk. "Not a friend, exactly. But someone who knows him well—who's known him for a long time. He needs someone strong enough to fight with him. And he's already declared you as his to protect."

"He's declared half the world as his job to protect."

"He has." Blue nodded. "But that's not what I said, is it?" She gestured to the cross, and Maria cut her gaze away. "That little bit of gold is blessed, you know. It's special. And though Cara couldn't believe in herself enough to fight, in the end, she believed in you. So make sure you're willing to fight for her...and more than that, make sure you're willing to fight for Warrick. He deserves that, after all these years."

"Look, I—" Suddenly realizing Blue had used Cara's name, Maria glanced up sharply—but no one was standing there. The woman was gone.

She flagged down another waitress, the twin to the one who poured her champagne. "Can I have another drink?"

"Of course," the woman smiled. "More champagne?"

"Not even remotely," Maria said. "Tequila, chilled, twist of lime. The best bottle you have."

The woman moved off, her smile remaining perfectly curved, and Maria returned to the study of the room. The game plan tonight was simple. The undercover cops in the room wouldn't be bagging Takio tonight. Warrick had been clear on that point. At best, the LAPD would be taking down Takio's lieutenants, the men he surrounded himself with most closely. Those, according to Warrick, would be human. They would know enough to tank the organization. Takio couldn't be taken by the authorities, no matter how hard they tried. If Takio allowed it, it was only because he was planning something far worse. He needed to be banished again…this time, for good. For Cara, and for the sake of hundreds of thousands of people like Cara that his operations had harmed throughout the centuries.

She smiled grimly as a glass and full bottle of tequila was set down in front of her, the waitress deftly serving her before moving away. Maria picked up the glass and took a quick, shallow drink, savoring the sharp, angry liquid as it scorched down her throat.

Okay, mostly for Cara.

The clock ticked on another fifteen minutes, the night not so much wearing toward midnight as building up to it with an energy that set the entire room to hopping. Everything seemed sharper, harder as the night progressed, and Maria's adrenaline amped with every new knot of people that came in the door. But still there was no Warrick, and the VIP table at the far end of the room remained empty as well.

Where was Takio?

Finally, there was a rustle of movement at the club's entry, a murmur of excitement that rippled through the room like a living thing. Maria straightened in her seat, but once again, she was doomed to be disappointed. A woman walked into Morpheus, probably one of the most striking of anyone in the club, and that was saying something. Her body was tall and lithe, her hair long, straight, and pure white. Her features were porcelain perfection. But unlike Blue, with her hard-focused energy, this woman appeared languorous as she walked, waving with relaxed ease to her fawning public. She was beautiful and entitled and luxe, everything Maria was not. And Maria couldn't take her eyes off her.

"It's starting."

Maria jerked her gaze away from the opening to Morpheus and connected with Warrick's hard stare. Like Blue and the woman who'd just made her entrance, he looked like he belonged in clubs like Morpheus. He was dressed in a suit that probably cost more than a month's salary—and not one of her month's salary either. It was the color of dark steel, single-breasted and open to reveal a deep blue silk shirt that bared a swath of his deeply tanned skin. His shirt cuffs were visible at the edges of his jacket sleeves, and a platinum watch glinted from his right wrist. He was easily the most arresting man in the room, and he was sliding into the seat next to her, leaning toward her to brush a kiss against her cheek.

"Are you ready? Because it will move quickly now."

"You're kidding," Maria said, her voice equally low. "That's Takio? He's taken on the—glamour or whatever to look like a woman now?"

"A woman?" Warrick scowled. "What are you talking about?"

"Her." Maria jerked her head to the right, where even in her periphery vision, she could see the woman in the ice-white bandage dress making her way across the floor. "She just got here."

Warrick glanced up casually, then his entire body seemed to freeze in place. His face blanched, his eyes went flat, his mouth opened, then shut—then his lips curled into a hard, implacable snarl.

"Um..." Maria hazarded, feeling the menace flow off him in waves. "You okay?"

"Holkeri, you *bastard*," Warrick seethed.

Warrick struggled to keep himself under control—struggled and failed mightily. He knew that Holkeri had survived millennia for a reason. He'd been called to defend humans from the demon on more occasions than any other, and he'd taken intense delight in carving pieces out of the demon every chance he could.

But in all those times, Holkeri had never revealed that he'd been holding back the ultimate prize from Warrick.

Serena had been one of the most beautiful of the Fallen, her gifts of music, laughter, imagination, and pure joy among the things that made anyone who saw her fall in love with her. When she'd come to Warrick with her plans of leaving the angelic plane and walking among the children that God loved so dearly, not as mystical phantasms but as flesh and blood, able to teach, to guide, to savor the best of both worlds without the extremes of either...

Warrick grimaced. He'd been entranced by her, willingly blinded, and, in truth, already chafing against the bonds of his role in the heavens when something deep within him yearned for more. Serena had promised him a way to reach that more, a rebellion against the strictures they'd felt were holding them back, a path to new possibilities—farther away from the unending source of the creator's love, but not so far that they couldn't find their way back one day. Not so far that they couldn't still bask in his approval, merely in a new and different and boundlessly more interesting way.

She'd leapt; he'd followed.

And it had been *glorious*.

"Earth to Warrick? You all right there?"

Maria's voice cut across Warrick's intensity, and he looked down to realize his hands were gripping the thick steel tabletop hard enough to leave impressions in the smooth surface. He released his hands, running his fingers over the faint grooves. He could already feel the kindling of his rage — because this was part of it. The part where he left marks of his anger on the world around him. Never again would humans suffer for his rampage, sure, never again would bones break and screams fill his ears. But rage didn't exist in a vacuum. It left a trail. A trail of conquest to some.

For him, only shame.

"No," he answered honestly. Because he was bound to do so.

"Who is she?" Maria asked the question quietly, and for a moment, all Warrick wanted to do was turn from it, turn from her, retreat. But Holkeri would not have brought Serena here unless he'd needed her. Warrick needed to focus on that, understand it. Use it.

"Her name is — was — Serena. I haven't seen her since the end days of the war, when so many of our kind were swept away."

"Is she Fallen?"

"Once." Warrick's mouth tightened. "One of God's most favored angels, fallen to become one of the humans' most celebrated guides, a bright star in the darkness for all to follow. That was her goal. And she would have achieved it — she was that bright, that strong. Her gifts that many. Art, music, stories, magic. Were she a human, she would have been a queen. As a Fallen, she was nearly a goddess...and there came a time when that was not an easy path to walk."

"Yeah, I deal with that all the time," Maria put in drily.

But Warrick's gaze had turned inward as he conjured up memories he'd long since put to rest. "She couldn't dim her beauty even when it grew wise to stay in the shadows, was convinced of her supremacy among the humans, the Fallen, and even the angelic host. Her pride — as it was for so many of us — was her greatest sin and her ultimate downfall."

"Pride? How so?"

"She believed what others wanted her to believe, what she in time wanted to believe, that in the end, her one life was more important than the lives of God's children, His chosen. She was celebrated and honored and loved and despaired over. She was untouchable, and armies would rage and serve and die in her wake. When the end times came and the humans rose up in their fear-stoked outrage to sweep out the gods who wished to control them, that should have proved her undoing. But she would not be undone."

Maria pulled over a bottle of clear liquid and sloshed it into a glass. "Here. You need this more than I do."

Warrick lifted the glass to his lips, tasted the harsh but strangely sweet slide of liquor as it chased down his throat. The sudden jolt of fire, then spreading heat — that was what humans craved so much. In their vices, in their lives.

Not only humans either.

"She didn't make it to the point of human banishment, refused to be sent beyond the veil, separated from those who had for so long adored and revered her. She could fight, she decided. She would make a stand. She would return one day to rule the mortal realm as she once had led it with her ethereal strength. I, also Fallen, also in danger, pleaded with her to change her course. I believed I loved her, and I placed that love at her feet. Willed her to find another way. But she wouldn't listen to me. And then I was trapped and offered as sacrifice to appease the humans in her place, banished beyond the veil by those I had pledged to serve."

"Trapped," Maria whispered. "They tried to capture you?"

"They did capture me. With chains and lash and magic. I was placed in a cage, wheeled out as a spectacle for a roaring crowd. But I was still Fallen." Warrick could hear the bleakness in his voice. "I could still see. And there, in the shadows, I could see that it was Serena who had betrayed me. Serena — and beside her, Holkeri. Only then did I realize that he'd become a demon. Only then, did I realize that he planned to make Serena one too."

"Uh-oh," Maria said.

"The rage that filled me then was unlike anything I had ever experienced before. It was not heady or pure, it was not filled with righteous fire. It was a black and living thing, a twisting menace. It roared in my blood and broke all my bones, remolding me in its image."

He shook his head and took another long pull of his tequila, then set down his glass, not objecting when Maria filled it again. "I don't remember bursting free from the cage, I don't remember the people at all after that. I could only focus on Holkeri."

"Holkeri? Not the chick?"

His lips curved into a smile. "In my hubris, I assumed that Serena was the weaker one. That she must have been duped, beguiled."

"We really have to work on your sensitivity training."

Maria's wry, sarcastic comments should have

goaded Warrick to anger — might have, in another time, another place, coming from another human. But he knew what she was doing, attempting to pierce the veil of his memories that had for so long suffocated him like a shroud. She sought to misdirect and defuse his anger, his pain, so that he could view those memories more dispassionately. But there was no denying what he'd done. No denying all the children of God he had hurt, killed. His damnation was testimony enough for that.

"Holkeri was still standing there as I came up upon him, standing and laughing in the fire. The entire village was now in flames. There was so much screaming all around, torment, pain. Fear. I'd brought that to the humans. That was my legacy. Not my truth, not my strength, not the art of war. But the utter despair of debilitating, paralyzing fear. I was damned before I reached Holkeri, smote down, becoming the creature the humans already believed I was. But if I was demonized for my rage, I was also born of it." His lips twisted into a dark smile. "I was banished that very hour, but not before I held Holkeri beneath the fire long enough to sear his bones so deeply that no glamour he could ever effect would truly mask his monstrous form from his own kind."

Maria opened her mouth to speak, then shut it.

"Serena was gone. And in a matter of minutes, I was wrenched away from Earth on the magic of humans who did not realize their own strength. It was a lesson I didn't need to learn twice, but the damage, of course, had already been done. Still…" He tipped his glass to the stricken-looking Maria. "Holkeri saw me coming that first time. He hasn't seen me coming in all the times since."

"And tonight?" Maria managed.

"Tonight, he knows I'm here. Ordinarily, I would

fear for the future of the man called Nico, if he in truth tried to lie to his master. Demons who have committed the sin of murder develop a taste for it. Holkeri certainly has. I haven't."

He grimaced. "But after this night, there won't be enough of Holkeri to harm another child of God again." He turned to regard Serena. She was surrounded by human men and women, a protective circle understood by no one as well as him. "And any who throw in their lot with him shall suffer the same."

CHAPTER EIGHTEEN

Maria didn't opt for another hit of tequila and instead switched back to her flute of faux champagne, her eyes still on the door. "Holkeri hasn't shown up, right?" she asked. "He's not in some glamour I'm missing?"

Warrick stirred out of his unhappy trip down memory lane and leaned back in the banquette, scanning the room. "No. Other than Serena, there are humans and spawn, and—"

He frowned, going slightly still. "I thought you told Harris to place only a few operatives on-site. I count fully a dozen."

Maria winced. The problem with demons, it seemed, was you couldn't hide from them. "I think you're overestimating the amount of influence I have in my job. I can make recommendations, even strong recommendations, but it's not like I can tell the chief of police that a known drug kingpin is going to be making some kind of potentially lethal move in a public nightclub in the heart of his city and have him be all 'you know, why don't you handle this yourself.'"

"And he still let you come?"

"The man's not an idiot." Maria shrugged. "He came to the same conclusion you did. As far as bait goes, I'm the real deal." She felt the cool eyes of the woman she now knew as Serena on her once again. "Speaking of, your ex-girlfriend is totally picking up on the chum in the waters. How is it she hasn't figured out you're sitting beside me?"

Maria didn't miss how Warrick's hands tightened on the tequila glass, but he didn't grip it tight enough to shatter it. He was more or less under control, at least for the moment. "There are two possibilities. One is that my glamour is sufficient, or that my proximity to a warded human is enough distraction that the combination proves sufficient. The other is that she has long since forgotten me."

Maria snorted. "I think we can safely rule out option two." She searched her own emotions, assessing her reactions for weakness. She wasn't exactly jealous of Serena, she decided. The woman had betrayed Warrick, and while he appeared still deeply in need of therapy over that betrayal, he also had the benefit of an entrenched hatred for Holkeri that was keeping him laser-focused. That was good.

Another flurry of activity at the front door had her going tense — and a quick glance showed her she wasn't the only one. The operatives littered throughout the room straightened slightly in their lounging conversations, tilting glasses, chatting it up...all of them no doubt packing. Someone must have used an awful lot of influence to get the owners of Morpheus to put all their guests at risk.

Then again, this was LA. Some of the people on this floor would have gladly paid tens of thousands of dollars for the publicity that was going to ensue if anything interesting went down. Assuming they didn't end up dead.

Her gaze swiveled to the front door. "Please tell me that those guys aren't off-limits," she said under her breath. "We're going to have to give LAPD and the Feds something."

"They're human," Warrick said. "Lieutenants of the la Noche operation, most of them already lit on some drug mix I can't discern. Not enough to be noticeable but…enough to impair them as the night goes on."

"Really." Maria eyed the men. They didn't look drugged. They looked like what they were: well-dressed thugs. Well-dressed thugs who were also packing, she was sure of it.

"Yes." Warrick nodded. His voice was harsher now, and she glanced at his right hand, which had abandoned the glass and was now gripping the table. "Apparently, you're not the night's only distraction. If Holkeri puts up these men as a screen, human scum to be sacrificed but not by his hand, he could slip away."

Then Warrick hissed out a word that was probably a curse, but not in any language Maria had ever heard. She waited a beat, then slid her own gaze to the doorway. The lieutenants had scattered in a loose circle, hands in pockets, stances easy, your basic group of guys looking to party. But there was no denying their focus on the man who'd just walked in the room. The man she'd only seen in grainy photographs, his face always turned away from the camera.

Or had it been turned away?

"Cameras? He seriously doesn't care?"

"He doesn't care. No camera can capture him, or any demon, not even with today's technology. Holkeri doesn't have to hide. His essential nature provides more than enough disguise for humans."

Maria nodded, focusing again on Takio—or Holkeri, as Warrick knew him. She vividly remembered the way Cedo had described him, but this man was no hideous creature slinking into the room, a horror to everyone who gazed upon him. To her, Takio looked exactly like he sounded. A Eurasian male, middle height, middle weight, wearing an understated black suit that was no doubt insanely expensive. His face was startlingly attractive — with tawny skin stretched over high cheekbones, and flashing dark eyes that had a faint purple glow to them, now that she was looking for it. He glanced around the room with what seemed like sincere approval, but Maria was positioned too far away from the door for him to see her, she thought.

Had Cedo truly been that wrong about Takio? Or had he merely been able to see him through the eyes of a demon, the truth of Takio's appearance something that could not be hidden anymore from his own kind?

Without another word, Warrick stood and left her table. She felt his loss as almost a visceral jolt, but she understood it. As powerful as his glamour was and regardless of how strong Maria's ward seemed to be, Warrick couldn't run the risk of being identified before he was ready to make his move. Instead, she studied Takio's expression, seeing the steel beneath the easy smile. She had a feeling he was very much a shoot-first, ask-questions-later kind of guy.

Regardless, whatever he saw in the pulsing lights of Morpheus seemed to please him, and he proceeded to enter the room with a loose-limbed swagger. Two silver-clad waitresses greeted him inside the door, one with the martini glass filled with clear liquor, the other gesturing for him to accompany her forward, apparently to his table. As he moved through the room, there were the usual greetings and fawning, and Takio seemed to take it all in stride. He was a celebrity here, Maria realized. This wasn't her turf, exactly, but the cops who patrolled the heart of the city weren't idiots. How was it that, up till now, they had missed the preferred nightclub of one of the most notorious gang lords in LA?

Her gaze swiveled back to the men now watching Takio. Plausible deniability was definitely in the guy's favor. With Takio playing it so close to the vest, these cops couldn't tie him to any specific crime. Takio might be a suspected drug lord, but nothing had ever stuck to him. He was a free man.

Finally, Takio reached the VIP sanctuary that was twin to the sea of glittering beauty where Maria currently claimed her very own island of solitude. Then, with a move of smooth, almost languorous grace, he turned and saw her...truly saw her.

In that moment, Maria understood what must have helped fuel the man's unprecedented rise as a criminal kingpin—both now and in however many previous centuries he'd lived. The pull of his gaze was unlike anything she had ever experienced before, even with Warrick. Despite herself, Maria wanted to stand, to cross over to this man, to put her hand in his and see what he had to say to her. Not because she was eager to take him down either. But because she wanted him to notice her, wanted him to pay attention.

Unbidden, an image of her cousin sprang to mind. Beautiful, wild Cara, whose star had burned so fast and bright. Had she met Takio in the course of her work? Was he the reason she'd been recruited so easily into la Noche, willing to sacrifice her own body, selling herself as a mule to make this man richer?

Cara's cross seemed to burn against Maria's neck, and from sheer force of habit, she lifted her hand to grasp the small, slender icon.

Across the room, Takio smiled, nodded to her. He turned to one of the men standing beside him, issued instructions. Maria swallowed as the man turned her way, and suddenly, she wished she'd taken that last slug of tequila. This was what she'd been waiting for, though. She had to be pulled into Takio's web, had to be placed squarely in danger. Until those two things had happened, Warrick couldn't make his move. And until Warrick could make his move, everyone in this nightclub was at risk.

This would work, Maria thought. They'd nail Takio to the wall. And that made everything she'd endured — all her training, her waiting, her tracking, her pain…worth it.

None of this is worth it.

Warrick stood in the shadows of one of the ridiculous purple Christmas trees, glaring out as he saw one of Takio's lieutenants approach Maria. She played her part to the tee, the perfect combination of delighted, favored human, with no indication of the steel of the cop beneath.

Maria stood and followed the lieutenant, but Warrick was sure her cover was already blown. Takio would have done his homework on her. Once he'd decided to look, it wouldn't have taken him long to figure out who she really was, especially now that the Citadel had gone up in flames and his operation had been routed there. Maria would never be able to work in that neighborhood again as an undercover cop, but she'd done her job, and now Warrick would do his. The gangs would reform, a new leader would take hold, but it wouldn't be Takio. And that was all he could do. Humans had to fight their own battles.

But this battle was his. Had been his since he'd been first condemned. Inevitably, he'd send Holkeri back beyond the veil a little more damaged than before, a little more desperate. Inevitably, Holkeri would come back.

Each new time Warrick would be summoned to rout the demon, he reminded himself that the rage that continued to burn within him still served a purpose. And that if he removed Holkeri from that equation completely, he risked the loss of that purifying rage. It had been rage that had condemned him, after all, but also rage that allowed him to become the best at what he did: leading the Syx.

And what was a twisted hero without the villain who drove him?

That was what he'd told himself, over all these long years. On some level, it was what he believed. But now, watching the human he'd come to prize more than anything else in all creation walk toward Holkeri with a fierce smile on her lips, a determined grace and strength to her stride, Warrick realized he'd been a fool. Far better for him to have lost his rage centuries ago than to allow Maria to spend even a moment at risk from this despicable excuse for a creature of God.

If anything happened to her, Warrick couldn't survive it. Not anymore. It would break him far more deeply than his original damnation.

For his part, Takio seemed to understand that he was the center of the show. He watched Maria approach him with a feral, needy grin stretching across his mouth, a grin that went deeper than his glamour to paint itself onto the elongated, demonic form that hovered beneath the glittering illusion of his handsome, sculpted face, his elegant clothes. He was intent, far too intent, as if he was the one so close to a coveted prize, as if he was on the verge of claiming final victory.

Warrick was also concentrating so fiercely that the voice, when it came, was as shocking as a spear to the gut.

"He told me you would come here tonight. I didn't

believe him."

Warrick turned and regarded Serena, seeing both the transcendently beautiful glamour she presented with barely a ripple of need, to the horrific, withered crone beneath. She had still appeared to be Fallen when he'd seen her last, by Holkeri's side at the breaking of the world. She'd not yet been held accountable for the sin that would so damn her.

But when her condemnation had come, it'd been a doozy.

"So you do miss me." She preened as he said nothing, but merely stared at her. "I didn't believe Holkeri when he told me that either."

Warrick blinked, gradually forcing his attention back, realizing almost too late that Serena didn't fully understand the added benefit of his enforcer status. How could she, not being an enforcer herself? So she didn't know that Warrick could pierce the glamour of any of his brethren as easily as he could see through a light mist. There were no secrets he didn't have access to, not among his own kind. No demon could hide from him.

"I expected you to be more…surprised, though," she said, when Warrick would have turned his gaze back to Takio and Maria. "Both now — and then."

He refocused on her. "I didn't realize you were no longer Fallen," he said, his words low and harsh.

Serena's laugh was equally grim. "That night? Neither did I. It was only after you were sent beyond the veil that I felt the change upon me, the fires twisting my limbs, scourging my skin. Then I too was caught up in the wailing lament of the humans." She said this last with a sneer, the expression rendering even her impossibly beautiful glamour an ugly shroud. "I would have been thrust into the Nothing with you, were it not for Holkeri."

Warrick scoffed a laugh. "Holkeri is the betrayer who got you into this mess."

"No," she said, and her words were emphatic— emphatic and not even the slightest bit desperate. This was not a creature struggling to believe the lies she told herself, Warrick realized. This was someone certain in her position, her strength. This was someone who knew she was right. "Holkeri showed me what you were not willing to accept. That the humans we'd been allowed to teach were graceless wretches unworthy of the love the Father had showered upon them. That even as they accepted our teaching, learned from us, grew and thrived and reached never before heights in their own abilities because of us, even then they were plotting to overthrow us, to shut us out. He showed me this, and I saw it with my own eyes. It was the truth."

"Of course it was the truth," Warrick snapped. As Serena's brows shot up, he swiveled his gaze back toward the opposite side of the room, seeking out Maria. It was easy to do. Her light gleamed brightly beneath the strange glow of Morpheus's décor, making her a beacon in the room. In contrast, Takio stood like a hunched-over troll beside her, little more than a lumpy smudge.

Warrick returned his gaze to Serena's dark, fathomless eyes. "Humans are not pets or playthings, Serena. They think. They struggle. They aspire to greater things. It was only a matter of time before they acted against us—even if the Fallen weren't their primary target."

"They turned on their own *gods*," she retorted, and in that word, Warrick wondered if she might have gone a little mad after all. "They had no *right*."

This was a lament as old as time itself, and one Warrick had no patience for. "Why did you listen to

Holkeri? He was no friend to you."

"He was my only friend," she said, her voice taking on the mantle of indignation. "He was the one who came for me, when you had been thrust away in smoke and fire. I was being pulled away as well, to be banished, stuck into the Nothing, perhaps never to return, and what would my precious Fallen status do for me then? I would still have been lost. And so he pulled me back, and I let him pull me, helped him wreak his vengeance against the mortals who dared do this to us, steeping myself in their blood."

Now it was Warrick's turn to stare at her. "You weren't there, though," he insisted. "When I returned to avenge the humans that Holkeri was murdering, to stop him from killing more — you weren't there."

"I *was* there." She fairly spat the words. "There to see you reemerge as the accursed sword of God, to watch you exact your vengeance and wallow in your rage. There to watch you take your wrath out on Holkeri, when you had no *right* — "

"And where did you go after that?" Warrick rumbled, cutting her off.

"I healed him," she hissed. "Then and every time after. With the core of humans who still worshipped at my feet, I was there to guide them in summoning Holkeri from his prison, to gather up his broken body, heal him, and hear his spoken truth. That you had forgotten me. That you had never loved me, despite all your promises. Despite all I'd done for you."

"You betrayed *me*." Warrick couldn't help it, he could feel the banked embers of his rage lighting anew. "You handed me over as a sacrifice to save your own sorry skin. I thought you'd been banished after that. I thought it was done. There is no way for me to find you beyond the veil, and that's where I thought you had been sent."

221

"You could have *tried*," Serena snarled. "You could have, every single time you returned to this plane. But you didn't. And now, with the release of the horde on the earth once more, I no longer have to hide. None of us do. Holkeri's new drug will return us all to our rightful place."

Warrick saw it then, the hungering gleam in her eye, the endless, aching need. It would never be enough for her to have the love, the support of one soul—not his, not Holkeri's. She needed all of them. So she'd lived in the shadows of the world for millennia, furtive and waiting for just such a catastrophe as the release of the horde. And she was ready to take advantage of it.

Serena's gaze darted behind him, and her mouth creased into a dark smile. "Once again, you are too little and too late, Warrick."

CHAPTER NINETEEN

Maria stood in front of Takio, her mind racing. She could sense the LAPD and DEA operatives moving into place around her. She knew that Warrick and Serena were now together a few feet beyond a stand of purple-and-silver Christmas trees. But despite her best efforts, she couldn't seem to fully focus on the man—thing—whatever it was standing directly in front of her.

"Maria Santos, at last," Takio said, his face creasing into a mobile smile. "I knew Nico had lied when he said you'd been taken out by my pets in the Citadel. I somehow think I would have felt it, you know? That I would have known I'd taken yet another life of one of God's most precious children." His gaze narrowed on the cross hung around her neck. "And that explains yet more. Stupid and careless of Cedo not to pay attention. But once again, Cedo is barely one step above spawn. Very helpful to the extent he can be...but not an especially good thinker."

She didn't respond to that. It wasn't a question, and more to the point, Takio seemed to be gearing up for something, something she needed to brace herself for, without being distracted by his babble.

"And then, once I had your name, it really didn't take long to realize that you were no stranger to the dregs of humanity that walked the streets of this city. That you were right at home with those barely surviving on the scraps they were willing to accept, thrown at their feet while they scrabbled like dogs, attacking each other in their attempts to get ahead, to survive at the expense of those they supposedly held dear."

He leaned closer to her. "You've been busy today, but so have I. Cedo has too, once I put him to work. You want to know what he was able to get out of your poor, crippled aunt? The mother of sweet Cara?"

Maria swallowed. Her aunt wasn't crippled. But from the glint in Takio's eye, he was waiting for her to walk into that trap. In her mind, she could see the beautiful older woman, strong and stoic and still so ready to offer a laugh, a warm meal, a long hug when nothing else could help. Aunt Adelle had lost her daughter, she would always tell Maria. She had lost her sister. But she would not lose her faith.

Maria wanted to close her eyes. What had Cedo done to her aunt?

"So you're not going to play?" Takio pouted. "Well, I'm feeling generous tonight. Your beloved, now unfortunately broken, aunt told Cedo everything, eventually. About how proud she was of you, how much she hoped to see you soon, even though you'd moved all the way up to Sylmar and she'd long since fled Compton for that pretty home in Santa Ana. She had no idea you'd been back to the neighborhood, wouldn't believe it. You wouldn't be that foolish, she said. There were bad people there. Dangerous people."

Maria's anger simmered, lightning hot. She looked at Takio and remembered the face of Cara, remembered her eyes, her mouth, her belly torn open because of this man's thugs. She knew Takio was taunting her, knew he was trying to get her to do something rash, foolish. But what? What could she possibly do to him? Her tension was stretching tighter, and still they stared each other down.

"It was the work of five minutes to find the rest. Your records in Sylmar are hardly private. Any of us could have discovered it if we'd wanted to look for it. No one wanted to look until now, of course. No one thought it necessary to look. Because in the end, you're like any human. Cattle. Dogs. You're nothing and no one we have to care about—except..." Takio grinned, shaking a finger at her. "Except we were wrong about you in another way too. A way that the mother of dear, dead Cara gave away without even realizing."

There it was. One of the operatives shifted his location, zeroing in on the largest of Takio's lieutenants. They'd made a positive ID, and the guys were lit up on some sort of drug, Warrick had said. What would be the odds they'd still have those drugs on their persons? And they were humans, so humans could take them down.

Takio seemed like he was waiting for Maria to respond, and she decided to string him along. She needed the time. When Takio finally struck, there would be a very narrow window of opportunity to apprehend his men in the midst of them performing the acts of violence that would justify their immediate arrest.

"Okay, I'll bite," she said, and from the way Takio straightened, practically quivering with excitement, she wondered whether he was high on his own drugs as well. "What else did you learn about me, Takio?"

"Do you even know what that cross around your neck is?" he asked, then answered his own question before Maria could reply. "It's a symbol of protection, nothing more. But on you—because of the faith you placed in it, it became more. It gave you strength to break the arm of a creature who should have pounded you into dust."

"Well then, it looks like God was on my side."

"Oh no, not God," Takio sneered. "That's the thing. The symbol is His, but the strength? That's all human. And it's that kind of strength that we can harvest. Harvest and synthesize. Here we've been looking for a Fallen all this time...when I didn't need one. I only needed someone like you."

"I don't think so." Maria held his stare. "My breaking some idiot demon's arm won't get you any closer to getting your wings back."

"You're wrong. You can't even begin to know your skills...your potential. And you're—nothing! Mere cattle. So for you to stand up in even the slightest way..." He drew in a deep, satisfied breath. "The blood of a righteous human. Of course."

"Uh-huh." Another operative slid over, positioning himself as Takio's second lieutenant took up his stance. "You need a cigarette or something?"

His lips curved into a knowing smile. "I'm going to need a little more than that. All this time we'd been trying to figure out how humans could ingest our special drug—when we *knew* it would render them as useless as the meanest spawn. We never considered the possibility that humans could improve the drug itself. This changes—everything. With the perfected formula, we strike. And when we strike...we rule the world."

Time...time, Maria thought, as she let Takio prattle on. She needed more time. Time to get Takio's men snared, and time to get Takio himself away from all these people. "What if I went with you right now?"

"Sadly, we can't leave quite yet." Takio shook his head. "I need you on hand to settle my other issue. There is a thorn that refuses to leave my side, and it's well past time to remove it."

Anger suddenly flared in Maria, sharpening her

focus. The kind of anger that had burned inside her when Cara had died in her arms, only then she'd been too young to understand it. The kind of anger she'd felt when the demons had attacked her in Sycamore Park. She'd done something then.

And she would do something now.

Maria gripped the tiny cross hanging around her neck. "Sword of God, defend me," she whispered, staring into Takio's eyes.

For a long moment, it seemed like nothing happened.

Then the world exploded around her.

Takio lunged for her, his hand curling around hers and wrenching it away from her neck so that the fragile necklace with its compromised clasp came with it, the cross spinning end over end to disappear in the glittering lights of Morpheus. Even as he moved, though, Maria reacted, instinctively fisting her right hand and punching Takio square in the jaw. To her surprise, the shot connected. Takio's head snapped to the side, his wide eyes rolling.

Unfortunately, he seemed to recover just as quickly, regaining his position as Maria scrambled away. Only now, everything looked different.

Maria gasped in horror as she spun, taking in the room with literally new eyes. Without Cara's cross around her neck, or perhaps simply because she'd attacked the ancient demon, Maria saw everyone not in their elegant glamours, but…as they really were.

And they were nightmares.

Fully a third of the partiers inside Morpheus were monstrous in appearance—and not only those hanging with Takio's crew. Some were gyrating on the dance floor, others were leaning up against the bar, still others were looming over humans who looked like a mix between being starstruck and scared out of their lives.

Maria could well understand why. The demons looked *exactly* as they had been depicted in mythological art since the dawn of mankind—their heads were animalistic in nature, with long snouts and pointed ears, some with hair, some with horns, all of them with arms and legs too long for their torsos. They squatted more than they stood, a few even sporting tails and some with wings pinioned tightly to their backs.

She wheeled again and saw two demons lurching forward, one slightly before the other. The demon in pursuit was the most fearsome creature she'd ever seen—a gargantuan bone-white beast with a head that was more animal skull than anything remotely human, vicious bone horns sticking straight up from the brow ridge, and a body with powerful arms and legs. From the creature's backside, a long, viciously barbed tail writhed and slashed. It was monstrous in the true sense of the world, and it was also…female. Or what Maria thought must have passed as female in the demon realm, the creature's bare-breasted chest now streaked with blood.

Serena.

But that meant that creature in front of Serena, the one racing toward her even now—was Warrick. Warrick, the most beautiful man she'd ever seen—tall, strong, invincible. Proud and true.

The creature that had replaced him was an abomination.

With the thick, oversized neck and shoulders of a rhinoceros, Warrick's body tapered into long, powerful arms and knuckle-dragging claws. His haunches—there was no other way to describe them—were also thick, matted with heavy patches of hair. Hair covered his torso too, a thick furring that emphasized his apelike appearance. His roar was apelike as well, a ululating howl that made Morpheus shake all the way down to its steel girders. That roar came out of a head she couldn't even fully process—the head of a lizard, a dragon, cruel and pointed and fierce, with amber glowing eyes and a yellow tongue that snaked out as Warrick rushed toward her. Toward *her*.

Maria whipped around, trying to dispel the horror she had seen, only to find it replaced with a fresh catastrophe as Takio's men—humans all—pulled out guns.

The operatives burst into action—

And she was shoved to the side, straight into the flailing limbs of demons she knew immediately were spawn.

Warrick leapt over the nearest table and raced toward Takio's enclave the moment he saw the demon reach for Maria's neck. This was the moment he'd been waiting for, the act of aggression against his protected that he needed to justify his act of blasting the demon beyond the veil. Only, once again, Warrick didn't want to banish Takio as much as he wanted to make him suffer, the way he'd always wanted to make him suffer since he'd first returned as an enforcer.

But Takio had always been smart—very smart. Smart enough that it'd been hundreds of years since Warrick's last shot at him. And this time, he wasn't alone.

As he arrived at Takio's table and pushed Maria free from the demon's grasp, Warrick caught her eye as she turned toward him for the barest moment, her horror and fear so strong as her gaze raked across him that he instantly knew the truth. She could see him—truly *see* him—his true self revealed without the glamour that even the basest of demons were granted to hide their ugliness from the children of God.

Somehow, impossibly — she could see him.

Warrick didn't have time to process that as Takio and Serena squared off to attack. Neither demon was making any pretense of holding on to anything but the barest minimum of their glamour, though most of the humans still in the club wouldn't remember what they saw except in the deepest depths of their nightmares. Instead, Takio and Serena were focusing all their energy on Warrick.

They attacked at once. Under the combined onslaught of their teeth and claws, Warrick went tumbling, grateful for the relative space of the VIP section. He came up and fended off their second attack by hurling throwing stars at them, but this only gave him a temporary reprieve. He had his knives, though, and he had his wits. He was used to fighting multiple demons at once, but not used to those demons being as old and as canny as he was. And usually, he had another member or three of the Syx as backup or to run a distraction, if nothing else.

But this battle was his alone to face.

Of the two, Takio took more risks. He lunged forward, leading with his mouth, and clamped his long jaws around Warrick's leg, rending muscle and sinew, cutting deep into bone. Warrick screamed, and if Takio's plan had been to trigger his rage, the demon was succeeding. Fury billowed up and out of him like a poisoned geyser, and in a flash, Warrick had buried a knife up to its hilt in Takio's thick hide, shaken off the bastard, and had gone for his head, both of his large hands squeezing around the demon's thick, muscular neck. Takio reached up with knifelike talons, the sharp points of his claws digging into Warrick's hands until

Warrick cried out with frustration.

Not to be outdone, Serena slashed and battered at him from the side, her long, graceful claws digging chunks out of his flesh with each pass, her scorpion's tail rising up behind her to jab forth, delivering stinging blows to Warrick's back. He was a demon built to live forever, virtually unkillable. But he had never faced opponents like Takio and Serena.

Still, he could not, would not summon the Syx. If Warrick was going to pass this test, he would have to do it alone. His future — the Syx's future — was lost anyway if he did not. Serena gave a lashing swipe with her tail, then fell back, unbalanced by the ferocity of the move.

The moment's reprieve was all Warrick needed. He rushed at Holkeri's shoulder first, sending the smaller demon sprawling

All around him in Morpheus, people were screaming, running. A single shot was fired, and then the air was filled with exploding capsules of hissing gas, setting off another panic.

He grinned. Good. Finn had gotten to the LAPD after all, had convinced them that what mattered most in what was going down at Morpheus was that people were evacuated, that the local and federal operatives they'd assigned not lose control. Real tear gas could cause significant damage to its victims; no one wanted that. Especially since the only victims who would succumb to it were human. Instead, the colored gas rolling out of the canisters was about as harmful as dry ice.

The distraction of the gas did its job in another way, though. The spawn, confused by the panicking people around them, didn't know where to turn or who to fight. But Holkeri's human lieutenants tightened in a circle surrounding Holkeri, determined to protect their leader. That gave the LAPD a target, and they capitalized on it, moving in quickly with guns and, at closer range, military clubs. The crunch of metal shattering bone ricocheted over the loud house music and the screams.

Serena jabbed at him again, and as Warrick turned to confront her, another figure burst from the gas cloud and ran straight for Holkeri — Maria, he realized, armed with a pistol that she used to pump a full round into the demon's chest. While ordinarily the demon wouldn't be harmed by anything issued from the hand of a human, Maria nearly glowed from within, lit with righteous fury. Holkeri went down in a heap, and Serena screamed, lunging past him to get at Maria.

Warrick blocked her path. She turned on him, her cold ice-white eyes blazing with hatred and fury, toxic bile spewing from the fleshy lips stretched over her jaws "You dare to look at me that way," she howled. "You dare!"

"I dare more than that," Warrick growled. Thrusting his hand forward, he grabbed Serena by the neck and nearly broke it in one swipe, hurling her to the floor. Her hands and feet pumped, her tail jabbed and darted, but it was her eyes that Warrick focused on, eyes that were panicked and frightened at last. Warrick stared back into those eyes, all his rage shattering into a thousand crystalline shards.

"I return you, broken child of God, to the Nothing," he said above her howls, invoking the ancient name of the space beyond the veil that Serena loathed so much. "May you find healing in its eternal embrace."

"Warrick—" Serena reached up, desperate now, clawing at his wrist, her talons digging deep as her body convulsed once—twice—then she burst out in an explosion of light, pulsing Warrick back until he staggered and fell.

"No!" Another roar filled the space, and Warrick scrambled to his feet to see Holkeri lunging forward even as Maria lifted her gun and blasted him again at point-blank range. The demon leapt through the air anyway, and Warrick took the full weight of his body, the two of them rolling end over end until they crashed up against the low wall of the VIP entrance. And once again, Warrick's hands shot out, pinioning the demon whose purple eyes glowed now in complete madness. All he had to do was squeeze —

And yet again, he stopped — gasped. His rage once more sluicing away. Because it had no place here.

Every time he had banished Holkeri, the demon had returned. Maybe...maybe this time it would be different, because this time, Warrick would not play judge and executioner. This time, he wouldn't act in anger, eager to see Holkeri punished. This time, it would be different.

"I return you, broken child of God, *not* to the Nothing," Warrick gritted out as Holkeri's eyes flew wide. "But to the Father's embrace. May he have mercy upon you."

"You dare!" Black, murderous hate flooded out toward Warrick with the creature's tortured gasp, and then Holkeri convulsed, his body nearly ripping free from Warrick's grasp. The demon didn't explode — he imploded, the desecration of his life leaving nothing but a black hole in the space of this plane. Then that too was gone.

Warrick sank back to his heels, his lungs heaving. His face wet with blood and soot.

And, unaccountably...tears.

"It's done," he whispered, though no one could hear him above the screams. "It's done."

CHAPTER TWENTY

Maria watched Warrick out of the corner of her eye as the detectives and federal agents continued to work the scene. He appeared beaten and broken, but she knew that was how he was supposed to appear. Takio and Serena had apparently fled in the madness that had followed the gas release, which had resulted in a few patrons hyperventilating, but no other issue. Takio's lieutenants had been rounded up and, sure enough, carried enough illegal drugs on them to warrant their arrest. Maria had no doubt they'd be flipping on each other within the hour.

The spawn and other demons that had been on the premises had not all been blasted to kingdom come, but those that were left had fled on foot at the first opportunity. No humans had died. Other than Warrick, no one had been seriously injured. He looked exactly like the role he was playing, a special operative who'd been charged with taking down a known felon. To anyone else, he'd been beaten, physically and mentally, by the exchange. Because Takio still walked free. A BOLO would be issued for both him and Serena, but the official assessment was that the head of la Noche had been cut off the snake. Even if it grew another one, it wouldn't be growing one here.

Eventually, Maria worked her way over to him. "You okay?"

Warrick visibly flinched as she touched him, and she scowled, frustration knotting her stomach. His glamour was now firmly back in place, and she'd blocked the image of what he'd looked like before out of her mind. Almost.

"Here," he grunted. He held up a bloody hand in offering to her, something held tight in his fist. She obligingly held out her own hand, and her cross and chain dropped into it. Warrick's palm where he'd gripped the medal had been burned to a bloody mass.

"Warrick," Maria muttered, shaking her head.

"Put it on," he commanded, his voice low, though he wouldn't lift his head to look at her. "I don't..." He shuddered. "It helps you tolerate my presence, it would appear."

Maria blinked, then glanced around the room. Sure enough, the demons and spawn who still remained in the room looked more demon than human to her, their glamour now more like loose-fitting clothes if she looked at them longer than a few seconds, probably because the adrenaline spike of the fight was still racing through her blood. But Warrick...

"It's not like that with you," she said, infusing her voice with as much confidence as she could manage. "You're — back to looking like you always look. Exactly the same. Well..." She smiled as he glanced up, the look in his eyes almost heartbreaking. "You're a little more banged up than I'm used to seeing you, I'll give you that."

"We've got medics." A brusque detective walked up as Warrick struggled to his feet.

"I'm all right," he said, waving off the hovering EMT who stood behind the detective. "I look bad, but it's all pretty superficial. At least Takio didn't have a gun."

"Didn't gut anyone on the way out, either, which is his usual MO." The detective shrugged. "Makes my job easier. We're going to need to question you, sir. Are you up for that now?"

Warrick was, of course, and Maria submitted to a second round of questioning as well, and a call from Stan, who tightly informed her that he could find absolutely no one to corroborate Warrick's story of his clandestine unit within the DEA.

"He's going to have a target on his back for a while, but no one is arguing about the assistance he's provided the unit, and no one can say for sure he isn't telling the truth about being in some sort of black ops unit—at least not yet. But he's going to be expected to come clean sooner rather than later. He probably shouldn't plan on leaving the city."

"Uh-huh. You want to be the one to tell him that?" When Stan didn't reply, she sighed. "Kidding, Stan, kidding. I'll let him know. How's Jack?"

"Somewhere in Oklahoma by now. And Maria, we checked on your aunt in Santa Ana, as you asked. She's fine—well, almost fine. She suffered a fall, she said, and we checked that too. Earlier this afternoon, EMTs were called to her villa because of a fall she sustained in her kitchen. She was cooking and became overwhelmed with the spices or something like that. She passed out, and when she came to, she called for help."

"She…passed out." Maria closed her eyes, her hand stealing to her pocket where she'd stuffed Cara's necklace. "That's all she remembers?"

"That's all that was reported. EMTs noted delusional statements consistent with a concussion, called a cousin who said they'd go with her to the hospital, bring her home. But she suffered some lacerations to her leg, a banged-up knee. Nothing more than that."

Nothing more than that. Maria didn't know if that were true or not, but her aunt was an honest woman. "You got a copy of those delusional ramblings, by any chance? In case there's more to it?"

Stan paused, and she winced, regretting the question. The last thing she needed was for her handler to think she'd gone around the bend. "You know what, never mind," Maria said. "I'll check on her myself later. Anything new with the Citadel?"

She glanced over to where Warrick was sitting, answering another round of questions with two agents. He'd consented to some first aid, apparently, because his face had been cleared of blood, and a bandage was applied to his temple. He looked angrier now, less defeated, and as he spoke, he gestured in violent surges. Both agents hung on his every word, and Maria smiled. He'd probably done this sort of thing thousands of times over the past several hundred years, explaining the disappearance of a bad person to people who were used to finding bodies at the scene of a crime.

"We're getting more by the hour," Stan informed her with grim satisfaction. "First, there were the assholes at the Citadel, who were so shell-shocked by the place blowing up that they couldn't confess fast enough. Apparently, they were convinced that the explosion had let something free, something that was after them." He chuckled. "Whatever works. We did our best to agree that there were several unaccounted-for predators at the complex, and our descriptions matches the stories that the la Noche guards are spitting out. We haven't found anyone that fits those descriptions, fortunately. The residents were harder to nail down. Family services is there now, and it's an absolute mess. But while the adults won't talk, the kids are, for once. And though the shit they're saying went down sounds too weird to be true, there's too many of them all saying the same thing. It's going to keep us busy for a while."

"But it's a good bet I'm done with this job."

He snorted. "That would be a good bet. It's likely a good bet you're done with undercover work in the city, you want my take on it. Your face is known now. Especially with the media circus at Morpheus. You can go back to being a cop...but not an undercover one."

A cop. Maria realized again that she'd not given nearly enough thought to what she would do next, after this job was done. There was always — only — finding Cara's killer. Bringing him to justice. Nothing ever mattered, other than that. Nothing could matter.

So now that Takio was as close to dead as she could ever understand him to be...who was she?

"Thanks, Stan. I'll check in when I'm back in Sylmar. Or when I'm down here again for more questioning."

"Do both." The call ended, and Maria pocketed her phone, striding quickly to where Warrick now stood, shaking hands and accepting cards. The agents let them go a short while later, and they left the club, walking through a corridor of plateglass windows. She peered down. Several stories below at street level, a ring of news vans circled the hotel.

"We're not leaving tonight," Maria said firmly, but Warrick didn't respond. He also, thank God, didn't object when she guided him to the elevator and hit the button for their floor. They made the short drop to the Emperor's level, exited, and managed not to bleed on anything as they returned to their room.

Warrick roused himself when they reached the door. "I'll check first."

"Of course," Maria murmured, keying open the door and pushing it open. Warrick passed by her, and for a moment, she thought he was going to slam the door shut, locking her out. But he didn't. He padded into the sitting room, then the bedroom, then finally, the bath.

"Clear," he said, his tone muffled.

"Good." She stepped inside the room, closed and locked the door, throwing the extra bolt. She didn't know if hotel locks would keep demons at bay, but she wasn't interested in being disturbed.

When Warrick strode back out of the bathroom, however, his face haggard, she pointed him toward the sitting area.

"We gotta talk," she said.

Warrick winced. He didn't want to have this conversation with Maria, didn't want to have any conversation, really, but he couldn't avoid it. She'd held up her end of the bargain. Holkeri was banished, and all Warrick's rage had emptied out of him in the wake of Holkeri's and Serena's departures from this plane. It'd left a blank hole behind, and that was something he was going to have to live with. He rubbed his chest, a move Maria didn't miss.

"What's wrong?" she asked sharply, coming up to him, but he shook his head.

"Nothing. Tired."

Her brows went up, and she peered at him as she pushed him gently backward until he sank into the overstuffed chair. Not the couch, he noticed. He rather liked the couch.

Instead, Maria took up position on the low coffee table, regarding him intently as she settled her elbows on her knees. "Demons get tired?"

The question was so unexpected, Warrick barked a laugh, then winced again, hiding the reaction from

Maria before she demanded that he strip. His body would heal. It needed time. The glamour, of course, could usually heal immediately. He'd gotten used to appearing beat up enough so that medical professionals, such as the EMTs upstairs, didn't ask too many questions — they saw what they expected to see, until he was released from their care. Then he healed himself in short order. He'd done so on the way down to this floor in the elevator, and even now looked almost normal. But the flesh and muscle beneath — he did have a physical form, as horrific as it appeared. That form had been ripped to shreds by Takio's talons, Serena's barbs. It would take...a while for him to recover from that, though he would, he knew, eventually heal.

He resisted the urge to rub his chest again, over his heart. Mostly heal, anyway.

When Maria didn't say anything further, Warrick glanced at her, frowned. "You're still not wearing the cross."

"The chain broke." She shrugged, and when he moved to hold out his hand for it, she waved him off. "No, you can't solder it together with your pinky fingers, but thanks," she said. "I'll put it back together. I don't need it right now. It did its job. It found you."

He blinked at her, and the empty space in his chest ached worse. "I came because you called me. Because of your strength and the strength of Cara's faith."

She nodded. "And you did what I needed you to do. You...banished, or whatever you want to call it, Takio, and as a bonus, took out the female demon as well, Serena or whatever." She shook her head, the look in her eyes going distant. "I know you said they existed, but I confess I didn't really believe in the idea of female demons. That's totally sexist, I know."

His lips quirked into a grim smile. "You should

probably check out some sensitivity training."

"Noted. But she was about a million times uglier than Takio was, I gotta tell you. She looked like someone had been in a particularly bad mood when she was hatched."

Warrick sighed. "The demonic form isn't something that you're cursed with, it's the form you believe you deserve to take. The more powerful you feel you are, the worthier of attention, respect—the more horrific you become as a demon."

"As punishment?"

"Not at all. As reward. Even demons remain God's children, and they have a pecking order. The uglier you are by human standards, the more humans cannot help but fear you. Serena craved that fear as much as she craved attention. Her form was designed to inspire the worst of nightmares. She got her wish—but found she no longer wanted it in time, as most demons do who cannot stay wrapped in the protective thrall of their outrage. By then, of course, it was too late. So yes, you could say she was cursed, but she was cursed by her own hand."

"No wonder you guys are messed up," Maria muttered, and he brought his attention back to her.

"You saw what I truly am," he said simply. She shook her head.

"No. I *see* what you truly are. And for a few minutes when you were busy saving the planet from two of the worst scourges of humanity, I saw what you had to become in order to do your job. And, yes, it scared me."

Warrick tightened his jaw, his throat unaccountably working. "I know."

"See, I don't think you do," Maria said. She reached out and took his hands, her own seeming impossibly frail in his as she held on to him tightly. "I wasn't scared because of your enormous shoulders and your hairy body or your freakishly long, double-jointed arms and legs. I wasn't scared because your hands were as big as boulders and your head looked like something out of a monster magazine. I saw all that, Warrick. I saw it. I saw you."

He held himself rock steady, the hole in his chest gaping larger. "I know."

"You keep saying that, but you're still not getting it." Maria's eyes were wide now, glistening with a sheen that hadn't been there before. "All those things—that wasn't the problem. The problem was every time Takio took a swipe at you—you *bled*. Every time Serena pumped that godforsaken tail forward, catching you with her barb, you jerked like you'd been struck with an electric cattle prod. They *hurt* you, Warrick. They took chunks out of your flesh and sliced you all the way to the bone. They burned your skin and singed your hair and gouged pieces from your arms, your legs, your"— she gripped his hand more tightly—"paws. I was scared because I not only didn't want you to die, I didn't want you to be hurt. I don't care what body you inhabit, you idiot. To me, you are Warrick. You came into my life to save me, to protect me and protect the girl who died in my lap fifteen years ago, and from the moment you first touched me, you pledged to keep me safe and whole. And I..." She shook her head hard, and the tears slipped free of her lashes to trail down her face. "I can't keep you whole, Warrick. I'm not strong enough. Even with Cara's cross, I am good for like one punch—that's it. I'm *useless.*"

The anger in her voice at this last admission rang so deep that Warrick found himself lifting his own hands to Maria's face, pressing his thumbs to her cheeks to brush the tears away. "You're not useless, Maria," he whispered. "You're not even close. You are a child of

God. You walk in His grace."

"Well, I would rather walk next to you," she said softly.

"No!" The anger returned then, quick and hot, and Warrick jerked himself away from Maria, clearly shocking her.

"Are you even *listening* to yourself?" he asked, hating that he'd brought the quick rush of surprise and embarrassment to her face. "Humans have been saying such things to demons for millennia. It is *exactly* that sentiment that keeps humans in our thrall. You seek out the other, the expression of all that is not you. Demons scratch that itch."

"What are you talking about?" Maria stared at him, clearly shocked. "I couldn't give a shit about a bunch of demons. I don't care about them. I care about you."

"They are who and what I am. They are all of who and what I am. I can aspire to nothing more than that heaving, bleeding, raging freak you saw in the dance club upstairs. That's as good as it's going to get."

"And I say you're wrong. Full stop," Maria said. She stood then, briskly, and moved over to the couch, settling back on it and grabbing the remote.

Warrick frowned at her, nonplussed. "What...what are you doing?"

"Trying not to beat the shit out of you," she growled. She gestured toward the back of the hotel suite with her hand. "You're going to play the martyr card, I can feel it coming on, and I am so pissed off at you right now, I want to wallop you with my well-warded fist. So you take your sorry-ass, heaving, bleeding, raging freak body back to the bathroom, and you take a shower and throw yourself in bed. And maybe, if you're lucky, I'll wake up from my nap in the middle of the night and join you."

"I'll take the couch," Warrick said stiffly,

automatically, and Maria rolled her eyes.

"And you have spent way too long on the other side of the shroud."

He blinked. "The veil."

"The veil, whatever," she said, waving the remote again. This time, she hit a button, and the screen flashed to life. Warrick winced at the noise of it, his ears still burned to a crisp from Serena's poison.

"Go, Warrick," Maria said again, her voice flat and angry. "You try to move me from this couch, and there *will* be hell to pay."

Chapter Twenty-One

Maria awoke curled in a heavy layer of luxurious hotel sheets topped by a pillowy white comforter and immediately knew she was alone. Warrick had also moved her from the couch to the bed without her ever knowing it. *Ass.*

She sighed, rolling over to peer at the clock. 7:00 a.m. Bright sunlight trickled in past the heavy blackout shades, but otherwise, the room was still plunged in darkness. The TV was off in the main area of the suite too. She didn't remember turning it off, didn't remember Warrick emerging from the bedroom to pick her up and carry her in here. She doubted he'd slept at all. Her gaze drifted to the wingback chair opposite the bed.

Slipping out from beneath the comforter and wrapping it around her, Maria padded across the thick carpet and checked the main room of the suite. No Warrick. She turned toward the chair. Sure enough, the chair had been moved slightly, at least judging by the indentations in the carpet.

Biting her lip, Maria sat in the large chair, curling her feet up beneath her as she rested her head against the comforter-cushioned fabric. Warrick had sat here, watching her for, what—how long? Hours, anyway.

She'd probably passed out while Warrick was still in the shower, and, being Warrick, he'd decided that the enormous couch wasn't big enough to serve as her bed. She glanced to the small table beside the chair and saw something else. Her slender gold chain, with its small golden cross. Perfect and pristine.

She picked it up, settling it once more around her neck and resetting the clasp. "Idiot," she whispered, another line of tears trickling down her cheek.

But where had Warrick gone? She didn't know anything about him, not really. His cover story was nowhere near the truth, and hadn't he said he'd be sent back "beyond the veil," whatever the hell that meant, now that his summons was done? Though judging from the number of demons she'd seen in Morpheus, she didn't see how his summons could ever be done. What could possibly keep him on Earth other than the eternal churn of demons behaving badly?

She had no idea. She had no idea about anything anymore. She merely felt...bereft.

It took another hour, but eventually, Maria uncurled from the chair, drifted through the motions of getting cleaned up in the obscenely large bathroom, then wandered back into the main part of the hotel suite. The bag Finn had brought Warrick's weapons in still lay on the floor behind the small dining table, and her jeans and shirt were still piled on the counter, along with her boots and a small, crisp stack of hundred dollar bills. Enough to get her home, she thought. Warrick thinking of everything, except for what mattered most.

Maria sighed. It made more sense to wear the casual clothing instead of her party dress, she supposed, though she had no interest in discarding that. She'd already lost one set of clothes to this job.

This job.

She blew out a long breath as she returned to the bedroom for her dress and boots. She needed to go back to her apartment in Compton, clean out whatever she was going to clean out, and leave the rent payment on the kitchen counter. She should go by Lucy's to say goodbye too, but—not yet, she thought. Not yet. They'd ask about Warrick, where he'd gone, and she had nothing to tell them. In fact, maybe she should stay away from the neighborhood in Compton altogether for a while. Her rent wasn't due until January. Christmas was coming. No one would question her getting out of town.

Christmas. It was only a couple of weeks away now. She should go down to Santa Ana, stay with her aunt, like she did every year. Together they'd go to Long Beach, visit the ocean where they'd spread Cara's ashes all those years ago, the bright and laughing girl forever able to play in the sea. And after that…

After that, she simply didn't know.

Maria dumped her clothes on the table and snatched up her high-end jeans and T-shirt, dressing as she moved around the hotel suite for a final recon. They'd brought very little in; they'd take even less out. Her gun had been bagged the night before by the cops, and she had no idea what Warrick had done with his knives and throwing stars. The other, smaller weapons were still tucked in her pocket, and of course, she had her party clutch from the night before.

She squinted to the sitting area, located the purse, and dumped out her phone. No calls, no messages. Burner phone, but still. It was a burner phone that at least Warrick and Finn knew about. One of them could have reached her. She checked the caller ID, saw only her outbound calls to Stan. There was no point in calling him again—he wouldn't know where Warrick had disappeared to, and he wouldn't be happy she'd lost

247

him.

Maria tucked her phone in her back pocket, then trotted back up the few steps to the front of the suite and picked up Finn's plastic bag. Not exactly an overnighter, but it looked close enough to a shopping store bag that she could probably pass for a tourist. She smoothed the bag out, rolling her eyes at the image of the brightly lit Eiffel Tower, fireworks going off in the background, behind the big, happy balloon. Leave it to Finn to find the most ridiculous bag possible. She slid her clothes and party purse into it and left the room.

Maria made it out the front doors of the hotel without anyone bothering her, though both the hotel registration clerks and the concierge seemed to be giving her the side-eye. She glanced at herself in one of the hotel's plate glass windows — she looked the same as she ever did. Better clothes, admittedly, but otherwise the same.

She reached the corner and turned, then turned again, unsure where to go. She should get an Uber back up to Sylmar, but she wasn't ready to face her real life again. She believed Stan — she wouldn't be able to continue undercover work, but the idea of returning to her job as a straightforward beat cop… What would that be like? Everything she'd ever hoped and dreamed about was tied up in avenging her cousin's death. Now…

Maria glanced up, then squinted as she made out the distinctive spire down the street, instantly recognizing the silhouette. Her lips twisted. A Catholic church, of all things to catch her attention.

Well…it couldn't hurt.

She jogged the short distance up the boulevard and turned down North Las Palmas Avenue, turning once more onto Sunset. The church loomed high, more elaborate than she would have expected for downtown LA. There was something about the city that had always seemed so secular to her, but here was this church, right in the center of everything.

Maria climbed the short flight of stairs to get to the main cathedral doors, then tried them. To her surprise, they opened easily. She slipped inside the building and through the ornate vestibule, pushing open a side door into the main part of the church, and walked a short way down a narrow aisle. She stopped then, taking a moment to appreciate the building's serene beauty. Large windows lined the walls, casting bright sunlight down on the rows of pews. The altar stood atop another set of stairs and behind an honest to God communion rail. She didn't think they made such things anymore, but the church looked like it had been built more than a hundred years ago, and it was so beautiful, the current parish family probably didn't want to do anything to modernize the aesthetic. Some things were meant to be renewed, while some things were meant to be old…even in Los Angeles.

Maria's gaze drifted to the huge stained glass windows, their brilliantly glowing images catching the morning light. Saints and angels, penitents and true believers. She thought again of Warrick, fighting, bleeding, pierced and broken, all to protect his latest summoner in a millennia of service to pay for his crimes. Would he ever stop paying?

"Good morning." The voice was rich and welcoming, and Maria turned to see a man approaching her with a broad smile. His eyes were a deep brown, almost as dark as his skin, and he wore a simple clerical collared black shirt and black pants. In his hands, he carried a well-worn book, undoubtedly a Bible. "Our next mass isn't until this evening, but you are welcome to pray in seclusion if you would like. Or, if you have any questions…if there is anything I can help you with, it would be my gift to do so."

His kind smile proved to be Maria's undoing, and she tightened her hold on her plastic shopping bag, as if it was the only thing of solace left in the world.

"Can demons be forgiven of their sins?" she blurted.

The question was out before she could stop it, and the priest's eyes flew wide, his brows climbing his broad forehead. Maria lifted a hand to her mouth as she felt herself flush with embarrassment. "I'm sorry," she said quickly. "I truly am. I—I don't know why I asked that."

"No apologies are necessary for a question that comes from the heart," the priest said, recovering with easy grace. He half turned as if to gesture her forward, deeper into the church, then seemed to reconsider, squaring himself to Maria. "I sense you're not comfortable in a house of God. Do you know why?"

"I'm not…" Maria glanced around, then sighed. "I guess I haven't been here for a while. Not *here* here, but—"

He smiled. "I understand. And when did you stop visiting God in His house? You were young?"

"Ten," she said. The priest made a soft sound of distress, and she rushed on, wanting to do better by her aunt. "I mean, I still went to church, every week. But…God and I sort of stopped talking then." Saying the words out loud almost made her want to cry. "My mom had died, then my cousin died. I had a hard time forgiving God for all that."

"As any child would." The priest nodded. "As any man or woman would either. When death parts us from those we hold most closely, it's we who feel ripped from our moorings, not the children who return to Him. You speak of a demon, but it's the same for any creation of the Father. We yearn to journey home. If we travel too far away from that home, we forget the way. But though we may have forgotten, that doesn't mean the way has stopped existing. The path remains for those with the courage to walk it. Ever and always."

He smiled at her, his eyes filled with kindness. "So to answer your question, yes. God can do anything, even forgive a demon his sins. Of course He can."

Maria found she couldn't do anything but nod back at him, ridiculous tears once more building behind her eyes. Watching her keenly, the priest smiled at her again.

"You are a child of God too," he said, his words so quiet, she didn't know if he was saying them aloud or if they were merely ringing in her head. "One who walks in His light, scattering that light wherever you go. As such, you are blessed. And anyone you love is equally blessed. The Father would have it no other way. You must believe that, and you must only believe that." He gestured to Maria's neck. "The cross you wear. Do you know its significance?"

She frowned. "It's a cross. It means, I don't know, God loves us."

"A Celtic cross, more aptly — given the circle behind the crossed bars. The Irish were quite fond of that design. Even before they knew of the Christian God, they used that circle as one of their earliest representations of divinity. But though your cross is simple, I can sense its power. It's been profoundly blessed."

Maria pinned her gaze on him. "Do you know — do you know by who?"

The priest smiled benevolently. "Does it matter? Or does it only matter that *you* bless it — by the fact that you're wearing it now. Wearing it and imbuing it with your faith. That has always been the greatest strength of God's children, after all…our faith." He reached out and

251

tapped her bag. "The answers you seek are closer than you know, dear child."

With that, he turned and walked away, and Maria turned as well, blindly moving back down the aisle, her eyes now clouded with tears she could no more understand than she could stop. When she reached the front steps of the church, she angrily brushed those tears away, sucking in long, gasping breaths as she felt the sun on her face once more, the breeze lifting her hair.

As her sight cleared, Maria looked down at her bag with its cheerful burst of fireworks beyond the Eiffel Tower and its soaring hot air balloon.

And then, finally, she noticed the scrawling script beneath in the archway of the Tower, meant to look like the building itself...

Paris Las Vegas.

"Whoa, whoa, whoa, buddy, take it easy."

Finn's voice barely penetrated Warrick's fog. He bent over, lungs heaving as he gasped for air. They were running in the late hours of the morning, on a trail that ran through the mountains and down to the Colorado River, deep within the Lake Mead nature preserve. They'd reached the part of the trail that was too steep to climb for most runners, but Warrick wasn't most runners.

Now he stared at the river, watching it cascade through cuts in the rock it had forged over tens of thousands of years. Finally, something in this world that had been here longer than he had... something that, unlike him, *could* stay.

Finn heaved himself up beside him, following Warrick's gaze toward the river while trying hard not to look at him directly, Warrick noticed. Finn was no fool.

Well, not entirely a fool. "You're way too messed up, my brother."

"It's not worth talking about," Warrick snapped. He'd watched the human sleep for hours, the ache in his chest not abating. That hadn't happened before either, like so much else afflicting him. But the job was done, and when the summons came from the Syx for him to return to Las Vegas, he'd accepted it, steeling himself for their scrutiny.

To his surprise, they hadn't noticed his fractured mental state. They'd been too busy losing their minds over his body.

And that was fair enough. Warrick simply wasn't recovering the way he typically did after a fight. He was healing, yes — but more slowly, and with far more pain. As if his body had forgotten the way back home. He'd stared at himself in the oversized mirrors of their temporary domain in one of the casino hotels on the Vegas Strip, noting every scar, every gash and rent. That was also different, he decided. The scars on his demonic form. He didn't mind them, exactly, except...

He gritted his teeth. Except the scars reminded him of Maria. What she'd seen. What she'd loathed in him.

He'd slept for nearly a day — something else that had never happened before — and then he'd raced out of the hotel like a man possessed, desperate to breathe, to burst free of the trap of his own skin. It itched and burned, his bones seeming to shift beneath the weight of an expectation he couldn't fully understand. Only in the harsh, hot sun and fragrant trees of the preserve had he found the solace he craved...and he'd pounded down every trail he could find.

Finn had fallen into step with him before he left the casino, Stefan and Hugh following at a more careful distance. Gregori and Raum had remained at the casino to run interference if needed. They all knew something was wrong with Warrick, and they were the Syx. They would fight for him, suffer for him, or suffer *with* him, if it came to that. They would also die for him, if such a release was allowed.

It wasn't.

And neither was it allowed that the Syx could remain on this earth longer than the archangel suffered it. Suffering being the operative term here.

Warrick drew in a shallow breath, and Finn looked at him sharply. "You know, it'd help if you dialed back the glamour. I can't see what I can't see."

Warrick hung his head. "I can't. I don't seem to have full control over my glamour right now. It's not as easy to shift back and forth." He'd realized that when he'd been on his knees in the Morpheus's VIP section, his body ravaged from the attacks of Serena and Holkeri. He'd managed to reinforce his glamour once his energy wasn't diverted to attacking the demons with all his strength, but for the first time since he'd taken on this form at the breaking of the world, it had been challenging to make the shift. He'd tried going back and forth two or three more times once he'd returned to Vegas, and it still wasn't a smooth transition. "I don't know if it's because I'm healing more slowly."

"What was in that barb that Serena jabbed you with? You have any clue? Because if she had it, others could too. That would suck."

Warrick shrugged. "No idea, but I will say it's nothing I want to encounter again."

Finn pursed his lips. "We could...I don't know. Test your blood? Make some sort of antidote?" Even as he considered the idea, though, he shook his head. "Blood heals first, then the body. Whatever she dumped inside you, if it didn't kill you..."

"Then it's already gone. So I don't think that's it." Warrick blew out a long breath, looking at the surrounding trees, the steep, striated canyon, the river far below. "I think being too long on this plane is the issue. It's fine as long as we're strong. But in the past, we healed in our own bolt-holes, held in stasis until we were called again. We didn't stick around here."

"Well, of the two, I vote for the longer healing time and better views."

Warrick smiled, knowing Finn was only trying to cheer him up. It was what Finn did.

"But think about it," Warrick continued. "Earth was a different environment before the first war. With the flooding of the world, Atlantis disappeared beneath the ocean's surface and the skies were rent. All that humans could do, all that the gods could do—changed. Then with the setting of the veil, the atmosphere thickened, weighing everything down. No one lived as long, ran as far, was built as strong. Humans dwindled in size for all that they grew smarter, until the tide turned once more and they gained mass and height. Our own brothers could not hide so well for those many years."

"The Fallen." Finn's lips twisted. "You think they're still out there, living—what, in the shadows? They're way too big to do that, too noticeable."

Warrick shrugged. "They have to be. If demons could survive this long, surely the Fallen could too."

Finn scowled. "Fantastic." Unlike the rest of the enforcers, Finn had not been judged by God for his sins but by his own brethren. Judged and condemned in the cataclysm that broke the world, horrified by his descent into the demon realm, but also—also unlike the rest of them—shocked by it. Were Finn to be faced with one of the Fallen today...pure, pristine, whose eyes had not seen all he'd seen, whose hands had not been bathed in the blood of his own accursed kind...Warrick was pretty sure how that would go.

It wouldn't be pretty.

"Where to now, my brother?" Finn asked, his voice sounding a touch bleaker now, as if he too had gone down the path of Warrick's thoughts, had stood on the edge of that abyss.

Warrick cursed himself. As leader of the Syx, it was his job to keep his men strong. To do that, he needed to be stronger, himself. He shouldn't let Finn dwell on all that could not be changed, not when so much of their existence was out of their control.

He stood. "Now, we need to find our vehicle again." He frowned, turning to scan the trees. "Which might be a problem. You remember where we left it?"

"Ah…not exactly." With a startled laugh, Finn fished in his pocket until he found his phone. He held it up for Warrick to see. "No bars."

Warrick lifted a brow, and Finn grinned. "No bars, no service, no way to track our way back home. I guess we'll have to—"

The call came with the same brutal force that it always did, sweeping them up in the maelstrom of urgency, need, power. Not a human call, not this time— there was nothing plaintive or desperate about it. Instead, it was a cold, soulless demand, as ancient as it was impossible to ignore.

Warrick turned. Finn was already falling back, his body still solid, still substantial, but still definitely remaining behind.

Screw that, Warrick decided. Where he went, so went his brothers. If not to fight with him…then to mourn his death.

He stuck his hand out, and Finn dove for it, the power of their connection giving Warrick a jolt of unexpected strength.

A second later, they disappeared from the clearing in a bolt of pure white light.

CHAPTER TWENTY-TWO

Maria clutched her tote bag as she walked through McCarran International Airport, already amazed by the number of slot machines she'd passed since she'd exited the boarding ramp. Festooned with Christmas decorations, the machines jangled and rang, nearly every one of them occupied by gambling hopefuls. Some of them having just landed as she had, posing for laughing, high-energy selfies as they eagerly started their preholiday sojourn in Sin City, the rest with the wry, rueful smiles of those having gambled their way through their vacation already, and who now were facing the return to reality.

It was Tuesday morning, and the place was jam-packed. What must it be like on the weekend?

As close as Maria lived to Las Vegas, she'd never visited the gambling paradise. She'd never had the money to lose, for one, and she simply hadn't fallen in with the kind of friends who could take off for a few days and ramble around looking for ways to go broke.

She twisted her lips, eyeing the crowds of people thronging toward baggage claim. She hadn't fallen in with friends, period. She'd always been too focused on the larger picture. The ultimate prize. Even Jack, with whom she'd been so comfortable, had been a means to an end.

While Warrick…

Maria sighed. She skirted the baggage carousel — she had nothing but her carry-on, and that was barely half-full as it was. It'd taken her a day to get a flight, collect her real ID, her credit cards, spending cash and at least check in on her apartment in Sylmar. But now she was here. In Vegas. With nothing but a hotel name to go on.

"Stay focused," she muttered. She didn't know what Warrick would say when she found him — if she found him. But she couldn't stay in LA and not at least try. As it was, she seemed to be drifting along like a ghost without him. And maybe that was because of his ridiculous assertion that she was swept up in his demon thrall, but…

She wouldn't know if she didn't see him again.

Maria had begun searching the overhead signs for directions to taxis and public transportation, when her gaze fell on a woman so startling in her appearance that Maria nearly stopped dead…would have stopped dead, actually, except for the crowd of people pushing her forward.

The woman was tall — easily six foot four, with a boldly platinum swing of hair beneath a sharply cut chauffeur's cap. She wore aviator sunglasses, even though she was inside, and her lips were painted a shocking cherry red. The black jacket and deep-cut white blouse that made up her chauffeur's uniform stretched tightly across her ample breasts and skimmed her long waist before flaring out over her hips. At that point, things got even stranger, as the uniform devolved into a glittering sequined skirt barely reaching to mid-thigh. Beneath, miles of long legs ended at shiny black platform stilettos with four-inch heels.

But perhaps most shocking of all was the sign the woman held, which contained a single word:

WARRICK.

The chauffeur spotted Maria almost at the same time Maria saw her, but allowed her an extra moment to catch her breath. Maria got the impression she needed to do that a lot.

"Maria Santos!" The woman finally called out, her wide, mobile mouth splitting into a grin as Maria managed a nod. When Maria still didn't move, however, the chauffeur strode over with her sign and her platform heels and her sequins.

"I simply could *not* be happier to meet you. Do you have any bags?" The woman's gaze fixed on Maria's overnighter, then her shirt. "Sweet Mother Mary on a shopping spree, we have work to do with you, child."

"I'm sorry?"

Maria glanced down. The woman did too.

"The jeans are primo, but the rest—" The chauffeur sighed heavily. "Don't you worry about a thing. We'll get you taken care of. But right now, we've gotta motor."

"I—what?" Maria's brain suddenly kicked into gear, and she shook her head, even as the chauffeur turned and gestured her toward the open sunshine of the Las Vegas morning. "Wait. Who are you?"

The woman's manicured brows leapt behind her glasses. "My apologies, you're absolutely right." She slipped her sign under her left arm, whipped off her glasses, and tucked them into her…well, her bra, then held out her right hand. Maria found herself drilled with eyes the color of whiskey, thickly lashed with expertly applied makeup. "Nikki Dawes, your official chauffeur and tour guide for the magical mystical wonderland of Las Vegas," she said, grinning even more broadly when Maria still hesitated. She winked. "And, more to the point, your ticket to finding the lovely and eternally cranky Warrick. We're ever so slightly in a time crunch on that, however, so choppity choppity."

Nikki Dawes waggled her fingers, which were long-fingered and ungloved, the flash of her bright red nail polish flawlessly matching her lips. Maria shook her hand, and the woman's smile only deepened, her eyes going wide and appreciative as she held on to Maria a little longer than was strictly necessary.

"Oh, this is going to be good," Nikki breathed, and Maria pulled her hand back. Had she just revealed too much, somehow?

"You mind telling me how you know me?" Maria asked, but she saw no reason not to follow the woman. Whether or not this Nikki Dawes was friend or foe, she knew more about where Warrick was than Maria did. That was all that mattered right now.

"I'll give you the short version, sweet pea," Nikki said, striding out into the heat of the day. Since it was December, it was remarkably comfortable—though Maria could sense the dryness of the desert around her. Nikki pulled a key fob out of her bra, extracting her glasses as well and resettling them on her face. "There's my car."

They approached a beautiful Lincoln Town Car, and Maria blinked as she saw someone sitting in it—then blinked again. "Oh." She said. "I thought…"

Nikki waved the fob. "Hologram. One of—well, never mind. A tech geek friend designed it for me, and let me tell you, it makes pickups at McCarron a hella lot easier. Hop in the back, and I'll give you the 411." She glanced again at Maria's bag as she opened the back door and tsked as she gestured Maria inside. "We have got to get you a new tote, minimum. Or at least get you a Members Only jacket to match it."

"Hey," Maria retorted, clutching the bag close. She'd had it a long time, but not that long. Still, she obligingly slid into the back of the cab. Nikki trotted around to the driver's side and hopped in. Then she threw the car into gear, ripping out of her parking space and into the flow of traffic with a move that seemed more at home on the streets of LA than in a city in the middle of the desert. Slammed into the corner of the car, Maria finally felt herself relax. Insane cabbies, she was used to.

But Nikki's next question had her sitting up short. "Okay, so whaddya know about what Warrick's doing in Vegas?"

"I don't know anything," Maria protested. "It was only a guess that he was here, a bag his friend Finn gave us that had Paris Las Vegas on it." She'd looked up the casino online, and it was definitely one of the nicer bits of kitsch on the Strip. "Is that where we're going?"

"That would be negative, though it would've been a good place to start. The rest of the Syx are staying there right now."

"You mean Finn."

"I mean six of the hottest damned demons you've ever seen in your life, baby doll, and Warrick is right there at the top, if I say so myself." She grinned at Maria in the rearview mirror. "We had a thing for like, a minute. But ultimately, I wasn't his type. And now that I'm meeting his type, I totally agree."

Maria's face must have registered her confusion, because Nikki cackled as she cut the wheel hard, slewing across two lanes of traffic and into a sharp turn. "So, let's get you squared away. You got that Warrick's a demon, and you're down with that, right?"

"I saw him."

"More on that later. In addition to the demons of the world, and sweet Jesus, are there a crap ton of them these days, there are humans with psychic abilities. You familiar with those?"

"You mean like telephone psychics?"

Nikki barked a laugh. "We'll start there, and we'll call them Connecteds. We got a whole mess of Connecteds here in Vegas, including the granddaddies of them all, a group called the Council."

"The Council." Maria nodded, though her mind was starting to fray at the edges.

"The Arcana Council, if we're being exact," Nikki clarified. "Think of them as a board of directors for Magic, Inc., responsible for keeping the company going. Only, they've mostly been a pain in the ass up to this point, but that's another story. What's important now is that one of the Council members, a guy by the name of Michael, as in Michael the Archangel—"

"Michael the Archangel?" Maria blurted, her gaze snapping sharply to Nikki's face in the rearview mirror. "As in the real archangel of God? He's on this Council?"

"He is. And all the members of the Council are embodiments of the Major Arcana cards of the Tarot— please tell me you know Tarot."

"Ah…a little?"

"Well, brace yourself. You'll get to know it a lot, you hang around here for long. Michael is the Hierophant, and that means he can drop the hammer on the demons, including—especially—the Syx. He's the guy who says who among them stays on this earth and who goes."

"Wait a minute." Maria frowned. "You said there was an influx of demons recently, but if Michael can say who stays and who goes, can't he simply wave his magic sword or whatever and send all the demons away?"

"You'd think that, but he's more interested in humans dealing with the issue. Which is generally the case with anyone on the Council." Nikki waved off Maria's grimace. "Like I said, they can be a pain in the ass. But what we're now figuring out is that Michael can absolve a demon of his sin, if he so chooses. And that's sort of like a get-out-of-demon-jail-free card."

Maria felt her eyes go wide. "So that demon becomes an angel again?"

Nikki lifted her right hand, waggling manicured fingers. "Sorta kinda. He'd still be Fallen, but with this special sanction, he can stay on Earth. Which means he can keep fighting the demon hordes but also have someplace to crash when he's done. Being a Fallen is a totally different kettle of whack from being a straight up demon enforcer, however, and it requires more of a — commitment, I guess you would say. A Fallen can stick around, but he's got to really *want* to stick around. For a better reason than because he wants to do his job. He's got to long for something that is on this earth, something that will tether him to it."

Nikki looked up at the rearview mirror. It was once more impossible to see her eyes through her shades, but Maria could feel their intensity anyway.

"Something like you."

Maria made a face. "You might have noticed Warrick left me behind. I — I saw him in his demon form, and he decided that I couldn't possibly want him after that." She scowled, shaking her head. "He's wrong."

"Of course, he's wrong." Nikki snorted. "Demon or not, he's a dude, and dudes can be idiots sometimes. So that means we gotta help him get a clue. And by we, I mean you, baby doll. And we don't have a lot of time."

Warrick staggered under the weight of so much pain, he'd already fallen to his knees.

"You alone were summoned," Michael said again. "You alone stand trial."

"I am a *Syx*. We fight together." It wasn't the first time he'd uttered the words. They came back on him in a horrific cacophony of noise, the words running over, around and through each other, the trick of the demon mind trap obviously still a favorite of the archangel's. And he could see that, despite Michael's fury, Finn still stood guard at the front of the chamber, for all he could no longer see Warrick. Because Warrick was trapped in a hell of the Hierophant's making.

Another blast of energy knifed through him, another memory unlocked. So much death. Every one of his banishments coming back to confront him with wing and talon and claw, every banishment where he'd allowed his rage to get the better part of him, where he'd left a mark not only on the demon he'd imprisoned beyond the veil, but on the humans that demon had left behind. Over and over again, he'd seen the damage he had wrought—sometimes intentionally, sometimes not. Even in his work with the Syx, in his commitment to do his worst solely against the worst of his kind, he was not blameless in his actions. He'd never remained behind long enough to see that damage, to suffer the guilt of its effects.

He'd never remained behind.

As if the archangel could read his thoughts, a mocking laugh rolled over Warrick. "You say you wish to remain bound to this earth, demon, dedicated to your mission. But it is not so simple as that. You have reveled in the carnage of your role but not its true impact. You have destroyed without discernment, banished without mercy or healing. It is not enough."

Though he wanted to point out the irony of the archangel accusing him of being merciless, Warrick bore down. "I can serve on this earth or from beyond the veil," he growled. "But those of the Syx who would stay should not be held accountable for any decision leveled

265

against me."

"That is also not enough."

The blow came from nowhere, a searing blast of pain that caught Warrick under the chin and sent him sprawling backward. All at once, there was a demon on top of him, jabbing him with a thousand different jolts of electricity, arms and legs little more than naked filaments of fire. He remembered this guy. He'd been a bastard the first time around.

But this time, he saw more than the writhing, snarling beast. He saw the humans who'd gathered around the demon he'd been sent to destroy — and only now, for the first time, did he realize that they were more than momentary victims. That they'd needed him as much *after* he'd banished the demon who'd plagued them as before — perhaps more so.

Warrick winced as another wave of pain leveled him, finally able to see a glimpse into the uniquely human torment of being left behind, abandoned.

"You really want a life where you cannot escape the ramifications of what you do?" Michael taunted him. "Where the weight of the lives you leave behind never dissipates but serves as an anchor tying you to the frail, the weak, the desperate? That is your charge, demon. That has always been your charge, though you were too stupid to realize it when you chose to Fall."

Warrick blinked, bleary as he tried to zero in his attention on the archangel. He could barely see him through the screen of screaming humans, their eyes wide and panic-stricken, their mouths agape, their faces a wet and soggy mess of blood and salt and bile. Something was ripping at his legs now, tearing chunks out of his already abused skin, but he struggled to focus.

"What are you—" he managed, but he didn't need to complete the question, didn't even need the archangel to carry on his tirade. A tirade only he could hear.

"You did not Fall from luxury to luxury, you imbecile," the angel seethed. "You had a job to do. A job accorded you from the Most High, a way to serve when you were so ungrateful that you no longer thought you needed His grace. He created that opportunity for you, and you—especially you—*failed*. You believed more in your right for rage than you did your honor, all you owed the Father who brought you life and breath and power over all you surveyed. And with that rage, you fell anew."

The scales dropped from his eyes as Warrick saw the final insult paraded before him once again. Serena, beautiful Serena, tall and strong and still wrapped in the light and glory of her position as Fallen. Holkeri beside her, already descended into demon form. And Warrick, bound and chained, jabbed at by spears, stunned by rocks and clubbed, his face and body beaten and bloody, until it seemed that only his eyes had been spared, only his eyes that still gazed out to see the defilement of the pure and untouched Serena by the loathsome horror that was Holkeri. She couldn't see, he'd thought. She couldn't know.

And then she'd laughed. And he'd realized that she *could* see. She *did* know. And that she was already lost to him. Lost because of Holkeri's own lying tongue.

The archangel's voice burned across his mind like acid. "Had you loved her—truly loved her—you would have fought in the light of God for her, not succumbed to your rage. But love is pain, isn't it, demon? Love is so much harder than the cleansing heat of fury. Love is an agony that can break you so badly that nothing will ever put you back together again."

Warrick roared as the outrage once more overtook him. Beyond the shadows of humans clawing, beating, striking him, piercing him with blades and cudgels and knives, Serena stood once more, seeing him, witnessing his fall, eyeing him with disgust and malice that he who stood so far beneath her would have the audacity to love her and believe she could love him back.

Only it wasn't Serena standing there any longer. Instead, the Fallen's cool patrician features were replaced with dark flashing eyes, a tumble of rich dark locks, a body tall and strong and fiery with intensity. Warrick felt his heart turn over, its thuds painful and harsh.

"No," he whispered, though he couldn't speak, could barely breathe. Someone had placed a noose around Warrick's neck and was even now pulling it tight.

"Only now it isn't one of your own you loved, but a human—a human who truly sees you, Warrick Zarnaah, sees you in all your ugliness and rage. Sees you for the creature that you are."

"No—"

"Look into her eyes, and know the truth."

Warrick tried to tear his face away, tried to keep himself from staring at Maria—Maria, so clear and full and bright, it was as if she wasn't an illusion but standing right before him, staring at him in mute horror. Her beautiful face, her strong, hardened body, her internal fire and the light that burned mirror bright around her. But he could no more look away from her than he could become a creature who was worthy of her. And still he could do nothing but wish, *wish* he could be the person she believed him to be. Wish that she didn't see the hulking creature, but that she saw—something else. Something that wasn't him. Something he could never be.

Another muscle-rending bolt of energy scored through him, and he felt his body succumbing to the darkness, the emptiness of the Nothing.

"Warrick!" Maria screamed.

CHAPTER TWENTY-THREE

Maria didn't object when Nikki Dawes pulled her limo up to the Palazzo Hotel, though that was neither Paris Las Vegas, where she'd said Warrick and Finn were staying, along with the rest of their team, or Treasure Island, where she'd said Warrick was at that very moment.

"Sorry for the brief detour, but I got a deal now with the Palazzo, and the less money I have to spend on parking, the more I can spend on being fabulous," Nikki said. "Plus, as it happens, Treasure Island is right across the street, so this will actually be faster."

"I—sure," Maria managed, staring out at the throngs of people gathered in front of the hotel. No, not gathered. They were simply thronging, a knot of tourists who pushed forward as one motion along the holiday-themed Strip. "Is it always this busy?"

"We do pull in a lot of people for Christmas," Nikki said, flipping her platinum hair as she rummaged for something in the front seat. Outside their car, a respectful valet stood waiting to take the limo off her hands. "The weather is to die for, everybody's in a good mood, and hey, it's Vegas. There's no telling what might happen. Okay, here we go."

Maria turned her attention from the crowd outside

back to Nikki, blinking to see her straightening again in the front seat. The hat, jacket, and white blouse had disappeared, and she now wore a spangled tank top that perfectly matched her sequined skirt. Her sunglasses were now in her hair, and her grin widened as Maria stared at her. She looked like she could breeze out of the car and hit the runway.

"Am I underdressed?" Maria asked.

"Not for your job you aren't," Nikki said, winking at her. "But for this gig, I'm merely eye candy. It doesn't happen very often, so I like to take advantage of it when it does. Let's bounce."

Nikki meant that most accurately, as she propelled herself out of the limo and onto her platform shoes with a springy grace that didn't at all resemble Maria's clamber to get out of the vehicle. Still, no sooner had they exited the limo than Nikki was striding quickly across the walkway, joining the mass of tourists and heading toward, sure enough, Treasure Island.

Maria stared at the building as they approached, from the lagoon strung with Christmas lights not yet in full glittering display, to the curved cream-and-dark-tan façade of the building, instantly recognizable for all that she'd never been to the city.

"That's where Warrick is?" she asked, taking it in. "And the, ah, archangel?"

"It certainly is. More or less on the top floor. If you look close, maybe you can see them."

"What?" That made absolutely no sense, of course, but Maria found herself looking up to the absolute top floor of the building nevertheless. She craned her neck, squinting as the light hit the building exactly right, creating a dazzling reflection that almost made it seem…that nearly gave her the impression…

"Um…that's weird," she muttered.

"What's weird? Hey, let's go in here."

271

"I…" Maria shook her head. What she'd seen in the flashing sunlight before stepping into the shadow of the casino's front entrance almost looked like an extension of the building. But an extension that couldn't be possible, not even with today's construction techniques. It almost looked like an enormous white tower stretched up from the walls of Treasure Island, soaring up into the sky so high, she could almost imagine it touching the heavens themselves.

She glanced back to Nikki to find the woman grinning at her with particular focus. "What?" she asked.

"Not a thing, sugar plum." Nikki pulled her through the glass doors and into the opulent lobby of Treasure Island, equal parts kitsch and joy, and didn't stop until they'd passed the reception desk and were approaching a corridor of elevator bays that led to a distant casino.

"We gotta head to the white elevators," Nikki continued, her long, lacquered nails flashing as she dipped her fingers inside her camisole once more and pulled out a fully blinged phone—the entire case covered in blue and black sequins that somehow magically matched her outfit. "Can you snag one for me?

"Um—sure." Maria swung her gaze to the wall of elevators, squinted. "Except they're all in—oh." And, sure enough, sort of shoved in between the ordinary-looking elevator bays, there was a narrow set of white elevator doors. She stepped forward as Nikki typed furiously on her phone and hit the button.

As the doors shooshed open, she glanced back at her guide. Her guide who was now watching her with an almost gleeful expression. "We just go in?"

"We just go in," Nikki confirmed, and she strode forward, holding open the door to let Maria step inside.

"You sure you don't know anything about being psychic?" she asked.

Maria winced as the doors hissed shut, the noise from the casino suddenly cut short. "I guess I've never really given it much—hey!"

The elevator shot up with so much force, Maria stumbled against Nikki, who braced her as if she'd been doing this her whole life. No more than a blink later, the doors snapped open again and all conversation was forgotten. Everything was forgotten, in fact, except for the man who stood hunched over in the center of the room, his body lit on fire by what looked like a thousand volts of electricity sparking from the wires that bound him tight.

Maria dashed forward, leaving Nikki behind, but as she neared the center of the room, she crashed—literally crashed up against an invisible wall, a barrier thrown up between her and Warrick. It wouldn't let her pass but didn't stop the flow of heat and anger and sheer, unmitigated pain that radiated from the demon's shuddering form.

And it *was* his demonic form, at least in part—flashing with each jolt of electricity between the beautiful, powerful man whose arms had wrapped around Maria, holding her close, protecting her...and the horrific beast that twisted and writhed in sheer, unadulterated agony. Something flashed in front of her, and it seemed to almost catch Warrick by surprise. His entire body went rigid, his eyes rolled back in his head, and Maria's heart surged in panic.

"Warrick!"

With a cry of nearly inarticulate rage, Maria pounded her fists against the invisible wall before her, desperate to reach him. At the first crash, nothing happened, but at the second, it seemed the wall gave a sound, almost. A hollow booming that seemed to emanate from somewhere deep inside the heart of the building in which they were standing, a building that now seemed built to an impossibly large scale.

Maria banged her hands against the wall again, and this time, Warrick seemed to hear her. His head jerked forward, his body staggering drunkenly, his arms flinging wide to steady himself. Once again, he shifted between the horrific monster of his demon form and the glamour she knew so well, but Maria searched both, desperate for any sign that the attack was lessening.

It wasn't. If anything, her assault on the wall or Warrick's sudden awareness of her seemed to throw him into even more agony, his very skin catching on fire as Maria watched.

"No!" she cried out, and then, finally, she saw what lay beyond Warrick, the being standing at the far end of the chamber, watching Warrick suffer, as if the demon was some sort of gladiator put on display for his captor's sick, private enjoyment.

The figure looked almost human, but his skin was so colorless, it appeared translucent, his hair a nearly white blonde. Michael the Archangel—it had to be. Even at this distance, Maria could tell that his eyes glowed with an eerie, soulless light, and he was surrounded by a corona of bright yellow fire. None of this mattered to Maria, though—the only thing that mattered was the expression on the archangel's face: smug superiority.

"How *dare* you!" she screeched, throwing everything she had inside her into the accusation. With the powerful battering of her fists, Maria flung herself against the wall again, once, twice, her bones compressing, her skin on fire, her teeth rattling inside her skull with every impact.

"How dare you!" she screamed again. Finally, the archangel seemed to notice her, and with another full-body assault against it, the invisible wall suddenly gave way.

She fell into a maelstrom of fire, wind, and electricity — and even, somehow, a storm of pelting rain and ice. Warrick stood still trapped in its center, now fully in his loathsome demonic form, his mouth barely a gash in his ruined face, his eyes staring out at her with hollow, desperate horror.

And Maria ran. She ran toward Warrick with more urgency than she'd ever felt in her life, more desperate need, fully consumed by her desire to reach him, to stand with him, to help him stay strong. She didn't know what she could do — she didn't know *if* she could do anything, but she also couldn't imagine drawing another single breath if this magnificent creature, this fearless protector, this beautiful child of God could not draw that breath alongside her.

"You are *mine*," she cried as she finally reached Warrick, flinging her arms wide and nearly tackling him. "I will not let you go!"

Warrick spun with the momentum of Maria's body crashing into his, his arms grasping for her, his hands once more stretching out with fingers instead of heavy-knuckled claws. He wrapped his arms around her as his glamour took hold more fully, lifting her off the floor as it writhed with a thousand live wires.

And then suddenly, as quickly as the maelstrom had started, it was over, and a curtain of silence dropped on the room. For a long moment, there was nothing but the sound of his own tortured breathing and Maria's stifled sobs, as she buried her face in his chest and wept upon him, the sound so heartbreaking that Warrick stared down at her in shock, unsure of what to do.

"Speak, human." The archangel's voice rolled out over the space, filling every corner with its rich resonance, and Maria's head came up sharply. Warrick tightened his grip, but Maria didn't try to break free from his embrace, merely turned in it, his arms tight around her shoulders and her hands grasping his forearms, the pose reminding him instantly of when they'd stood together in the showers, the first time he'd ever truly touched her.

Funny. Her hair still smelled like sky.

But Maria's words brought him fully back into focus.

"Why are you doing this?" she demanded, as if she wasn't addressing an archangel, wasn't challenging the warrior of God. "He fights for you. He endures every trial for you. And he healed me when I didn't think anyone could."

Warrick stiffened, his gaze arrowing down at Maria, but he couldn't see her eyes. She stood firm in his embrace, drawing strength from him and giving strength to him in equal measure.

"Explain," the archangel intoned. And with that simple word, Maria's awareness seemed to come back to her of who she was speaking to. For just a moment, she froze.

"You don't have to answer him," Warrick rumbled, but she gripped his arms more tightly, lifting her chin, though her entire body trembled.

"Yes," she murmured back, equally soft. "I do."

She squared her shoulders, as if she was fully prepared to take on any and all who would listen — the archangel, standing implacable in his judgment...Death, who stared with cool, inscrutable eyes...his brother-in-arms Finn, who fairly blazed with fury and outrage...Nikki Dawes, the first human to remind Warrick in a millennia that he was understood. All of them stood as witness to the woman in his arms, the woman who even now lifted her voice high.

"I grew up knowing I was nothing," Maria said fiercely. "Knew it and accepted it as my due. My father hadn't stuck around to care for me, care for my mother. I grew up poor and alone. An outsider. The one bright light in my life was my cousin, and she died in my arms, the light going out of her even as she begged me to defend her. To call upon the protection of God and save her from those who'd struck her down. But I didn't make that call. I'd seen things no child should ever see. Not just the violence against my cousin, not only the death of my mother barely a year before, but a darkness that crept ever closer, every night. Things I couldn't unsee. When Cara died, all that mattered was that I avenge her. But I never realized I needed saving too."

Maria shifted then, pulling down on Warrick's arms until he loosened his hold and she could step forward, but she never dropped her gaze from the archangel. "When I summoned the sword of God to defend me, he came. He honored the call. But he didn't stop there. He treated me, for the first time in my life, like I was something special, something to be honored, cherished, and, yes, protected. And in him, for the *first* time, I found someone that I could honor too. And, what's more…" Maria swallowed. "I found someone who was strong enough to stand with me and against every darkness that sought to push out the light. I didn't realize how much I needed that. How much every human needs it, maybe."

She turned in Warrick's arms, then, no longer facing the archangel, but looking up to him. Her eyes were dark and wet, but her voice was resolute.

"And you gave me something else, Warrick, something you never wanted to give, something you were horrified that I even witnessed, much less remembered. You showed me the core of your vulnerable self. The image you thought you most deserved when you were struck down and turned into a demon. The creature who is as much a part of you as this beautiful being I see now, tall and straight and true. And I loved you for it. I *loved* you because in that one flash of vulnerability, in your horror and hatred for me seeing who you are, you still accepted that this was you. This was all of you. That you were mighty and you were frail and you were beauty and ugliness and sin and also forgiveness."

Warrick stiffened at her words, but now it was Maria who held on tight. "Yes, forgiveness, my beautiful warrior. You treated me as if I was a singular creature of God, not some castoff who should never have been born, not the little girl who failed her cousin and then spent half her life trying to somehow undo a wrong she could never make right. Not the woman who wondered if maybe she was going insane because she saw men with crazy eyes and shifting skin. You treated me from the first time you saw me as a woman worth protecting, and you gave me a gift that I had never been able to give myself."

She lifted her chin, her jaw set, her words defiant. "And I will never stop loving you, Warrick, even if you can't allow me to be near you. Not because you are a demon. Not because you are powerful. Not for any reason other than that your light has shone so brightly that it has given me a path to follow home...and *you*, you are that home."

For a long moment, no one spoke. Maria continued to stare fiercely up at Warrick, though how she could see anything, he didn't know, as much as her eyes were swimming with tears.

"Maria," he rumbled, his entire heart, his entire deathless life in the word, unsure of what else to say.

"Yes, Maria."

The voice was closer now, bolder, and Warrick blinked up to realize the archangel had left his dais at the far end of the room and was now right before them. Warrick looked around quickly. He could no longer see Finn, or Nikki, or Death. Beyond their tight circle of light, a howling wind now raged—a wind that Warrick knew too well. The veil. The Nothing.

"Maria Santos," the archangel continued. "You are a child of God who has been specially blessed by your faith and your dedication to others. Through this faith, you can see what you should not, do what most dare not. But you allowed your life to cling to vengeance, anger, seeking a revenge when that would never bring your cousin back. There is such great strength in you. But you chose to live in shadows. You were blind and needed to see."

Before Maria could defend herself anew, however, the archangel turned to him. "Warrick Zarnaah, you were among the Father's brightest stars, and yet you fell. And fell again. And continued to wreak your rage upon the children of God who could not understand, could not see. You were hidden and needed to be seen."

Warrick drew breath to protest, but Michael raised his hand, his face as devoid of expression as Warrick had ever seen it. "The horde must be fought, and we need able warriors to defend the earth from the scourge that overruns it. You—both of you—have proven you are up to the task. If you take the pledge to fight for the children of God, the path of Light is before you. You need only to walk upon it."

Warrick stared at him, and Michael held his gaze. And there, for the briefest instant, Warrick caught a glimpse of a vast chasm of pain held within the

279

archangel…

Then Michael was gone.

CHAPTER TWENTY-FOUR

Maria collapsed to the ground, heaving for air, desperate to be heard, to be known, to be understood...

Only to realize she was sprawled on the lush pile carpeting of an empty conference room.

Well, not quite empty. There were no table or chairs in the space, but Warrick lay crumpled beside her, moaning, and two other figures raced toward them seemingly from a long distance away. She blinked, recognizing Finn, then Nikki Dawes, and then—

She squinted. The third person in the room wasn't advancing but retreating. Blue, she thought with one dim portion of her mind. The woman who'd introduced herself as Blue, who'd known about her cross and her cousin...

As Warrick groaned again, rolling over to his back, Maria managed to pull herself up to her elbows.

"What was that?" she managed, but Warrick couldn't seem to do anything more than heave deep breaths, as if he hadn't drawn in a full lungful of oxygen in weeks.

Finn reached Warrick first. "My brother!" he gasped, dropping to his knees. He reached forward and patted down Warrick's arms, his shoulders, as if convincing himself that Warrick was still there.

Warrick flinched away, and Maria pulled herself up to her own knees, sitting back on her heels as Nikki strode up, then dropped a hand on her shoulder. The chauffeur—who clearly was much more than a chauffeur, gave a low whistle, but Maria's eyes were only for Warrick.

"What's wrong with him?" she asked Finn as Warrick grimaced.

"I'm fine," Warrick rumbled, but he sounded...different now, his voice deeper, clearer. He tried to sit up, but Finn pushed him back down.

"You're fine, but you're not all *that* fine," he announced. "These wounds... These are *your* arms, Warrick. This isn't damage to your glamour." He whistled. "Michael put you through the trial and...I think you passed. But dayum, I'd hate to see it if you failed."

"Hmm..." Warrick frowned down at his own body while Finn drew his hands together, bowing his forehead to the fingertips, in the perfect pose of a man praying. Before Maria could figure out what he was doing, the entire room seemed to shudder, the air snapping taut.

And suddenly, four more giants surrounded him.

"Oh, I do love my job," Nikki said happily, even as she crouched down to bolster Maria, who had fallen to her backside and instinctively scrambled away. Nikki leaned close to her, gave her a little hug. "Maybe we should give the guys a moment, baby doll. From what I saw of your memories, this is going to be good."

Maria, wide-eyed, could only stare.

Warrick vaguely understood that the rest of the Syx

were there, and, wincing, he looked up at them. But there was something wrong with his eyesight. It wasn't so much that he couldn't see, it was as if everything was so much brighter than it was before, brighter and diffuse, with no hard edges.

"Is he hurt worse now than he was?" The voice sounded like an angelic choir, and Warrick blinked, focusing on Raum.

"Not worse," Finn offered as Warrick staggered upright, leaning on his fellow demon as if he'd just survived a bar fight. "But different this time, for sure. He's got no glamour, from what I can see."

"This is — temporary," Warrick gasped, finally able to grasp the gift he had been given…the gift and also the challenge. "A…taste. The smallest taste of the life we'll lead after we all pass the archangel's test. It is what it means to be Fallen once more." He grimaced, thinking of Holkeri's drug, understanding now more than ever why Holkeri had been so desperate to reclaim that state of grace.

"A taste, huh?" It was Stefan who stepped forward first, leaning in to squint at him. "Well, you're taller, anyway. And you look like you've been beat to shit. That's not all that tasty."

Gregori stood back with his arms crossed. He was the biggest of them all, the strongest. And his words were sonorous enough to move the bones of the world. "There's no longer any illusion to your form," he said thoughtfully. "What's cut bleeds. What's broken must knit. There's no covering it up, no smoothing out the edges to ease the experience of the humans who see. The price of protection is high in this state."

"I'm not sure this taste is all that worth it, then." It was Hugh who spoke up now, his jaw tight. "I may not have been Fallen all that long, but I don't remember it being that easy for me to be injured, I'll tell you plain."

But Warrick merely smiled. As he took in his men, his sight still far too crystal bright, every nerve ending on fire, every sense spinning, he knew what he was feeling. He remembered. The others — and he himself — had taught themselves long ago to forget, to drown out what was true in the fury of their fight against the demon horde. This was what it meant to be Fallen, he realized.

This was what it meant to be back in the light.

As quickly as the change came over him, it receded again. He sensed it going — not with bereavement or even anger, but with full and clear-eyed knowing. If all of them reached their redemption, then each of them would see this light, feel this energy. If even one of them didn't reach it…

He straightened, his full strength and glamour returning to him as Finn fell back with a hiss and the other Syx straightened.

"What the hell?" Finn blurted, but Gregori was now nodding. Gregori, whose gaze had never faltered — whose gaze never did.

"You passed the archangel's test," he said simply. "The first among us all."

Warrick looked down at his hands. He could see the monstrous shadow of his demonic form, the heavy paws, the gnarled claws. But even that was fading, leaving only normal-sized hands and fingers behind. Once more, he stood clad in the same running gear he'd been wearing when Michael had summoned him, as if nothing had happened.

And yet everything had happened.

Because Maria was here, with him. As if she had no wish to be anywhere else.

She'd come for him, he thought. She'd taken his rejection of her, his abandonment, and she'd come for him all the same. And in his greatest privation, she'd attempted to fight for him. To give what he didn't wish to take from her, but which she'd willingly offered anyway.

Her life. Her truth.

Her love.

Now Warrick turned toward her as she stood beside Nikki. He held Maria's gaze, smiled. "I am the first among us all," he agreed. "But not the last."

Maria didn't speak as they moved across the room, toward the elevators, said nothing as they whisked down the long flights to the first floor of the Treasure Island. By the time they reached the floor and exited the elevator, the rest of the Syx had disappeared, Nikki along with them.

"They all...left?"

"Ordinarily, we must be summoned to travel anywhere, beholden to the humans who need us most, or constrained to return to our cells beyond the veil," Warrick said. "On this plane, however, we can return to our base when the job is done."

"And Nikki?"

He chuckled. "Nikki Dawes is a miracle unto herself. What's more, we owe her and her friends a debt of deepest gratitude. If she chose to travel with the Syx, then they were honor bound to let her."

Maria nodded, smiling too. "Will I see her again?"

"I don't think you'll be able to avoid it."

She curled her hand into Warrick's, and together they walked through the Treasure Island lobby. When they stepped out of the casino, though, she blinked. "It's night. We were in there longer than I thought."

"The city is always better at night," Warrick said. He

pulled her into his arms and gestured to the Strip. "What do you see?"

Standing there, his arms wrapped around her, Maria stared down the Technicolor wonderland that was the Las Vegas strip. The cacophony of color dazzled her eyes, but she knew what Warrick was asking her. It was the same thing Nikki had asked, and she lifted her gaze up, taking the enormous lit constructs above the casinos. "I see towers," she said finally. "Glittering lights high above the hotels — way too high and too…insubstantial to be real."

She felt him tense and glanced up at him. "You're telling me they're real?" she asked, though it wasn't really a question. She was beginning to understand that there was far more to this world than she'd ever realized, far more that she would learn at Warrick's side.

"Because you can see them, yes. They are real," he said, and there was something in his voice that caught at her, causing her to look more closely. Warrick's profile was sharply defined against the bright backdrop of neon lights, but he was staring too intently off into the distance.

"What?" she asked.

"You can see them, like you saw me. Because you have been blessed by All That Is, and, more importantly, you accepted that blessing. And now you're beside me, which is more than I ever thought would be possible, more than I could have dreamed."

Maria swallowed hard, forcing herself not to tear up. "Well, get used to it," she managed. She stood on her tiptoes and pulled Warrick's face down to hers, reveling in the intensity of his gaze as he stared back, as if there was no one else in the world but her. "Because I'm not going anywhere."

"Yes," Warrick said, and though the admission

seemed to cost him, he looked deep into her eyes, and his face suddenly glowed with such beauty it took her breath away. In that moment, Maria could see what Warrick was capable of, see what he would become, and see what—if they both were strong enough, if she stood with him and for him and loved him with all her heart—what the future held for him. For him, and for them both. Together.

There is such great strength in you…and the path of Light is before you. Those had been the words of the archangel. That had been his promise.

His promise and his challenge. One she was more than willing to take.

"Together," she whispered, and she didn't miss the hard flare of longing in Warrick's eyes, the glint of determination and might. This was her beautiful, terrible demon. This was her Fallen. This was her path of Light.

Maria lifted her face to Warrick's and sealed her future with a kiss.

DEMON FORSAKEN

~ Coming July, 2018 ~

It's beginning to look a lot like Christmas—only Finn of the Syx has to travel to Cleveland to tangle with an enemy he'd long thought dead: the Fallen angel who'd condemned him to eternal torment more than six thousand years earlier. Now that angel's back, and targeting a human, whose high-tech security company is definitely more than it seems. So when no-nonsense, hard-edged Dana Griffin unexpectedly finds herself in need of a little celestial intervention...Finn's just the demon for the job.

To keep up with the latest news on the Demon Enforcers, visit me at http://www.jennstark.com!

Acknowledgments

Demon Unbound has been so much more of a labor of love than I expected, as it made me truly reconnect with the magic of All That Is. Thank you so much for letting me share this new tale with you. As always, my thanks to Elizabeth Bemis for her beautiful work on my books and my site—including my series of covers, which I absolutely adore. My editorial team of Linda Ingmanson and Toni Lee saved me as always, and as always, any mistakes in the manuscript are most definitely my own. My thanks to Edeena Cross for her careful beta read, and to Sabra Harp, who helps remind me of everything I've forgotten. Special thanks too, to Geoffrey, for encouraging me to go where angels fear to tread. It's most definitely been a leap worth taking.

ABOUT JENN STARK

Jenn Stark is an award-winning author of paranormal romance and urban fantasy. She lives and writes in Ohio. . . and she definitely loves to write. In addition to her Immortal Vegas urban fantasy series and Demon Enforcers paranormal romance series, she is also author Jennifer McGowan, whose Maids of Honor series of Young Adult Elizabethan spy romances are published by Simon & Schuster, and author Jennifer Chance, whose Rule Breakers series of New Adult contemporary romances are published by Random House/LoveSwept and whose modern royals series, Gowns & Crowns, is now available.

When she's not creating fictional trouble for herself, You can find Jenn online at http://www.jennstark.com, follow her on Twitter @jennstark, and visit her Facebook author page and keep up on all the latest news at http://www.facebook.com/authorjennstark.